Dear TO ME

BRIDES OF WEBSTER COUNTY 3

WANDA E. BRUNSTETTER

BARBOUR BOOKS

An Imprint of Barbour Publishing, Inc.

Print ISBN 978-1-63058-739-0

eBook Editions:
Adobe Digital Edition (.epub) 978-1-63409-435-1
Kindle and MobiPocket Edition (.prc) 978-1-63409-436-8

All scripture quotations are taken from the King James Version of the Bible.

All Pennsylvania Dutch words are taken from the *Revised Pennsylvania German Dictionary* found in Lancaster County, Pennsylvania.

This book is a work of fiction. Names, characters, places, and incidents are either products of the author's imagination or used fictitiously. Any similarity to actual people, organizations, and/or events is purely coincidental.

Cover design: Mullerhaus Publishing Arts, mullerhaus.net

Published by Barbour Books, an imprint of Barbour Publishing, Inc., P.O. Box 719, Uhrichsville, Ohio 44683, www.barbourbooks.com

Our mission is to publish and distribute inspirational products offering exceptional value and biblical encouragement to the masses.

Printed in the United States of America.

DEDICATION/ACKNOWLEDGMENTS

To my dear friends Diane and Phil Allen,
whose love for the wildlife that come into their
yard prompted me to write this story.

Be ye therefore followers of God, as dear children.
EPHESIANS 5:1

Chapter 1

Melinda Andrews hurried across the grass, eager to arrive at her favorite spot. Just a few more steps, and there it was—dappled canopies of maple, hickory, cedar, and pine towering over a carpet of lush green leaves and fragrant needles. She drew in a deep breath, relishing the woodsy scent. The sun had tried all morning to overcome the low-hanging clouds. It had finally made an appearance, and Melinda planned to enjoy each moment she could spend here.

She slowed her pace and crept through the forest, being careful not to snag her long, dark blue dress or matching apron on any low-hanging branches. After a while, she came to a clearing with several downed trees. "This looks like the perfect place for me to sit and draw," she murmured.

Taking a seat on a nearby log, Melinda pulled her drawing tablet and pencil from the canvas tote she'd brought along. "Where are you, deer friends?"

The only movement was the flitter of leaves as the wind blew softly against the trees.

Melinda spotted a cluster of wild yellow crocuses peeking through a clump of grass. Spring was her favorite time of the year, with new life bursting forth everywhere. She lifted her pencil, ready to sketch a tan-colored rabbit that had hopped onto the scene, when two does stepped into the clearing.

"You're so beautiful," she whispered.

The does lifted their heads in curiosity as a hawk soared high overhead.

Melinda watched the deer nibble on leaves while she sketched their picture. Her stomach rumbled, which caused her to think about the lemon sponge cake Papa Noah had made last night. She'd had a sliver of it for breakfast this morning, and it had been delicious. She thought her stepfather was the best cook in all of Webster County, Missouri.

Melinda had been six years old when her real father had been hit by a car and killed. Shortly after his death, her mother had given up her career of telling jokes and yodeling among the English. She and Melinda had caught the bus from Branson to Seymour and come to live with Grandpa and Grandma Stutzman in the Amish community where Melinda's mother had been raised.

Even though Melinda had been young back then, she remembered many things about their arrival in Webster County. She especially recalled meeting her aunt, Susie Stutzman, for the first time. Susie was Grandma's youngest child, and she was a year older than Melinda. Melinda and Susie had become friends right away and had remained so ever since.

Melinda smiled at the memory of seeing her aunt dressed in a long blue dress with a small white *kapp* perched on top of her head. "Plain clothes" is what Mama had told Melinda. "My folks follow the customs and rules of the Amish church, and they live differently than we're used to living."

Melinda hadn't minded wearing the unusual clothes, for it seemed as if she were playing dress-up at first. The strange rules and numerous jobs Grandma Stutzman had expected her to do were the hardest part. She remembered, too, that Mama hadn't seemed too happy when they first came home—not until Noah Hertzler had started hanging around, taking an interest in her. Melinda had figured Noah would be her new daddy even before Mama had said she loved him. She'd been real pleased when they'd decided to get married.

Melinda lifted her face to the sun as thoughts of marriage made her think of Gabe Swartz, who had begun courting her a few months ago. Gabe had hazel-colored eyes with little green specks and brown hair that curled around his ears. He was tall and slender, yet strong and able-bodied. Melinda had developed a crush on him when they were attending the one-room schoolhouse down the road.

When Gabe, who'd been a year ahead of Melinda in school, graduated from eighth grade and began learning the trade of woodworking under his dad's tutelage, she missed seeing him every day and looked forward to their every-other-Sunday church services, where Gabe and his family would also be in attendance. Now Gabe, who had recently turned twenty, worked full-time at his father's woodworking shop.

When Melinda had finished school, she'd begun her vocational training at home with her mother, where she learned various household chores that would prepare her for marriage. Then a year ago, she'd begun working part-time for Dr. Franklin, the local veterinarian. At first it was just cleanup work, as well as feeding, watering, and exercising some of the animal patients. But later, when the doctor realized how much Melinda cared for the animals and noticed her special way with them, he had allowed her to assist him with minor things. Melinda had done everything from holding a dog while it received a shot or had its nails clipped, to giving flea baths and bringing animals from their cages into the operating room.

"You've been blessed with a unique gift," Dr. Franklin had told Melinda the other day while she held a nervous kitten about to receive its first shot. "Have you ever considered becoming a veterinarian's technical assistant or even a vet?"

Melinda had to admit that the thought of becoming a vet had crossed her mind, but she figured it was an impossible dream. Not only was she lacking in education, but going to college and then on to a school of veterinary medicine would mean leaving the Amish faith. Since she'd been baptized and joined the Amish church a year ago, it would affect her whole family if she left the faith and became part of the English world.

Melinda remembered several years ago, before their old bishop died and John Frey had taken his place, a young man named Abner had left home during his running-around years, and he'd ended up coming back a few months later, saying it was too hard being away from his family. As a young woman, her own mother had left the Amish faith for ten years, trying to make a name for herself in the entertainment business.

It would probably break Mama's heart if I left home the way she did when she was my age, Melinda thought. *And what would it do to my relationship with Gabe?* She shook her head. *No, becoming a vet is most likely just an impossible dream. I'll probably never leave my home here in Webster County.*

"I can't believe Melinda's not back yet." Faith placed a sack of flour on the counter and turned to face her mother and youngest sister, who sat at the kitchen table. "She said she was going for a short walk and would be here in plenty of time to help with the baking, but she must have lost track of time."

Susie, Faith's sister who had recently turned twenty, sighed. "Knowing Melinda, she's most likely off taking care of one of her critters or out in the woods sketching pictures of the deer."

Faith nodded. "You're probably right. My daughter has been taking in injured and orphaned animals ever since she was a little girl. It's not gotten any better since she became a young woman, either. Sometimes I wonder if Melinda will ever grow up."

"Just because she likes helping animals doesn't mean she's not mature," Faith's mother put in. "She wouldn't be able to work for Dr. Franklin if she wasn't grown up enough to make good decisions."

Faith wrinkled her forehead. She didn't know why her mother was sticking up for Melinda. She sure hadn't taken Faith's side of things when Faith was Melinda's age. *Of course,* Faith reasoned, *back then I was headstrong and disobedient, running off to do my own thing in the modern world. Mama only saw me as a rebellious teenager, not as a mature woman who made good decisions.*

"Be that as it may," Faith said as she pulled out a rolling pin, "Melinda's showing her immaturity this morning by not keeping her word and being here to help us with the baking."

"Would you like me to go look for her?" Susie offered.

Faith pursed her lips and finally nodded. "That's a good idea, since she's obviously not planning to come back anytime soon of her own accord."

Susie stood. "I'll check the barn first. If she's not there, I'll head for the woods."

As Susie scurried out the door, Faith moved over to the table and took a seat across from her mother. "Since we don't have the help of either of our daughters at the moment, why don't the two of us sit and visit over another cup of tea?"

Mama smiled and pushed back her metal-framed glasses, which had slipped to the end of her nose. "Sounds good to me."

"You know, it's not just Melinda's preoccupation with her animal friends that bothers me," Faith said while pouring her mother a cup of tea.

"What else is bothering you?"

"I'm concerned because Melinda's been acting kind of strange."

Mama's eyebrows lifted as a deep wrinkle formed above her nose. "Strange in what way?"

"Besides the fact that I have to stay after Melinda to get her chores done because she's too busy tending her animal friends, she seems to be off in her own little world. It's like her thoughts are somewhere else most of the time."

"I think you need to be more patient with

Melinda. From what I can tell, she and Gabe Swartz are getting serious. I think it's just a matter of time until they become betrothed." Mama smiled. "Once that happens, I'm sure Melinda will settle down and act more like the mature woman you want her to be."

Faith poured herself a cup of tea and took a sip. "I hope you're right about that, Mama. *Jah*, I surely do."

Susie had gone a short ways into the woods when she spotted Melinda sitting on a log with her drawing tablet. Susie was tempted to scold her niece for wasting time and trying to get out of work she should be doing, but she figured if she said too much, she and Melinda would probably end up arguing. Ever since Melinda had been a young girl, she had enjoyed spending time with animals. Susie used to think that once Melinda grew up, she would focus on the important things in life. But no, Melinda kept drawing and daydreaming, shirking her duties at the house, and causing her mother to send Susie after her on many occasions.

A twig snapped as Susie took a step toward the log. She halted and held her breath. Should she sneak up on Melinda and take her by surprise or make a loud noise so Melinda would know she was coming? Deciding on the latter, Susie moved closer and cleared her throat.

Melinda, engrossed in her artwork, didn't budge.

Susie held her hands above Melinda's head and clapped. "Hey!"

Melinda jumped, and the deer she'd been drawing bolted into the protection of the thick pine forest.

"Thanks a lot!" Melinda spun around and glared at Susie. "You've scared away my subjects, and they probably won't be back. Leastways not anytime soon."

"Sorry about that," Susie mumbled. She glanced at Melinda's drawing tablet and couldn't help but be impressed with what she saw. Despite the fact that Melinda drew well, was it really necessary to spend every free moment—and some time that was stolen—sketching her woodland friends?

Melinda stood and shook her finger at Susie. "I don't think you're one bit sorry. You look rather pleased with yourself, Susie Stutzman. I'll bet you clapped and hollered like that on purpose, just to scare away my subjects. Didn't you?"

Susie nodded slowly.

"Why?"

"Because your *mamm* has been looking for you, and your mamm and my mamm need our help baking pies for Sunday after church at my folks' house."

Melinda groaned and flopped down on the log.

Susie pursed her lips. "I also knew that if I just whispered in your ear that you were needed in the kitchen, the deer would have stayed put, and you'd have kept right on drawing."

Melinda pushed a wayward strand of golden blond hair away from her face and tucked it into the bun she wore at the back of her head. "How did you know where to find me, anyway?"

Susie wrinkled her nose. "You're kidding, right?"

Melinda shrugged. Her gaze traveled around the wooded area, and she said, "Just listen to the music of the birds. Isn't it the most beautiful sound you've ever heard?"

"It's nice, but there's other—"

"Do you smell that fresh pine scent from all the trees?"

Susie nodded and drew in a deep breath as the woodsy aroma filled her nostrils. "It does smell nice in the woods," she admitted.

"It's so peaceful here, don't you think?"

"Jah, but there are other things I'd rather do than sit in the woods for hours on end." Susie took a seat on the log beside Melinda. "What draws you to these woods, anyway?"

"The animals that live here, of course. Every creature God created is special, but the ones that live in the woods fascinate me more than any others."

"There's a big difference between *fascinated* and *fanatical*."

Melinda snickered. "Fanatical, is it? Since when did you start using such fancy words?"

Susie shrugged. "I've been reading a novel about a young woman who likes to solve mysteries. Her mother accuses her of being fanatical."

"You'd better not start shirking your duties because you're reading too much, or your mamm will become *fanatical*."

"Who's going to tell her—you?"

"Of course not. You know I'm not one to blab anyone's secret."

"No, but you sure do like to change the subject."

"What subject was that?"

"The one about animals and your love for them. Ever since you were little, you've been playing nursemaid to any stray animal that came near your place." Susie shook her head. "I just don't understand it."

"Do you think me wanting to care for animals is a bad thing?"

"I suppose not, unless it's all you think about." Susie turned her head sharply, and a wisp of hair slipped out from under her kapp and fell onto her cheek.

Melinda pointed to Susie's hair. "I thought it was only me who didn't get her bun put up right."

Susie snickered. "I guess that's one thing we still have in common."

"What do you mean? There are lots of things we both like."

Susie elbowed Melinda gently in the ribs. "Jah—lemon sponge cakes, barbecued beef, and Aaron Zook's new puppy, Rufus."

"I'm wondering if it's Aaron you're interested in and not his dog."

Susie's elbow connected with Melinda's ribs a second time. "You're such a kidder."

"I wasn't kidding."

"Aaron's more like a *bruder* to me than anything."

"He's like a brother to me, too. His mamm and my mamm have been friends a long time. Her *kinner*, Isaiah, and I have grown up together, so I could never see Aaron as more than a brother." Melinda scanned the woods again. "I wish those deer would come back so I could finish sketching their picture."

Susie stared at a noisy crow circling overhead. "You and Gabe Swartz have been courting several months now, right?"

"That's true."

"Do you think you'll end up marrying him?"

"That all depends."

"On what?"

"On whether he asks, and whether I decide to—" Melinda halted her words then slipped her drawing tablet and pencil into the canvas tote at her feet. She jumped up and grabbed Susie's hand. "We'd better go. It wouldn't be good to keep our mamms waiting any longer, you know."

Gabe whistled as he swiped a piece of sandpaper across the door of a new kitchen cabinet. He was alone at the shop today. His dad had gone to Seymour to pick up some supplies he had ordered. Gabe figured it might be some time before Pap returned, because when he went to town he usually headed straight for the fast-food restaurant and bought a juicy cheeseburger and an order of fries. And he'd often drop by Lazy Lee's Gas Station and chew the fat with whoever was working that day.

Gabe smiled. He liked being alone in the shop. It gave him a chance to try his hand at making a few new things without his dad holding him back or scrutinizing every little detail.

When I'm done with this door, I think I'll start making that birdhouse I plan to give Melinda for her birthday next month. She's always feeding the birds and taking care of any that get hurt, so I'm sure she'd like to have another birdhouse—maybe a feeder, too. He rubbed his chin thoughtfully. *Maybe I should make a birdhouse with a feeding station attached. I'll bet she'd like that.*

A vision of Melinda's pretty face popped into Gabe's mind. Her golden blond hair and clear blue eyes were enough to turn any man's head. He had been interested in her since they were both children. But it wasn't just Melinda's pretty face that had made him fall in love with her. It was Melinda's spunky attitude and zest for living he found so appealing. She had always been adventurous, wanting to explore new things and eager to learn all she could about birds and animals. Gabe still remembered how nervous he had felt months ago when he'd asked her stepfather for permission to court her.

The cowbell hanging by a rope on the front door jangled, and Gabe looked up, his musings halted.

Melinda's stepfather, Noah Hertzler, entered the room. "*Wie geht's?* How's business?"

"I'm doing well, and so is the business. How's your job at the Christmas tree farm?"

"We've been keeping plenty busy." Noah looked around. "Where's your *daed*? Is he around someplace?"

"He went to Seymour to pick up some supplies. Probably won't be back for a few hours yet."

Noah chuckled. "If I know Stephen, he's having lunch at his favorite burger place."

"No doubt, but I don't know why Pap would choose fast food over barbecued ribs, baked beans, or hillbilly chili."

"I have to agree, but each to his own."

"Jah. Everyone has different likes and dislikes." Gabe moved over to the desk in the center of the room. "What can I help you with, Noah?"

"Thought I'd see if you could make a birdhouse for me to give Melinda for her nineteenth birthday next month."

Gabe inwardly groaned. There went his plans for Melinda's special birthday present. He didn't have the nerve to tell Noah that he had intended to give her a combination birdhouse-feeder. Now he would have to come up with something else to make for Melinda. Maybe he could whittle a miniature fawn, since she seemed so taken with the deer that lived in the woods behind their place.

"I'm sure I can have a birdhouse done for you in time for Melinda's birthday," Gabe said. "Is there a particular size or color you'd like it to be?"

Noah shook his head. "You're the expert; I'll leave that up to you."

Gabe smiled. He liked being called an expert. Most folks who came into their shop thought Pap was the professional woodworker, and many saw Gabe as merely his dad's apprentice. Someday, though, Gabe hoped to have his own place of business, and then nobody could think of him as an amateur in training.

Noah leaned against the desk and visited while Gabe wrote up the work order. "You think you'll take over this shop when your daed's ready to retire?" he asked.

Gabe looked up. "I'm not sure. I might want to go out on my own some day." He covered his mouth with the palm of his hand. "My daed doesn't know of my plans, so I'd appreciate it if you wouldn't say anything to him about it."

Noah shook his head. "It's not my place to do the telling."

Gabe breathed a sigh of relief. Did Melinda know how fortunate she was to have such a nice man as her stepfather? *I wouldn't mind having Noah for my father-in-law,* he mused. *That is, if I ever get up the nerve and find the right time to ask Melinda to marry me.*

Chapter 2

How come we had to bake so many pies today?" Melinda asked her mother after Grandma Stutzman and Aunt Susie left for home. "Won't some of the other women be bringing desserts on Sunday?"

"It was your grandma's idea to have a pie social after church, and she wanted to furnish all the pies," Mama said as they finished cleaning the kitchen. She handed Melinda a sponge and pointed to the table, where streaks of flour and globs of gooey pie filling stuck to the oilcloth covering.

Melinda gave the table a thorough cleaning then dropped the mess into the garbage can under the sink. "If church is going to be at Grandpa and

Grandma's, why did we do the baking over here and not at their house?"

"Melinda, weren't you listening when I told you this before?" Mama asked in an exasperated tone.

Melinda shrugged. "I—I guess not."

"Your daed's busy with other things today, and I didn't want to leave Grandpa Hertzler alone in the *daadihaus* all day with his memory not being so good. No telling what might happen if he were left by himself for any length of time."

"That's right," Melinda's eleven-year-old brother, Isaiah, said as he came up behind their mother. "Remember the last time we left Grandpa alone in the grandfather house while we went to Bass Pro Shops in Springfield? When we got home, he wasn't there, and we found him down the road at the schoolhouse." The boy snickered. "I still can't get over seein' Grandpa on one of them swings, talkin' to Grandma like she was right there."

"Grandpa's memory loss is no laughing matter, Isaiah. Your daed and I are watching him closely, and if he gets any worse, we'll take him to see a specialist in Springfield." Mama shooed Isaiah away with the cotton dish towel she held in one hand. "Now get back outside and see that the rest of the wood is chopped before your daed gets home."

"Okay, I'm goin'." Isaiah grabbed a handful of peanut butter cookies from the ceramic jar on the cupboard then headed out the back door.

"That boy," Mama muttered as she ran water into the sink. "It'll be a miracle if I'm not fully gray by the time he's grown and married."

"If he can ever find a wife who'll put up with him." Melinda thought her young brother was a bit spoiled. The fact that Mama wasn't able to have any more children after Isaiah had been born could account for the fact that she didn't always get after the boy the way she should. At least that's how Melinda saw it.

"Isaiah's young yet," Mama said. "There's still plenty of time for him to grow into the kind of man a woman would want to marry."

Melinda's thoughts went to Gabe, the way they usually did whenever the subject of marriage came up. Was he the man she would marry? She cared deeply for him, but what would happen to their relationship if she left the Amish faith to become a veterinarian? Would he understand her desire to care for animals in a more professional way? Of course, she hadn't made up her mind yet about going English. There was a lot to think on and a good deal of planning to do if she did decide to pursue a career in veterinary medicine.

Pushing her thoughts aside, Melinda glanced at her mother, engrossed in the job of washing dishes. Mama's once shiny blond hair had turned darker, and a few streaks of gray showed through. Even so, she seemed youthful and full of energy. Mama had a zest for living, often telling jokes and yodeling whenever the mood hit. Of course, this usually happened when Grandpa Stutzman wasn't around. He found yodeling an annoyance, even though many Amish in their community liked to yodel.

I enjoy yodeling, too, Melinda thought as she wiped down the refrigerator door where some gunk had also splattered. *But I'll never yodel when I'm in the woods, because it would probably scare away the deer.*

"Did you read your Bible this morning?" Mama asked.

Melinda sucked in her lower lip, searching for words that wouldn't be a lie. She hadn't been doing her devotions regularly for some time, even though she knew she should. "I'll do it this evening before bed," she promised.

"I have found that in order to stay close to God, I need to spend time with Him in prayer and Bible reading," Mama went on to say.

"I feel close to God when I'm out in the woods."

"That may be, but spending time in nature is not the same as reading God's Word."

"I know, and I'll read some verses tonight."

"Jah, okay. In the meantime, would you check on that last pie we've got baking?"

Melinda set the sponge on the table and went to open the oven door. When she looked inside, it appeared as if the apple crumb pie was done. Just to be certain, she poked the tip of a knife through the middle. "The apples seem tender enough, so I think it's ready," she announced. "I'm sure it won't be nearly as good as the ones Papa Noah bakes, though." She pulled two pot holders from a drawer and carefully lifted the pie from the oven. "Should I turn the propane off?"

"Go ahead. I won't need the stove again until supper time."

Melinda set the pie on top of the stove while she turned the knob on the propane tank. She was thankful her folks didn't use a woodstove for cooking the way some Amish in their community did. Wood cooking was too hot to her liking, and it could be dangerous.

Melinda remembered once when she was young how her mother had caught the kitchen rug on fire after a piece of wood fell out of the firebox. Fortunately, Mama had been able to throw the rug and the wood outside before anything else caught fire. The whole kitchen had become a smoky mess, and Mama's cake had been ruined. Melinda had been forced to sit outside in the cold until the smoke cleared.

Melinda picked up the pie again and started across the room. While it cooled on the kitchen table, she planned to go out to the barn and check on the baby goat that had been born a few days ago.

She'd only made it halfway to the table when the back door swung open and Isaiah rushed into the room, all red-faced and sweaty. "My dog broke free from his chain again, and he's chasin' chickens all over the yard!"

Before either Mama or Melinda could respond, Hector, Melinda's favorite rooster, flew into the house, squawking all the way. Isaiah's hound dog, Jericho, followed, nipping at Hector's tail feathers. The rooster screeched and flapped his wings, and the two animals darted in front of Melinda, causing her to stumble. The pie flipped out of her hands and landed upside down on the floor with a *splat*.

Jericho screeched to a halt and sniffed the apple filling. The critter must have realized it was too hot to eat, for he let out an ear-piercing howl and ducked under the table. Hector crowed raucously as he strutted around the room, and Isaiah stood howling.

"Ach!" Mama shouted. "Get those creatures out of my kitchen!"

Melinda didn't know whether to laugh or cry. The pie was ruined, and Hector could have gotten hurt, but the whole thing really was kind of funny. "You'd better get your dog," she told her brother. "After I clean up this mess, I'll take Hector outside and put him in the chicken coop."

"Better yet, I'll clean the floor, and you can take the rooster out now," Mama said sharply.

Melinda frowned. "It wasn't Hector's fault Jericho broke his chain and chased the poor bird."

Mama tapped her foot. "I don't care who was

at fault. We have one less pie now and a big mess to clean."

Melinda bent down and scooped Hector into her arms. Isaiah grabbed his dog by the collar, and they both hurried out the door.

"As much as I like animals," Melinda muttered, "I have no use for that mutt of yours. He's dumber than dirt."

"Is not," her brother retorted. "Why, I'll have you know that the roof of Jericho's mouth is really dark, which means he's a smart one."

"That's probably just an old wives' tale you heard somewhere."

"Maybe it's not. Why don't you see what the vet has to say about it?"

Melinda shook her head. "I'm not going to bother Dr. Franklin with something so silly."

"It's not silly, and it'll prove once and for all that Jericho's not *dumm*."

"I'll think about it," Melinda muttered. Didn't her little brother realize she had a lot more on her mind than finding out if the color of a dog's mouth meant it was smart or dumb?

"What happened in here?" Noah asked when he entered the kitchen and found his wife down on her knees with a sponge and a bucket of soapy water, scrubbing away at a sticky mess on the floor.

Faith looked up at him and groaned. "My mamm and Susie were here earlier, and we baked some pies. But now, thanks to Melinda's dumm *hinkel* and Isaiah's spirited *hund*, we have one less pie to share during the social after preaching service tomorrow."

Noah hung his hat on the nearest wall peg. "Do I want to know why one of the chickens was in the house?"

"Isaiah was coming inside, and when he opened the door, the chicken ran in with Jericho right behind him. They had quite a tussle, and then they got in front of Melinda, causing her to stumble and drop one of the pies on my clean kitchen floor."

Noah bit back a chuckle. He could only imagine the disastrous scene. With all the critters Melinda had running around, something silly always seemed to be happening at their house these days.

"Do you think what happened here was funny?" Faith asked, tipping her head back and staring up at him with a pinched expression.

"What makes you think that?"

"You're smiling."

"I am?"

She nodded. "I don't see anything funny about this mess or about losing that pie."

"Would you like me to bake the replacement pie?" he asked, kneeling beside Faith. "I can make one quick as a wink."

"I know you can, and if you're sure you've got the time, I'd appreciate you doing that for me."

Noah reached out and tweaked the end of her nose. "For you, *schee fraa*, I've always got the time."

She grunted. "I'm glad you think I'm your pretty wife, but I don't feel so pretty right now."

"To me, you'll always be pretty." Noah patted her arm and rose to his feet. "Say, where are those two kinner of ours anyway?"

"Isaiah's supposed to be tying up his dog, and I assume Melinda's putting Hector back in the chicken coop like I asked her to do." Faith's pale eyebrows drew together as she frowned. "Of course, she should have been back by now, so I wouldn't be surprised if she's camped out in the barn, fooling with one of her animals."

"If she's not back by the time I get the pie put in the oven, I'll go check on her," Noah said as he grabbed one of Faith's choring aprons and tied it around his waist. No point in getting flour all over his trousers. He was just glad his dad was over at the daadihaus and wasn't here to see him wearing Faith's apron or making a pie. Even though Pop had relaxed his attitude some on men working in the kitchen, he still had no understanding of Noah's desire to cook and bake.

But he sure enjoys the fruit of my labor, Noah thought as he turned toward the cupboard to get the necessary ingredients. *Fact is, since Mom died, Pop's become almost like a child.*

"How was your day?" Melinda asked when her stepfather entered the barn and found her kneeling in the straw beside the new baby goat. "Did you get everything done that you wanted to do?"

He nodded. "I worked the first half of the day at the tree farm; then I stopped by Swartz's Woodworking Shop around noon. After that, I ran some other errands."

"Did you see Gabe?"

"Sure did. He was working alone at the shop because his daed had to go to Seymour."

Melinda was tempted to ask if Gabe had mentioned her, but she thought better of it. If Papa Noah knew how much she cared for Gabe, he'd probably tease her the way he did Mama whenever she was in one of her silly moods.

Melinda stroked the goat behind its ears as she thought about how sweet Gabe had been to her on the way home from the last young people's gathering. He'd asked if she was cold, and when she said, "Jah, just a bit," he had draped his arm around her. Melinda could almost feel the way his long fingers had gently caressed her shoulders. Even now, thinking about it caused her to shiver.

"Are you cold?" Papa Noah asked as he grabbed a brush and started grooming one of their buggy horses.

She shook her head. "Just felt a little chill is all."

"Spring has been fairly warm so far, but it does cool off in the evenings," he commented.

"That's for certain sure."

"I heard that you and your mamm did some baking today with Susie and Grandma Stutzman."

"Did you also hear what happened to one of the pies?"

He nodded.

Melinda moved over to the horse's stall. "The pies turned out fine until Isaiah's dog caused me to trip and fall." She groaned. "Now we have one less pie."

"That's not true." He reached under his straw hat to scratch the side of his head. "I just came from the kitchen, where I helped your mamm bake another pie. I don't get to bake as often as I used to, what with having so many other things to do, so it was kind of nice to spend some time in the kitchen."

Melinda smiled. She wasn't sure if Papa Noah had really enjoyed making the pie or if he was merely trying to make her feel better. "Mind if I ask you something?" she asked.

"What's that?"

"What will happen if Grandpa Hertzler's memory loss gets any worse? Will he have to move into our side of the house?"

"Maybe so."

"I wish there was something we could do to

make him feel better."

Papa Noah's dark eyes clouded over. "We need to remember to pray for Grandpa and be there whenever he needs us."

"I agree."

"So, how's that little kid doing?" he asked, motioning to the baby goat. "Is she getting along all right?"

"I think so. I thought at first she might need me to bottle- feed her, but her mamm seems to be taking care of her now."

"Glad to hear it."

Melinda swatted at a bothersome fly. That was the only bad part about being in the barn— too many bugs that liked to buzz and bite. "Say, Papa Noah, I was wondering if—"

"What's that?"

"Do you think you might have time to build a few more animal cages so I can take care of more orphaned animals?"

"I'm not sure I'd have the time for that right now, but I'll bet Gabe Swartz would."

"Should I ask him?"

"Don't see why not." He winked at her. "After all, a fellow bitten by the love bug is sure to do most anything for his favorite girl."

Melinda's mouth dropped open. "You know about Gabe and me?"

"Of course. You can't fool an old man like me. I've seen the way you two look at each other."

"You're not old, Papa Noah." Melinda placed

her hand on his arm and gave it a gentle squeeze. "You don't even have any gray hairs on your head."

He pulled his fingers through the end of his beard. "I've got some here, though."

She leaned closer for a better look. "Well, maybe just a few. But I still think you look plenty young."

He chuckled. "You sound just like your mamm."

"Is that a bad thing?"

"Of course not. If you were to follow in your mamm's footsteps all the way through life, it would be a good thing."

Melinda felt the heat of a blush cover her cheeks. *If Papa Noah knew what Dr. Franklin had suggested I do, he might wonder if I was preparing to follow in the footsteps Mama took when she left the Amish faith many years ago. He'd probably think Dr. Franklin was a bad influence, and he might insist that I quit my job.*

Chapter 3

Melinda hurried through her kitchen chores, eager to get outside. She planned to check on the baby goat and its mother, see that Isaiah's dog was secured for the day, and make sure all the chickens were doing okay. After yesterday's close call with Hector, she didn't want to see a repeat performance, and she was sure her mother didn't, either. Mama hadn't been happy about the loss of that pie.

"I'm going over to Grandma Stutzman's to help her clean," Mama said as Melinda passed her in the downstairs hallway. "Your daed, Grandpa Hertzler, and Isaiah loaded the pies into the buggy and will drop them over there before they head to Ben and Mary King's place to pick up the benches for tomorrow's church service."

"I'm glad Grandpa's going with Papa Noah, because I'll be heading for work soon, and it wouldn't be good for him to be left home alone."

Mama popped a couple of her knuckles, a habit she'd had ever since Melinda could remember. "I thought it was just Mondays, Tuesdays, and Thursdays you helped out at the veterinary clinic."

"It was, but Dr. Franklin thought I could learn some new things if I spent more time there, so I may be working some Fridays and Saturdays, too."

Mama sighed. "Learn more of what, Melinda? I thought you were only hired to clean the cages and feed the animals."

"I—I was, but sometimes the doctor lets me do certain things—like give a dog its flea bath or hold on to a nervous cat while it's being examined." Melinda shrugged. "He says the *gedier* are calmer when I'm there."

"You have a way with animals. Even unruly ones like Hector."

Melinda was on the verge of defending the poor rooster and reminding her mother that the incident yesterday was Jericho's fault, but Mama grabbed her black purse off a wall peg and headed out the door. "See you this evening. Have a *gut* day."

"You have a good day, too."

Melinda stood in the doorway, watching her

mother head down the driveway on foot. Since Grandpa and Grandma Stutzman lived less than a mile away, Mama often chose to walk there instead of bothering with a horse and buggy.

Melinda smiled at the way her mother held her head high, with shoulders straight back and arms swinging in perfect rhythm with the strides of her long legs. Soon Mama began to yodel. "Oh-lee-ay-tee—oh-lee-ay-tee—oh-lee-ay-tee-oh!"

Melinda cupped her hands around her mouth and echoed, "Oh-lee-ay-tee—oh-lee-ay-tee—oh-lee-ay-tee-oh."

Mama lifted her hand in a backward wave, and Melinda shut the door. She needed to get busy and clean her room before she left for the clinic. If there was enough time, she would check on the animals in the barn.

For the next half hour, Melinda dusted, shook her oval braided throw rug, pulled the colorful crazy quilt up over the four-poster bed, and swept the hardwood floor. Just as she was finishing up, she noticed her writing tablet on the dresser, and it reminded her that she'd forgotten about the note she was supposed to leave Gabe inside the old birdhouse near the front of her folks' property. She grabbed a pen from the drawer and hurriedly scrawled a message.

Dear Gabe,
    I got your last letter, and I do plan
    on going to the young people's gathering

tomorrow night. I'm looking forward to a ride home in your buggy.

I've enclosed a picture I drew of the baby raccoon Ben King found in the woods behind his place the other day. He said the critter's mother was killed, so the poor thing needs a home. I told him I would keep her, since the coon seems to have a problem with her eyes and probably wouldn't survive on her own. I've named her Reba, and I can't wait for you to see her.

I look forward to seeing you at church on Sunday morning. After the common meal, maybe we can play a game of croquet with some of our friends. Until tomorrow. . .

Yours fawnly,
Melinda

Melinda slipped the note, along with the picture of the orphaned raccoon, into an envelope and hurried out of her room. She made a quick trip to the barn and was pleased to discover that the baby goat was sleeping peacefully beside its mother. The kid's bulging tummy let a relieved Melinda know it had recently eaten. Too many times she had bottle-fed some animal because it was orphaned or its mother wouldn't take care of it. Not that she minded playing nursemaid, but it was better for the animal if its mother fed it.

"Sleep well, and I'll check on you both when I get home from work this evening," she murmured as she stroked the mother goat behind its ear.

Melinda left the goats and led Jenny, her favorite buggy horse, out of the barn then hitched her to one of their open buggies. Sometimes she wished they could drive the box-shaped, closed-in buggies most other Amish communities used, but when she and Mama first moved to Webster County, Mama had explained that the community she belonged to was more conservative than most. One of the things they did that separated them from other Amish was to drive only open buggies.

"These buggies aren't so bad in warmer weather," Melinda murmured, "but in the wintertime, it can sure get cold." She gave Jenny a quick pat, climbed into the driver's seat, and picked up the reins.

At the end of the driveway, Melinda saw the familiar gray birdhouse and halted the horse. "Just a few more minutes, Jenny, and then we'll be on our way."

Melinda hopped down and lifted the removable roof from the birdhouse. She was pleased to see that no birds had claimed it as their new home. She and Gabe had been sending each other messages this way since they'd started courting, and so far, the birds seemed to know it was off-limits.

She slipped the note inside and replaced the roof. "I just hope Gabe comes by before tomorrow and picks it up."

Melinda was about to walk away when she

caught sight of a small bird in some tall grass, chirping and furiously flapping its wings. She bent for a closer look and realized it was a fledgling blackbird that apparently couldn't fly well yet.

"I can't leave you here. Some big cat or hawk might come along and make you its meal." Gently Melinda picked up the tiny bird and set him on a low branch of a nearby tree. "There you go; be safe." She smiled, content with the knowledge that she'd helped another one of God's creatures, and hurried away.

Gabe shielded his eyes from the glare of the sun and pulled his buggy to the side of the road by the Hertzlers' driveway. *I sure hope there's a note from Melinda today.*

He hopped down and lifted the lid of the weathered birdhouse. To his surprise, a few blades of grass and a piece of string lay on top of an envelope. "Some bird must have decided to make a nest here," Gabe muttered. He reached inside, pulled out the grass and string, and tossed them on the ground. "That ought to discourage those silly birds from claiming this as their new home."

Unexpectedly, a sparrow swooped down, just missing Gabe's head. He ducked. "Hey, cut that out! This is Melinda's and my message box. Go find someplace else to build your nest."

Gabe stuck his hand inside the birdhouse

and retrieved Melinda's note. As soon as he had replaced the lid, he bent down, grabbed a small rock, and plugged the opening in the front. "That should keep you birds out of there."

As Gabe climbed into his buggy, he decided that, in all fairness to the birds, it wasn't right to shoo them out of a birdhouse that was built for them. He would add a separate compartment to the birdhouse he was making for Noah to give Melinda on her birthday. Then even if the birds decided to make it their home, he and Melinda would still have their secret place to hide messages—one without a hole in the front.

Gabe headed down Highway C toward Seymour, letting the horse lead while he read Melinda's note. He was pleased to discover that she planned to be at the young people's gathering on Sunday night and was looking forward to him taking her home afterward.

"I like a woman who knows what she wants," he said with a chuckle. "Especially if it's me she's wanting." Melinda's eagerness to be with Gabe made him believe she might say yes if he were to propose marriage. He just needed to find the right time and the courage to do it.

He studied the pencil drawing Melinda had made of the baby raccoon. It certainly looked like a coon, but he was concerned about her making a pet out of a wild animal. What if the critter bit or scratched her real bad? She could end up with rabies or something!

"That woman doesn't think straight when it comes to the animals she takes in," he mumbled. "She would cozy up to a bull snake if she thought it needed a friend. I think I'd better have a talk with Melinda and let her know I'm concerned."

When Susie stepped into the kitchen, she was surprised to see Faith sitting at the table having a cup of tea with their mother. "Wie geht's, Faith?" Susie asked. "I didn't know you were here."

Faith smiled. "I'm doing fine. I came over to help Mama clean house today."

"I appreciate it, too," Mama said with a nod. She took a sip from her cup. "Of course, we're not getting much done sitting here drinking tea."

"Well, you deserve a little break," Susie said as she grabbed her lunch pail off the counter and flipped it open so she could begin making her lunch. "I'd help with the cleaning if I didn't have to work at Kaulp's General Store today."

"If it makes you feel any better, Melinda won't be helping us, either, because she's working for the vet today."

"She's been working there a lot lately, jah?" Mama asked.

"A little too much, if you ask me." Faith's voice held a note of irritation, making Susie wonder if her big sister disapproved of her daughter working for the English vet.

"Why do you say that?"

Susie's ears perked up. That was something she'd like to know herself. She glanced discreetly over her shoulder and waited for Faith's response.

"All Melinda talks about anymore is either the critters she's caring for at home or the ones she helps Dr. Franklin with at his clinic." Faith set her cup down and popped a couple of knuckles, causing Susie to cringe. "Gabe Swartz and Melinda are courting, yet she spends more time with those silly animals than she does him." Faith popped a couple more knuckles. "Wouldn't you think she would want to concentrate on honing her cooking, sewing, and baking skills so she'll be ready for marriage, rather than trying to play *dokder* to a bunch of smelly creatures?"

"If I had a boyfriend, I sure wouldn't be thinking about any dumm old animals or trying to play doctor," Susie put in as she slathered two pieces of bread with butter.

"Do I detect a note of envy in your voice, daughter?"

Susie turned to face her mother. "I don't begrudge Melinda having a boyfriend; she has the right. I just wish I was being courted by someone, that's all."

"It will happen in due time," Faith put in. "Just try to be patient and wait on the Lord to bring the right fellow along."

Susie shrugged and turned back to her sandwich making. At the rate things were going,

Melinda would be married with a houseful of kinner before Susie had a boyfriend. It didn't seem fair that everything always seemed to go Melinda's way. It wasn't fair at all.

Chapter 4

On Sunday morning when Melinda and her family arrived at Grandma and Grandpa Stutzman's for church, Melinda spotted Susie on the wooden two-seater swing hanging from the rafters under the Stutzmans' front porch. Papa Noah and Isaiah headed to the barn to put the horse inside, and Mama and Grandpa Hertzler went into the house right away. Melinda stopped at the swing to speak with Susie.

Susie patted the seat beside her. "Why don't you sit with me awhile before everyone else shows up?"

"Don't mind if I do." Melinda sat down and started pumping her legs to get the swing moving again. The day was warmer than most April mornings had been so far, and the breeze from the motion of the swing felt nice.

Susie glanced over at Melinda with a puckered brow. "I see you've got dark circles under your eyes. How come?"

"I stayed up late last night caring for my animals."

"Which ones?"

"I've only got a couple I'm taking care of right now. One's a baby goat, and I've been checking to be sure the mother goat keeps feeding her little one." Melinda tapped her finger against her chin. "I also helped Papa Noah groom the horses and spent some time with my raccoon because she was acting kind of peculiar."

Susie's eyebrows shot up. "What coon? I didn't know you had a coon."

"I got her from Ben King. She's an orphan and nearly blind."

"That's too bad."

"At first, Reba wouldn't eat and kept bumping into the side of her cage. After I sat with her awhile, she finally ate a little and seemed much calmer."

Susie groaned. "I can't believe you'd lose sleep over some dumm critter or that you'd bother to name a wild animal."

"Reba's not dumb. Do you think your cat's dumb?"

"Of course not. Daisy's a good mouser. She also keeps me company and likes to cuddle."

"Well, there you go."

"Are you still planning to go to the young people's gathering at the Hiltys' place tonight?" Susie asked.

Melinda was thankful for the change in topic. She and Susie seemed to be arguing a lot lately—especially whenever they talked about Melinda's love for animals.

"Of course. I wouldn't miss it." Melinda smiled. "Gabe's giving me a ride home again. He said so in the note he left in our birdhouse the other day."

"You're sure the lucky one." Susie released a gusty sigh. "I wish I had the promise of a ride home with some cute fellow tonight."

Melinda stopped swinging and reached over to pat Susie's hand. "Your time will come. Just wait and see."

"Jah, well, I'm twenty years old. Many Amish women my age are married by now. I'll probably end up *en alt maedel*. Could be I'll spend the rest of my days working at Kaulp's and never have a husband or family of my own."

"You won't be an old maid, and I doubt you'll be working at Kaulp's General Store the rest of your life. One of these days you'll—"

Susie jumped up, jostling Melinda and nearly tossing her out of the swing. "Let's not talk about this anymore. Some more buggies have pulled into the driveway, and one of them belongs to Bishop Frey. Church will be starting soon, so we'd better get inside."

"You go on," Melinda said. "I'm going to sit here awhile and enjoy the fresh air. Once we're all in the house, it will be hot and stuffy."

"Suit yourself." Susie went in the front door, and Melinda resumed her swinging.

A few minutes later, John Frey and his wife, Margaret, stepped onto the porch. The bishop walked with a limp these days and was beginning to show his age, but he could still preach God's Word and lead the people. Melinda figured he would continue as bishop for several more years before he died.

"Guder mariye," Margaret said, as they approached Melinda.

"Good morning," she answered with a nod.

"Are you planning to be baptized and join the church soon?" the bishop asked.

Melinda could hardly believe the man had posed such a question. Was Bishop John's memory failing him the way Grandpa Hertzler's seemed to be? It was a shame to witness older folks forgetting so many things.

"I got baptized last year, Bishop John," she said. "It was soon after my eighteenth birthday."

The wrinkles in the bishop's forehead deepened, and he gave his long gray beard a couple of sharp pulls. Then he narrowed his eyes and stared at Melinda so hard she began to squirm. "Hmm. Well, jah, that's right, you were one of those I baptized last year."

Melinda realized the man's memory wasn't

going after all. His problem was probably failing eyesight. She had felt bad when her mother began to lose her close-up vision and started wearing reading glasses, but Mama had laughed and said, "It's okay. That's what comes with getting older."

Margaret smiled and adjusted her own metal-framed glasses. Then she clasped her husband's arm and said, "Shall we go inside now, John? The service will be starting soon."

The bishop yawned noisily. "Jah, guess we'd better."

As soon as John and Margaret stepped into the house, Melinda left the swing and headed straight for the barn. If she hurried, there would be time to see the kittens Susie's cat had given birth to a few weeks ago.

Inside the barn, Melinda took a seat on a bale of straw to watch Daisy feed her six squirming babies. *All baby animals are cute. Some more than others, but I enjoy each one,* she thought dreamily.

She drew in a deep breath, relishing the sweet smell of fresh hay. A horse whinnied from one of the stalls nearby, and a pigeon cooed from the loft overhead. *It's so peaceful here. Next to being in the woods, this is my favorite place to sit and relax.*

Sometime later, Melinda left the barn, but as soon as she closed the door, she realized that the preaching service had already begun. The chantlike voices of the people singing inside her grandparents' house filtered through the open windows. She hurried in through the back door and tiptoed down the hall. Backless wooden benches filled the large living room and spilled over into the parlor. The rooms were separated by a removable wall that was taken out whenever preaching services were held in this home.

As Melinda slipped quietly into the main room, a few people looked up from their hymnbooks and glanced her way. Most, however, stayed focused on the song they were singing.

Susie motioned Melinda over to the bench where she sat. There was an empty spot on the end, and Melinda figured her aunt had been saving it for her.

"Where have you been?" Susie whispered when Melinda took a seat.

"Out in the barn with Daisy and her brood. They're sure cute little things."

Susie shook her head.

Melinda clutched the folds in her dress. *She doesn't understand. Sometimes I wonder how Susie and I can be such good friends when we don't think alike on the subject of animals.*

She glanced across the room at the men and boys who were seated opposite them. Gabe sat beside his friend Aaron, and she caught him staring at her. He'd probably seen her sneak into the room, and she wondered if he thought she was irresponsible for being late. Would he say something about it later? More than likely, she would get a lecture from Mama on the subject of tardiness. She hoped she wouldn't get one from Gabe, too.

Gabe's friendly smile and quick wink caused Melinda's heart to flutter. It was enough to let her know he wasn't judging her. She shivered at the anticipation of spending time with him that evening.

Melinda's thoughts spun faster than a windmill blade whirling in a gale. Maybe if she could think of the right way to say it, she would open her heart and tell Gabe what Dr. Franklin had suggested she do. It would be good to tell someone what had been weighing so heavily on her mind these past few weeks.

A nudge to the ribs brought Melinda's thoughts to a halt. "You're not paying attention," Susie whispered.

"I am so."

Susie leaned closer. "You're paying attention to Gabe, but that's about all."

Melinda sat up straight and folded her hands. If her aunt had noticed her preoccupation with Gabe, others might have, as well. She was thankful Mama sat three rows ahead. Maybe she hadn't noticed Melinda's late arrival.

Melinda turned her attention to the front of the room, where Preacher Kaulp had begun the first sermon of the day. He spoke from the book of Proverbs on the subject of wisdom.

Wisdom is what I need, Melinda thought. *Wisdom to know if I should do as Dr. Franklin suggested and separate myself from those I love in order to become a vet so I can properly care for sick and injured animals.*

She closed her eyes. *Dear Lord, You know that Mama and Papa Noah already think I spend too much time with my animal friends. If they knew what Dr. Franklin wanted me to do, they would probably be upset with him. Oh, Lord, what should I do?*

❦

As soon as church was over and the women had begun serving the men their meal, Faith decided it was time to have a little talk with her daughter. She found Melinda on the porch with an empty platter in her hands. Apparently she'd just come from the barn where the men were eating.

"Hi, Mama," Melinda said with a smile. "I'm just heading back to the kitchen to get some more sandwiches."

"Before you do that, I'd like to speak with you a minute." Faith stepped in front of Melinda and blocked the door to the house.

Melinda's cheeks flamed as she stared down at her shoes. "Is it about me being late to church this morning?"

"Jah. This isn't the first time you've been late, either."

"I know." Melinda lifted her gaze. "I went to the barn to see Daisy's *busslin*, and I lost track of time."

Faith grunted. "I can't believe you would get so involved with a batch of kittens that you'd forget to come inside for church."

The color in Melinda's cheeks deepened. "Well, I—"

"You need to get your priorities straight, Melinda. Being in church is more important than spending time with some smelly animals."

"Daisy's kittens aren't smelly, Mama. They're sweet and soft as a downy chick."

"I don't care how sweet or soft they are. You should have been in church on time this morning."

"I'll try harder from now on."

Faith tapped her foot against the faded porch boards. "You're not a little girl anymore, Melinda. You need to start acting your age."

Melinda nodded.

Faith stepped aside, hoping she'd been able to get through to Melinda. This business of her fooling around with animals when she should be facing her responsibilities was getting old. "You'd better get those sandwiches now, or you'll likely get a lecture from the menfolk when you return to the barn."

"Okay, Mama." Melinda offered Faith a brief smile then hurried inside.

As Faith turned toward the porch steps, she spotted her friend Barbara heading her way with a coffeepot in her hands.

"You don't look so happy," Barbara said when she stepped onto the porch. "Is something wrong?"

Faith nodded. "I think I've failed as a *mudder*."

Barbara's eyebrows furrowed. "Ach, Faith, what would make you think that?"

"I've tried my best to raise Melinda so she'll become a mature, responsible woman, but apparently all I've taught her has fallen on deaf ears." Faith shrugged. "Either that, or I made some huge mistakes with Melinda somewhere along the line."

Barbara patted Faith's arm. "I don't think you made any mistakes. From what I've observed, both you and Noah have done a fine job raising your two kinner."

"Then how come Melinda's priorities are so messed up? And how come she's late to church so often these days?"

Barbara offered Faith a look of sympathy. "I noticed that she came in after the service had already begun, but I figured she'd been using the bathroom."

Faith shook her head. "She went to the barn."

"Why'd she go there?"

"To see a batch of busslin, of all things." Faith grimaced. "I have nothing against animals, mind you, but Melinda is consumed with them. It's getting so bad I'm beginning to think we live at the zoo."

Barbara gave Faith's arm another pat. "Is it really that bad?"

"Jah, it is. You should have seen the mess my kitchen was in yesterday after Melinda's chicken got into the house, with Isaiah's dog right on the rooster's tail feathers. Melinda ended up tripping over the dog and dropping a pie all over my clean floor."

Barbara's lips twitched, but then her face sobered. "No one ever said it would be easy to be a parent. Not even when our kinner are on the verge of leaving the nest."

"Puh!" Faith said with a wave of her hand. "At the rate Melinda's going, she'll be old and gray before she's ready to leave home and make a life of her own. For that matter, if she doesn't grow up and start acting more responsible, it's not likely she'll ever find a man who'll want to marry her."

"What about Gabe Swartz? Aren't the two of them courting?"

"Jah, but I'm not sure how serious they have become."

Barbara opened her mouth, but she closed it again.

Faith leaned closer to Barbara. "Do you know something I don't know?"

"No, not really. It's just that my boy Aaron's a good friend of Gabe's, and he's mentioned a couple of times how smitten Gabe is with Melinda."

"Well, if Gabe's really interested in my daughter, then he'd better be prepared to put up with all her critters." Faith grunted. "Either that, or he'll have to do something to make Melinda see where her priorities need to be."

Barbara lifted the coffeepot in her hands. "Let me put this in the kitchen, and then we can take a little walk. I think you need to talk about this some more."

Gabe was glad when the church service was over so he could be outside. Not that he hadn't enjoyed the sermons or time of singing, for he'd listened intently to the verse Bishop Frey had quoted near the end of his lengthy sermon. It was Proverbs 18:22: "Whoso findeth a wife findeth a good thing, and obtaineth favour of the Lord."

Those words made Gabe even more determined to make Melinda his wife, and if everything went well tonight, he might get up the nerve to propose. If Melinda accepted, he hoped they could be married sometime this fall.

From Gabe's vantage point under the shade of a walnut tree, he'd seen Melinda on the front porch awhile ago, talking to her mother, but now Faith was speaking to Barbara Hilty.

I wonder if Faith chewed out her daughter for being late to church. Melinda really ought to try harder to be on time to our services.

Gabe flopped onto the grass and leaned against the trunk of the tree. He was nearly asleep when he heard female voices nearby.

His eyes popped open, and he spotted Faith

and Barbara heading his way.

"I wish I knew what to do about my daughter," Faith said.

Gabe's ears perked up. He wasn't trying to eavesdrop, but he was curious to hear what Melinda's mother was saying.

"Sometimes, raising teenagers can be just as hard as when they were kinner," Barbara said. "I guess we'll be trying to steer them in the right direction until they get married and leave home."

"Jah," Faith agreed. "I just need to keep praying for Melinda and try to give her direction without being too pushy."

"I agree," Barbara said. "You know, my Aaron claims he's never getting married. It makes me wonder if he plans to stick around home and be told what to do for the rest of his life."

As the two women strolled past the tree where Gabe sat, he yanked his straw hat down over his eyes, plucked up a blade of grass, and stuck it between his teeth, hoping to look inconspicuous. Faith and Barbara continued on their way, apparently unaware of his presence.

Gabe drew in a deep breath and said a prayer for himself and Melinda. Someday, Lord willing, they would have their own kinner to worry about.

Chapter 5

It's nice of you to drive us to the young people's gathering, but I don't see why we couldn't have walked to the Hiltys' place. It isn't that far," Melinda said to Grandpa Stutzman as she settled herself on the buggy seat between him and Susie.

He grunted. "I won't have my youngest daughter or my granddaughter out walking in the dark no matter how close we live to the Hiltys."

Melinda glanced over at her aunt to gauge her reaction. Susie shrugged.

"I'll be back to pick you both up around ten," Grandpa said with a nod.

"Oh, Melinda won't be needing a ride," Susie blurted out. "She's already been promised one from—"

Melinda poked Susie on the arm. "Hush."

"Uh—what I meant to say was, I'll be the only one needing a ride home tonight."

"How do you know some young fellow won't be asking to bring you home?" Grandpa's bushy gray eyebrows lifted clear into his hairline. "Huh?"

Susie stared at her hands. "I don't know who it would be."

Melinda's heart went out to her aunt. It wasn't right that a woman Susie's age didn't have a steady boyfriend. Especially when she was so kind and pretty.

"How about I come by a little later than ten?" Grandpa asked, smiling at his daughter. "Just in case all the young men are too shy to ask and you find yourself without a ride."

Susie gave a quick nod. "I guess that would be all right."

As much as Melinda wanted to spend time alone with Gabe, she couldn't stand the thought of Susie being picked up by her father. It was bad enough he had insisted on driving them here. "If Susie doesn't get asked, Gabe and I will bring her home."

Grandpa chuckled. "Gabe, is it? I might have known."

Melinda covered her mouth with the palm of her hand. "I—I meant to say, Susie can ride with me and my date."

"I know," Grandpa said with a grin. "And if

Susie's okay with that, it's fine by me."

Susie shook her head. "I don't think it's a good idea."

"Why not?" Melinda wondered what her aunt could be thinking.

"I'm not going to be a fifth wheel on the buggy," Susie said with a shake of her head.

"It'll be fine. We'll drop you off first; then Gabe can take me home."

Susie sighed but finally nodded. "Jah, okay."

A short while later, they pulled into the Hiltys' driveway. Grandpa drove past the house and the harness shop, stopping the buggy near the barn. "Here you go. I hope you both have yourselves a real good time."

"Thanks, Papa." Susie hopped out of the buggy and sprinted toward the barn, where peals of laughter and chattering voices drifted on the night air.

Melinda turned to face her grandfather. "She'll be fine, Grandpa. You'll see."

"I know, but it sure would be nice if she found herself a beau." He picked up the reins. "Now go have some fun, and be sure to tell Gabe Swartz I said he's gettin' one fine girl."

Melinda's face warmed, and she leaned over to kiss her grandfather's wrinkled cheek. "I love you, Grandpa."

"That goes double for me."

She patted his arm then climbed out of the buggy. "See you soon."

"Jah." Grandpa Stutzman backed the horse up and headed down the driveway.

As Melinda hurried to the barn, the rhythm of her heartbeat kept time with her footsteps. She could hardly wait to see Gabe.

Gabe stood at the refreshment table, about to ladle some punch into a paper cup for Melinda, whom he'd spotted on the other side of the barn.

"Gettin' some sweets for your sweetie, are you?" Gabe's friend Aaron teased as he stepped up beside Gabe.

"What do you think?"

"I think you'd get down on your hands and knees and lap water like a dog if Melinda asked you to."

Gabe grunted and rubbed the side of his nose. "Would not. Besides, she's already got plenty of pets."

"Jah, well, she might want one more."

"Are you trying to goad me into an argument this evening?"

Aaron chuckled. "Who me? Never!"

"Jah, right." Gabe grabbed two peanut butter cookies, a handful of pretzels, and a wedge of cheese then piled them on a paper plate.

"Are you taking Melinda home tonight?"

"What do you think?"

"You sure do like to answer my questions

with a question." Aaron bumped Gabe's arm, nearly knocking the plate out of his hands.

"Hey, watch it!"

"Sorry."

"Are you planning to offer anyone a ride home?" Gabe asked, hoping to get Aaron out of his teasing mode.

"No way! I'm not ready to get tied down yet."

"Who said anything about getting tied down? You can take a girl home without proposing marriage, you know." Gabe wasn't about to tell his friend that a marriage proposal was in his plans for the night. If he did spill the beans, he was sure Aaron would only taunt him that much more.

Aaron snatched one of Gabe's cookies and bit into it. "That might be true, but as soon as you give some female a ride in your buggy, she starts thinking you want to court her. After that, the next thing on her mind is marriage." He shook his head. "I'm not ready for that. All I want is to own my daed's business."

Gabe lifted his eyebrows. "Is Paul planning to quit working at the harness shop?"

"Not yet, but someday he'll want to retire. When that time comes, I'll be ready to take it over. My real daed wanted me to have the shop he started, you know."

Gabe nodded. "I'm sure Paul does, too."

"Maybe so. Maybe not."

Gabe moved away from the table, and Aaron followed. "To tell you the truth, I think my daed still sees me as a little kid who doesn't know nearly as much as him about making things. It isn't easy being the youngest in the family, with four sisters who are all married and out on their own."

"What's that got to do with anything?" Aaron asked.

"Ever since I was little, Pap, Mom, and even my sisters have treated me like a *boppli*. I believe my daed likes being in charge of everything and telling me what to do."

"I'm not really treated like a baby, but my stepdad sure likes to order me around. The truth is I think our relationship was better when I was a boy."

"I guess in the eyes of our parents we'll never be grown up," Gabe said with a frown.

"You're probably right." Aaron bit off the end of one fingernail and spit it on the straw-covered floor.

Gabe wrinkled his nose. "That was so nasty. Where are your manners, anyhow?"

Aaron lowered his gaze and looked kind of sheepish. "Sorry. Nail biting's a bad habit that I probably should break. Least that's what my mamm thinks."

"So why don't you quit?"

"Maybe I will someday. . .when I have a good enough reason to."

"You mean when you find an *aldi*?"

Aaron shook his head vigorously. "No way! I don't need a girlfriend complicating my life."

"Well, Melinda's waiting for me, so I'd better get over there with this food," Gabe said, deciding it was time to move on.

Aaron thumped Gabe on the back a few times. "You do that, you lovesick *hundli*."

Gabe shrugged his friend's hand away. "I'm not a lovesick puppy."

"Okay then, you're a lovesick man."

Gabe swallowed a retort and headed across the room. Aaron was only funning with him, and if the tables were turned, he'd probably do the same. Right now, though, he had other things on his mind.

For the next couple of hours, Gabe relaxed and enjoyed visiting, playing games, and eating with the other young people. Shortly before things wound down, Melinda was called on to lead the group in some singing and yodeling. Her face turned red, but after some coaxing from Gabe and a few other friends, she finally agreed. While several others in attendance could yodel fairly well, nobody did it as expertly as Melinda.

Maybe that's because her mother used to be a professional yodeler, Gabe thought as he sat on a bale of straw and watched Melinda in action. She cupped her hands around her mouth as she belted out, "Oddle-lay—oddle-lay—oddle-lay—dee-tee. My mama was an old cowhand, and she taught me how to yodel before I could stand—yo-le-tee—yo-le-tee—hi-ho!"

Gabe glanced around the room and saw that

all eyes were trained on his girlfriend. He figured he was the luckiest man there and that the other fellows must surely be envious.

Susie was glad when the singing was over. Watching Melinda show off her yodeling skills was enough to make her feel downright sick. She left the table where she'd been sitting and moved over to the bowl of punch sitting across the room. *Funny Melinda. Cute Melinda. Talented Melinda. No wonder Melinda has a boyfriend, and no one's interested in me. I can't yodel worth a hill of beans, and I'm not nearly as pretty as Melinda. Truth be told, I'll probably be an old maid until the day I die.*

She grabbed a paper cup and was about to ladle some punch into it when someone bumped her arm.

"Oops. Sorry about that. I hope you didn't get any punch on yourself."

Susie turned at the sound of a deep male voice and nearly dropped her cup when she saw a pair of dark brown eyes staring down at her.

The tall, blond-haired Amish man grinned, revealing two large dimples in his cheeks. "What's the matter? Is there a cat around here somewhere?"

"Huh?"

"Well, you weren't saying anything, so I

figured maybe some old cat had stolen your tongue."

Susie's face heated with embarrassment.

"I'll bet you don't remember me, do you?" the young man asked as he folded his arms and continued to smile at her.

Susie swallowed a couple of times, realizing how dry her throat had suddenly become. "Jonas Byler?"

He nodded. "I'd just graduated from the eighth grade when I went to Montana to work for my uncle at his log furniture shop."

Susie ladled herself some punch and swallowed some down so she could speak. "You've changed a lot since then."

He gave a slow nod. "So have you."

Susie's cheeks burned hot under his scrutiny. Was Jonas staring at her in such a strange way because he thought she was homely as a horny toad? Of course, Susie didn't really think she was homely, just not real pretty and full of exuberance, the way Melinda was.

She took another swallow of punch. "Have you moved back to Webster County?"

Jonas shook his head. "Just came for a visit with my folks. They've come to Montana several times to see me, but this is the first time I've been home since I left ten years ago."

"Uh-huh." Susie didn't know why she felt so tongue-tied in Jonas's presence. It wasn't like she might have a chance with him or anything. Beside the fact that he was five years older than she, he would be going back to Montana again, and then it could be several more years before she would see him. He probably had a girlfriend waiting for him back in Montana, and by this time next year, he might even be married. So there was no good reason for her to be looking at him, wishing for something that wasn't going to happen. What she needed to do was grab a few cookies from the refreshment table, get back to her table, and forget she'd even spoken to Jonas Byler with the big brown eyes.

"I'll see you around," Jonas said, as he turned away from Susie.

Susie reached out a shaky hand and snatched a cookie. Then she turned and watched Jonas make his way across the room, where he took a seat beside Aaron Zook.

I wish he wasn't going back to Montana, she thought ruefully. *But then, even if he were staying here, he would never be interested in someone like me.*

She glanced over at Melinda, who sat next to Gabe, and a pang of jealousy sliced through her as sharp as a knife. Dropping the cookie back to the platter, she turned away. Her appetite was gone.

As Melinda sat beside Gabe in his open buggy, she closed her eyes and breathed in the sweet perfume given off by the trees and flowers bursting with spring buds. The temperature was just right this evening, and the full moon illuminated the road ahead to light their way.

"Are you sleeping?" Gabe asked.

She opened her eyes and smiled at him. "Just enjoying the fresh air and peaceful ride."

"It is a nice evening." He draped his arm across her shoulders, bringing them so close she could smell the pine-scented soap he must have used when he'd gotten ready for the gathering tonight. "Are you warm enough?"

"I'm fine."

They rode in silence for a while, with the only sounds being the steady *clip-clop* of the horse's hooves and an occasional *hoo-hoot* of an owl. Melinda thought about how things had gone this evening. Susie had hung around some of the other young women her age most of the evening, while Gabe stuck close to Melinda. Poor Susie never did pair off with any of the young men in attendance. Even during the time of yodeling Melinda had led and the singing of some lively songs like "Mockingbird Hill" and "Yellow Rose of Texas," Susie had appeared glum. "I Never Will Marry" seemed more like her song. Aaron's, too, for that matter, for he hadn't paired off with anyone, either.

When it came time for them to leave, Susie had informed Melinda that she'd found a ride home with Kathy and Rebecca Yoder. Melinda didn't argue, knowing once Susie made up her mind about something, she wasn't likely to budge. Besides, Melinda really did want to be alone with Gabe during the ride home.

"Say, Gabe, I was wondering if you might have the time to build me a couple more cages for my animals," she asked suddenly.

"I'd like to, Melinda, but right now Pap and I are really busy in the shop." He smiled. "I will try to squeeze it in when I have some free time, though."

"*Danki.* I'd appreciate that."

"Do you ever think about your real daed or find yourself wishing you and your mamm had stayed in the English world?"

Gabe's unexpected question startled Melinda, and she sat up straight. Did he have an inkling of what she was thinking about doing? Had Gabe spoken with Dr. Franklin recently? Could the vet have mentioned his suggestion that Melinda think about becoming a veterinarian? Surely he wouldn't have said anything, since she'd asked him not to mention the idea to anyone until she'd told her folks what she was thinking of doing.

"What would make you ask me such a question?" she asked, looking at Gabe out of the corner of her eye.

"If there's even a chance you might want to return to the English way of life, I feel I have the right to know."

Melinda drew in a quick breath. Since Gabe

had brought up the subject, maybe now was the time to discuss Dr. Franklin's idea. She squeezed her eyes shut, searching for just the right words, and when she opened them again, she was shocked to see a man standing in the middle of the road up ahead. He had his back to them, but she could tell by his dark clothes and straw hat that he was Amish. "Gabe, look out!" she hollered.

He pulled sharply on the reins. "Whoa there! Steady boy."

When the horse stopped, Gabe grabbed a flashlight from under the seat, and he and Melinda jumped down from the buggy.

The man in the road turned around, and Melinda's mouth fell open. "Grandpa Hertzler?"

Grandpa didn't answer. He stood staring at Melinda as though she were a complete stranger.

"He looks confused, like he doesn't know where he is," Gabe whispered.

Melinda nodded. "We've got to get him home."

"Levi, it's Gabe and Melinda," Gabe said, gently taking hold of Grandpa's arm.

Grandpa studied him a few seconds then turned to face Melinda. Finally, a look of recognition crossed his face. "What are you doin' out here, girl?"

"Gabe was giving me a ride home from the young people's gathering. We stopped the buggy when we saw you in the middle of the road."

She grabbed his other arm. "Don't you know how dangerous it is to be out walking after dark? Especially dressed in clothes that aren't brightly colored."

The confusion Melinda saw on her grandfather's face made her heart ache. He'd obviously wandered off their property and onto the road. She was sure Mama and Papa Noah had no idea where he was.

"Let's get into the buggy, and I'll drive you both home," Gabe said.

Melinda was relieved when her grandfather went willingly, but she could see by the frown on Gabe's face that he wasn't happy when Grandpa took a seat next to him, which left Melinda sitting on the outside edge.

She reached for Grandpa's hand and gave it a gentle squeeze. This buggy ride might not have been the romantic one she had hoped for, but at least Grandpa was safe. Maybe she and Gabe would have another chance to be alone soon. Maybe by then she would be better prepared to discuss her future with him.

Chapter 6

Good morning," Dr. Franklin said when Melinda stepped into the veterinary clinic one Monday morning a few weeks later. "How are you on this fine sunny day?"

"I'm fine. How are things going here?"

The middle-aged man's blue eyes twinkled. "I got a squirrel in this morning with an injured foot."

Melinda moved quickly to the counter where he stood. "How bad is it hurt? Will it be okay? What are you planning to do with it once you've doctored its foot?"

The doctor chuckled. "One question at a time, please."

"Sorry. I tend to be eager when it comes to helping suffering animals."

"I know you do, but your caring attitude is what makes you so special." He smiled as he held up one finger. "Now to answer your first question: the wound isn't real deep."

"That's good to hear. Do you know how the injury happened?"

He nodded. "I believe the squirrel had its foot stepped on."

She frowned. "Who would do something that mean?"

"I don't think it was done on purpose." Dr. Franklin reached up to scratch the side of his head, where several streaks of gray showed through his closely cropped brown hair. "Tommy Curtis brought the critter in, saying he'd found it lying beside a maple tree near his school. I have a hunch Tommy may have accidentally stepped on the squirrel."

"Will you keep it here until it's better?" she asked.

He grinned. "I thought maybe you'd like to take it home until it's ready to be set free, which should only be a few days from now, I'm guessing."

Melinda nodded eagerly. "I don't have many spare cages right now, but I did find an old one at a yard sale awhile back. I suppose I could keep him in that until his foot's healed."

"That's a good idea. I'll give you some ointment to put on the wound, and you can take the squirrel home with you this evening."

Melinda smiled as she donned her work apron. It felt good to know the doctor trusted her enough to care for the squirrel. Of course, if the animal's injuries were serious, she was sure Dr. Franklin would keep it at the clinic. "Guess I'd better get busy with the cleaning," she said.

"Before you get started, I'd like to ask you a question," Dr. Franklin said, stepping around the front of the counter.

"What is it?"

"I was wondering if you've had a chance to think over the things we talked about a few weeks ago, concerning you becoming a vet."

She nodded. "I have thought about it, but—"

"Have you looked at the brochures I gave you on the school of veterinary medicine I attended in New Jersey?"

"I did read through the information, and I've been thinking a lot about it." Melinda pursed her lips. She had hidden the brochures under her mattress so her mother wouldn't see them, since she wasn't ready to talk to her folks about this yet. "The thought of becoming a vet is appealing," she admitted. "But it would mean getting a college education, and that doesn't fall in line with our Amish beliefs."

The doctor's eyebrows drew together. "I've lived in Seymour for several years and know most of the Amish in the area. Yet I still don't understand all their ways."

"We believe the Bible instructs us to be separate

from the world," she explained. "We're not against basic education and learning from others, but our leaders feel that progressive education could lead to worldliness."

He took a step toward her. "So you're saying you've decided not to pursue a career in veterinary medicine?"

"No, that's not what I'm saying." Melinda swallowed hard. Just thinking about leaving home made her feel jittery, and talking about it with Dr. Franklin behind her parents' backs didn't seem right. "There's so much to be considered, and I haven't been able to think it all through. I haven't said anything to my folks about this yet, so I'd appreciate it if you didn't mention this to anyone."

"I understand. It's a big decision, so take your time, Melinda. I promise I won't say a word to anyone until you've made up your mind and have told your family what you plan to do."

She nodded. "When I do finally decide, I'll let you know."

Noah opened the door of Swartz's Woodworking Shop, and the odor of freshly sanded wood tickled his nose, causing him to sneeze. He was glad the work he did at Hank's Christmas Tree Farm didn't require sanding. He stepped into the shop and discovered Gabe sanding the tops of some kitchen cabinets.

"Wie geht's?" Noah asked.

"I'm doing all right. How about you?"

"Getting along fairly well." Noah smiled. "I was heading to work and decided to stop and see if you've finished that birdhouse I want to give Melinda for her birthday."

Gabe nodded. "I finished it yesterday. It's right over there," he said, motioning to the shelf across from him.

Noah turned, and in a few strides, his long legs took him to the other side of the room, where he lifted the birdhouse from the shelf. "This is real nice," he said. "You did a fine job making it. I'm sure Melinda will be pleased."

Gabe's grin stretched from ear to ear. "I hope so. And I hope she'll like what I made for her, too."

"What might that be? Or is it a *geheemnis*?"

"It's not a secret I'd keep from you—just from Melinda until Saturday night." Gabe opened the cabinet door behind him and withdrew a small cardboard box. He reached inside and pulled out Melinda's present. "I carved this little deer and glued it to a chunk of wood, thinking maybe she could use it as a doorstop."

"I'm sure whatever my daughter does with the deer, it will be one of her most treasured gifts since it came from you." Noah couldn't help but smile when he saw how red Gabe's face had become. It was obvious the young man was in love with Melinda. "Looks like you're doing a good job with those," Noah said, pointing to the cabinets Gabe had been sanding when he'd entered the shop.

"One of our English neighbors ordered them a few weeks ago, and Pap gave me the job of finishing them up."

"Speaking of your daed, where is he this morning?"

"Still up at the house. Mom wanted him to go over the checkbook with her. I guess she found a mistake when the statement came from the bank in yesterday's mail." Gabe nodded toward the door. "I'm sure he'll be here soon if you'd like to wait around and say hello."

"I would like to, but if I don't head out now, I will be late for work." Noah moved over to the desk near the front door. "If you will get my bill, I will settle up with you and be on my way."

Gabe nodded and scurried over to the desk.

A few minutes later, with the bill paid and the birdhouse tucked inside a cardboard box, Noah headed for the door. "I'll look forward to seeing you and your folks at Melinda's party on Saturday evening."

"We'll be there right on time."

Noah chuckled under his breath as he headed for his buggy. *Oh to be young again and so much in love.* He figured it wouldn't be much longer until Gabe and Melinda would be announcing their intentions to get married.

As Gabe resumed sanding the cabinets, he thought about Melinda's upcoming birthday and hoped the week would go by quickly. He was eager to give Melinda the little fawn, which had turned out pretty well.

Sure hope I'll be able to spend a few minutes alone with her on Saturday night, Gabe thought. *We haven't been able to be by ourselves since I took her home from the gathering and we discovered her grandpa standing in the road.* At the rate things were going, Gabe wondered if he'd ever get the chance to ask Melinda to marry him.

"From the way you're swiping that sandpaper across the cabinet tops, there might not be anything left by the time you're done. I'd have to say your thoughts must be on something other than work this morning," Pap said, stepping up beside Gabe.

"I was thinking about this coming Saturday night."

"Looking forward to Melinda's birthday party, I imagine." Pap's blue eyes twinkled when he grinned at Gabe.

"Jah."

"It was nice of her folks to include your mamm and me in the invitation."

"We've known their family a long time, so I guess it's only natural that they'd want all three of us to be there."

"Probably would have asked your sisters to come if they were still living at home," Pap added.

Gabe nodded, wondering if his dad knew he and Melinda were courting. He hadn't actually told his folks he was courting Melinda and planned to ask her to marry him, but he knew Pap was no dummy. Gabe figured his dad had probably put two and two together by now.

"Sure hope this nice weather holds out so we can have the party outside," Gabe commented.

Pap raked his fingers through the ends of his full brown beard, which was generously peppered with gray. "It's been a nice May so far. Makes me wish I had some free time to go fishing." He turned toward the rear of the shop with a shrug. "Well, time's a-wasting, so guess I'd best get back to work on that rocking chair Abe Yutzy ordered last week."

"Holler if you need any help."

"I appreciate the offer, but you'd better stick with the project you're working on now."

Gabe grimaced. "Say, Pap?"

"What is it, Gabe?"

"You think we might broaden the business to include more than just cabinets and basic furniture? I'd like the chance to work on some other things."

"I don't think so. We've got our hands full making what we do now."

Gabe gritted his teeth as his dad walked away. *Will he ever see me as capable? Will he ever let me try out some new things?*

He grabbed a fresh piece of sandpaper and gave the top of the cabinet a few more good swipes. *As soon as I get enough money saved up, I'm going to open my own woodworking business. When that happens, I plan to make a lot more things than just cabinets and a few pieces of furniture!*

When Melinda arrived home that evening with the squirrel she'd named Cinnamon, she headed straight for the barn. She set the cardboard box with the squirrel inside on a small wooden table and reached for a pair of leather gloves hanging on a nail. He wasn't tame like Reba seemed to be, and she didn't want to risk getting bitten by handling Cinnamon with her bare hands.

Melinda located the spare cage and reached inside the box to retrieve Cinnamon.

He didn't squirm or try to get away, probably because of his hurt foot. When she closed the door on the cage, she discovered that the latch was broken and wouldn't stay shut.

"I don't need you getting out, Cinnamon," Melinda muttered. "At least not until your foot is healed." She headed across the barn in search of some wire, but before she could locate it, Papa Noah stepped into the barn.

"Gut-n-owed," he said with a smile. "How was your day?"

"Good evening to you, too," Melinda replied. "My day was fine until now."

"What's the trouble?"

Melinda pointed to the cage. "The latch on the cage door is broken, and I was looking for some wire to hold it shut."

Papa Noah moved over to the cage. "Where did you get the squirrel, and what happened to its foot?"

"I got him from Dr. Franklin. Some English boy in Seymour found him outside the schoolhouse, and Dr. Franklin thinks the poor critter's foot got stepped on."

"Why isn't the vet taking care of him instead of you?"

"The doctor did all he could, but he didn't want to turn Cinnamon loose until the wound had healed properly." Melinda grinned. "So he gave him to me for safekeeping."

"Couldn't the vet have kept the squirrel in a cage there at the veterinary clinic?"

"He probably would have, but all of the cages are full of other animals right now."

Papa Noah grunted as he shook his head. "If you're not careful, you're going to have so many critters around here that they'll take over the place." He motioned to the cage. "I guess if you keep him in there it will be all right, but we'll have to wire that door shut."

"That's what I was about to do, but I haven't been able to find any wire."

"I know right where it is." Papa Noah headed across the barn and flipped open the toolbox sitting on a shelf.

In short order, he had the cage door wired shut. "I didn't make it too tight, because I know you'll need to be able to undo it so you can get inside to give the squirrel food and water," he said.

"Danki. I appreciate the help."

"Should we head for the house and see what your mamm's got for supper?" he asked, nodding toward the barn door.

"You go ahead. I want to check on the raccoon and the baby goat before I come in."

He shrugged. "Okay, but don't be too long. I'm sure your mamm could use your help in the kitchen. You know how upset she gets when you spend too much time taking care of your critters."

Melinda knew all too well how Mama felt about her animal friends. She'd never seemed to mind a couple of pets hanging around, but when Melinda had started bringing home creatures that lived in the woods, her mother had become less understanding.

"I won't be but a few minutes," she promised.

"Okay. See you at supper." Papa Noah lifted his hand and went out the door.

Chapter 7

Melinda couldn't remember when she'd been so excited about one of her birthdays as this one. It wasn't turning nineteen that excited her so; it was knowing she would be able to spend the evening with Gabe.

"I wonder what he'll give me," she murmured as she stepped into a freshly ironed, blue cotton dress in preparation for the big event. She was sure it would be something he'd made. Gabe could take any plain piece of wood and turn it into something beautiful.

The twittering of birds outside Melinda's open window drew her attention outdoors. At least she knew that Cinnamon, the squirrel Dr. Franklin had put in her care, wasn't chasing any of the birds. This morning, she'd let the critter out of his cage for a bit and later caught him trying to eat at one of the bird feeders. After that, she'd put him back in the cage, and he would stay there until his foot was healed and she could set him free in the woods.

A warm breeze coming through Melinda's bedroom window made the dark curtains dance. She drew in a deep breath and headed downstairs, excited that her guests would be arriving soon.

Outside, she discovered Papa Noah lighting the barbecue. He'd set up two large tables with benches, and Mama had covered them with green plastic tablecloths.

"It looks like we're about ready," Melinda remarked to her stepfather.

"Now all we need is our guests," he said with a chuckle.

"They'll be here soon, I expect." Melinda took a seat on the end of the bench closest to the barbecue grill, where she could feel the heat already rising from the hot coals. "Where's Grandpa Hertzler? I thought he would be out here already."

Papa Noah blew out his breath with a puff of air that lifted the hair off his forehead. "I'm not sure what to do about him."

"You mean his forgetfulness?"

"Jah. I reminded my daed this morning about your birthday party, but when I went over to his side of the house a few minutes ago, I found him asleep in his favorite chair."

"Maybe he's just feeling tired."

"I thought that at first, but when I woke him and suggested he get ready for the party, he gave me a bewildered look. He didn't seem to have any idea what I was talking about."

Melinda frowned. "It's hard to understand why some days he seems pretty good and other days he barely knows who we are."

"Your mamm made him a doctor's appointment in Springfield. I'm hoping they'll run some tests that will help us know what's wrong."

"Sounds like a good idea."

"I hear a buggy rumbling up the driveway," Papa Noah said, glancing to the left. "Why don't you see who's the first to arrive?"

Melinda stood. "Jah, okay."

When she rounded the corner of the house, she was greeted by Gabe and his parents, Stephen and Leah Swartz.

Gabe offered her a friendly smile. "Happy birthday, Melinda."

"Happy birthday," Gabe's folks said in unison.

"Danki." Melinda motioned toward the house. "Papa Noah has the barbecue fired up, and Mama's in the kitchen. So feel free to go out back or inside, whichever you like."

"I believe I'll go in the house and see if there's anything I can do to help Faith," Leah said.

"And I'll head around back and find out what kind of meat Noah's grilling," Stephen put in.

As soon as Gabe's folks left, he stepped up beside Melinda. "You sure look pretty tonight."

Heat radiated up the back of Melinda's neck and spread quickly to her cheeks. "I don't think I look much different than the last time you saw me."

He leaned in closer until she could feel his warm breath tickle her ear. "You're the prettiest woman I know."

"Danki, Gabe."

"Do you want to open my gift now or wait until later?" he asked, lifting the paper sack he held in one hand.

"I guess it would be best to wait and open all my gifts at the same time."

"Jah, okay."

Gabe leaned closer and studied Melinda so intently her toes curled inside her black leather shoes.

"Hey, Gabe! What are you up to?"

Melinda whirled around to face her brother. "Isaiah, you shouldn't sneak up on people like that."

"I wasn't sneakin'. I just happened to come around the house in time to see the two of you makin' eyes at each other."

Gabe ruffled Isaiah's hair. "You're right— we're caught."

"Why don't you go see if Papa Noah needs

any help?" Melinda suggested.

Isaiah squinted. "I've never figured out why you call him that. Can't ya just say, 'Papa,' without addin' the Noah part?"

"I was seven years old when Mama married Papa Noah. He's been like a daed to me all these years, but he's not my real father. So I've always thought it best to call him Papa Noah, and he's never complained or asked me to call him anything else."

"Suit yourself," Isaiah said with a shrug. "Guess I'll mosey around back and see what's cookin'."

"We'll be there soon," Melinda called to his retreating form.

Gabe reached for Melinda's hand and drew her aside. "As I was saying before Isaiah came along—"

Two more buggies rolled into the yard just then, and Gabe released a moan. "Guess what I wanted to say will have to wait until later." He gave Melinda's hand a gentle squeeze. "Maybe after the party winds down, we can take a walk."

She nodded. "I'd like that."

As Susie stepped down from her parents' buggy, she spotted Melinda and Gabe holding hands as they stood in the yard together. *Oh, how I wish I had a boyfriend,* she thought dismally. *If*

there was only someone to hold my hand and look at me with the tenderness I see whenever Gabe looks at Melinda.

"Something sure smells good," Susie's dad said, sniffing the air. "I'll bet Noah's been cooking up a storm."

"Besides whatever meat he's barbecuing, it's a pretty good guess that either he or Faith has made some other tasty dishes," Mama put in.

Papa smacked his lips. "When I talked to Melinda the other day, she said there would be a batch of homemade ice cream to go with the cake Noah baked for her birthday."

"That sounds good to me," Mama said with a smile. "Don't you think it sounds good, daughter?"

Susie shrugged.

"What are you looking so glum about?" Papa asked as he unhitched the horse from their buggy. "We're at a party—a celebration of Melinda's nineteenth birthday. You ought to be smiling, not frowning like you've got a bad toothache, for goodness' sake."

Susie forced her lips to form a smile. "Is that better?"

"Much." Mama nudged Susie with her elbow. "Let's head for the house and see if Faith needs our help with anything while your daed gets the horse put in the corral."

As they started walking toward Faith and Noah's house, Susie cast a quick glance in the birthday girl's direction. Melinda was so busy talking to Gabe that she hadn't even noticed them. Susie was tempted to stop and say a few words, but she decided Melinda might not appreciate having her conversation with Gabe interrupted. So she hurried to the house behind her mother, knowing the best thing she could do to get her jealousy under control was to keep her hands busy.

Melinda bit into a piece of moist chocolate cake and savored the moment. Her family and closest friends were here: Gabe and his folks; Grandpa and Grandma Stutzman; Susie; Barbara and Paul Hilty with their six children; and her immediate family—Mama, Papa Noah, Isaiah, and Grandpa Hertzler.

"Why don't you open your gifts now, Melinda?" Mama suggested.

Isaiah bobbed his head up and down and said, "Let's see what you got, sister."

Melinda blotted her lips on the paper napkin that had been lying in her lap. "Which one shall I open first?"

"Why don't you start with Susie's?" Grandma nudged Susie's arm. "Run on out to the buggy and get it."

Susie left the picnic table and hurried across the yard. A few minutes later, she returned carrying a small cardboard box, which she placed in Melinda's lap. "Happy birthday. I hope you like it."

Melinda opened the flaps on the box and grinned when a pair of pretty blue eyes stared up at her and a pathetic meow escaped the tiny white kitten's mouth. "She looks like a fluffy ball of snow," Melinda said as she lifted the kitten out of the box and nuzzled its little pink nose. "I think I'll call her 'Snow.'"

Susie grinned from ear to ear. It was the first genuine smile Melinda had seen her aunt give all evening. "I'm glad you like it, Melinda. It's one of Daisy's busslin."

"Danki," Melinda said.

"I can hold the kitten while you open the rest of your gifts," Susie offered. "That way you'll have both hands free."

Melinda handed the kitten to Susie, and Susie took a seat on the bench to the left of Melinda. Gabe occupied the spot to Melinda's right. "Who wants to be next?" Melinda asked, glancing around the table.

"I will." Papa Noah placed a cardboard box on the picnic table in front of Melinda. "I had this made especially for you, and after you see what it is, you'll probably know who made it."

Melinda lifted the flaps on the box. Inside she discovered an ornate birdhouse with a little door on it. She looked at Papa Noah and smiled. "Danki. I really like it."

"I'm glad you do, and now you can thank Gabe for all his hard work."

"You made this for me?" Melinda asked, glancing over at Gabe.

He nodded and smiled, looking rather pleased with himself.

She opened the little door on the birdhouse and peered inside. "What's this?"

Gabe's smile widened. "It's a separate compartment I added so we can keep sending notes to each other and not have to worry about the birds making a nest on top of our messages."

"That's a good idea," she said.

"Why don't you open mine next?" Gabe handed Melinda a smaller cardboard box. "I hope you like it."

With mounting excitement, Melinda tore open the box. Her breath caught in her throat when she lifted out a little carved fawn that had been glued to a small piece of wood. "It's beautiful, Gabe. Danki so much."

He smiled and reached under the table to take her hand. "I attached the piece of wood to the deer, thinking you might be able to use it as a doorstop."

"That's a good idea, but it's so nice, rather than using it as a doorstop, I might decide to set it on my dresser so I can look at it every morning when I first get out of bed."

Melinda was about to open the rest of her gifts, but the wind became restless and clouds raced across the sky. Minutes later, it started to rain. Everyone grabbed something off the table and dashed for the house.

There goes my walk with Gabe. It doesn't look like we'll get any time alone tonight, Melinda thought with regret.

"Whew! What a downpour," Mama said as they entered the kitchen. "It amazes me how swiftly the weather can change during the spring."

Melinda placed her kitten on the floor, and it scurried under the stove. The older guests found seats around the kitchen table, while the younger ones went to the living room to play games. Melinda, Gabe, Susie, and Aaron headed outside to watch the storm from the safety of the front porch.

"I like watching the way the *wedderleech* zigzags across the sky," Gabe commented with a sweep of his hand.

"I've always been afraid of the *dunner*," Susie put in.

"It's not the thunder that can hurt you," Aaron asserted. "It's those bolts of dangerous lightning you've got to worry about."

Melinda shivered and rubbed her hands briskly over her arms.

"Are you cold?" Gabe asked in a tone of concern.

"A little. Guess I should have grabbed a sweater before coming outside."

"Want me to get it for you?"

Melinda raised her voice to be heard over the thud of more thunder. "I'll be okay." She glanced nervously into the yard. "I hope all my critters are doing okay. Most animals don't like storms."

"At least we know Snow's all right," Susie put in. "She's probably curled up in someone's lap by now."

Aaron turned around. "I'm tired of watching the rain. Think I'll head back inside and see what the kinner are doing."

"Maybe I should, too," Susie said with a nod.

Melinda smiled. She figured their friends had decided to give her and Gabe some time alone. Gabe must have known also, for he reached for her hand and gave it a gentle squeeze.

As soon as Aaron and Susie entered the house, Gabe led Melinda over to the porch swing. Once they were seated, he pulled her close to his side. "Happy birthday, Melinda." He lowered his head and brushed his lips against hers.

Melinda melted into his embrace. Their first kiss was even sweeter than she had expected.

Suddenly the front door opened, and Isaiah stuck his head out. "Oh, yuck! I'll never kiss any girl 'cept Mama."

Melinda's cheeks burned hot as she shook her finger. "You say one word about what you saw here, and I'll tell Papa Noah that your dog ate out of a pie pan the other day."

"Aw, Jericho didn't hurt a thing." Isaiah

wrinkled his nose. "Besides, the plate got washed."

Melinda jumped up, ready to tell her little brother what she thought of his juvenile antics, but a flash of fur darted over her foot, raced across the porch, and dove inside the open doorway.

"Cinnamon!" she shouted. "How did you get out of your cage?"

Chapter 8

Melinda dashed into the house after the runaway squirrel, and Gabe followed right on her heels. He couldn't believe the way things were going tonight. First, the rain had put a damper on their plans to take a walk. Then Melinda's younger brother had interrupted them when Gabe was on the verge of proposing. Now a silly critter had come along and ruined things.

Pandemonium broke out as soon as they entered the living room. Not only was the squirrel skittering all over the place, but Melinda's new kitten seemed to be the squirrel's prey. The two animals circled the room, darting under chairs, banging into walls, and sliding across the hardwood floor. When Snow crawled under the braided oval throw rug, Cinnamon pounced on her. The kitten sailed out and zipped to the other side of the room.

"You get the cat, and I'll corner the squirrel," Gabe shouted to Melinda as he waved his hands.

Aaron, Susie, and the children, who'd been playing games in the adjoining room, came on the scene and became part of the chase, but no one had any luck catching either animal.

"Have you got any paper sacks?" Gabe called to Isaiah.

"I think there's some in the kitchen."

"Get four of the biggest ones you can find!"

When Isaiah returned a few minutes later, the older folks were with him.

"What's going on here?" Noah asked with a look of concern. "Isaiah said something about a squirrel."

"Cinnamon got out of his cage and ended up in the house," Melinda panted. "Now he's after Snow."

"The squirrel's gonna eat the cat!" five-year-old Emma hollered. When Cinnamon whizzed past the child, she jumped, squealed, and ran for cover behind her mother's long green dress.

"Settle down," Barbara said, taking hold of Emma's hand. "Let's go to the kitchen and let the others handle this."

"She needs our help."

"We're gonna have to trap 'em."

"They're just a couple of desperate critters."

"Come here, Snow."

"Easy now, Cinnamon."

Everyone spoke at once, and the animals kept circling the living room. Finally, Noah held up his hands. "Everybody, please calm down." He turned to Isaiah. "What are the paper sacks for?"

The boy shrugged. "I don't know. Gabe asked me to get 'em."

Gabe swiped at the sweat beaded on his forehead. "I figured if the four of us each took a sack, we might be able to trap Cinnamon or Snow inside one of the bags."

"I believe I have a better plan." Noah turned back to Isaiah. "Please go to the kitchen and get a broom from the utility closet."

Melinda's eyes grew huge as silver dollars as she grasped her stepfather's arm. "I hope you're not going to smack either one of my pets."

Faith spoke up. "Only one of them is a pet, Melinda, and I'm sure your daed wouldn't intentionally hurt either animal."

Grandpa Hertzler sank into the closest chair. "Would ya put that broom away? I hate housework; always did." He shook his head, and his white beard moved back and forth across his chest like the pendulum on the clock above the fireplace.

"We're not going to clean house, Pop," Noah said. "And I don't plan to do the animals any harm." He nodded at Isaiah. "Now hurry and get me that broom."

The boy shoved the paper sacks at Gabe and scurried out of the room.

Gabe handed one sack to Melinda, one to Aaron, one to Susie, and kept the one for himself. He crouched down and opened his sack, telling the others to do the same. "If either the cat or the squirrel comes your way, try to scoop it into your bag."

Noah shook his head. "I don't think that's going to work. I believe my way's better." He cupped his hands around his mouth. "Isaiah, where is that broom?"

"I'll see what's keeping him," Melinda's mother offered.

Just then, Isaiah dashed into the room, flung the broom at his father, and scuttled off to one side with an expectant look on his face.

"Somebody, open the front door!"

Melinda rushed to do as her stepfather had commanded.

Gabe groaned. Whatever Noah had in mind, he was sure it would fail. He remained on his knees, waiting for either the squirrel or the kitten to pass his way again. A few seconds later, Cinnamon skittered across the floor in front of Gabe's paper sack, and Noah's broom swooshed past the critter's bushy tail. Cinnamon took off like a flash of lightning and zipped through the open doorway.

With a pathetic meow, the cat darted under the sofa, and no amount of coaxing on Melinda's part could bring her out.

"Just leave her be," Noah said as he headed for the kitchen with the other adults. "She'll come out when she's good and ready."

As Gabe stood, his heart went out to Melinda. She looked so dejected, sitting with her head down and her shoulders slumped. What had started out to be a nice birthday party had turned into utter mayhem.

"Come on, the excitement's over. Let's head back to the dining room and finish those games we started," Aaron said to the others.

"I'm going to the kitchen to get more cake," Isaiah announced.

The children and teens filed out of the room, but Melinda stayed in a kneeling position as she continued to call her kitten. "Here, Snow. You can come out now. The squirrel is gone."

Gabe shifted from one foot to the other, unsure of what to do. He thought about offering to go outside and look for the squirrel but knew that would be ridiculous. Cinnamon was probably halfway to Seymour by now.

For lack of anything better to do, he flopped into a chair and sat with his arms folded, staring out the window at the pouring rain and streaks of lightning while he mulled things over.

"I can't believe the way Melinda carried on just

'cause her dumm old *bussli* got chased by an *eechhaas*," Isaiah said as he dropped into a chair at the kitchen table.

Faith turned from the refrigerator, where she'd gone to get a glass of iced tea for her mother. "Your sister did overreact a bit, but if she hadn't brought that silly squirrel home in the first place, the whole incident never would have happened."

"I'm just glad nothing happened to the bussli," Faith's mother put in as she pulled out a chair and sat down. "A wild squirrel is no match for a helpless little kitten."

Isaiah grunted. "If you ask me, Melinda cares way too much about all the animals she brings home."

Faith couldn't argue with that, although it wasn't as if Melinda's squirrel had gotten into the house and caused such havoc on purpose.

"I think we'd better find another topic of conversation," she said as she started across the room with the glass of iced tea in her hand.

Isaiah pointed to the chocolate cake sitting on the counter. "Can I have another piece of that?"

Faith nodded. "Help yourself."

Isaiah grabbed a hunk of cake and headed back to the dining room to join the other children.

Faith handed her mother the glass of iced tea then took a seat in the empty chair beside Noah. "There's still plenty of cake left if anyone wants some."

Faith's mother patted her stomach. "None for me. Thanks to Noah being such a good cook, I ate way too much supper."

Noah's ears turned pink. "It was nothing special."

"Jah, it was." Gabe's mother smiled. "But then, I would enjoy eating most anything I didn't have to cook."

Everyone laughed, and Gabe's father needled her with his elbow. "If you're hoping I'll start doing the baking and cooking, you'd better think again, Leah, because I can barely boil water."

"My wife, Ida, can sure cook up a storm," Noah's dad put in. "Fact is, she makes the best rhubarb-strawberry jam around."

Faith glanced over at Noah to gauge his reaction, but his placid expression gave no indication as to what he might be thinking. Was Noah embarrassed by his dad's apparent loss of memory, or did he think it best not to make an issue of it in front of their company?

"Ida couldn't come to the party tonight," Noah's dad went on to say. "She came down with a cold last night."

Faith's mother looked over at her with a strange expression, and Gabe's mother did, too. The men just sat there with stony faces. Finally, Noah stood and moved to the other side of the table, where his father sat. "You look tired, Pop. Why don't you let me walk you home?"

With a grunt, the older man rose from his chair and shuffled out the door behind Noah.

"The poor man's memory really seems to be failing him." Faith swallowed against the lump in her throat. She hoped nothing like this ever happened to her or Noah when they got old.

※※※

"Come, Snow. Here, kitty, kitty. Come out from under the sofa." When the kitten didn't budge, Melinda looked up at Gabe, hoping he might have a suggestion.

He shrugged. "You heard what your daed said. Leave the cat be. She'll come out on her own when she's ready."

Melinda released a sigh. "That could be hours from now. Snow's really scared."

"I'll tell you what," Gabe said as he scrambled to his feet. "Why don't we go out on the porch and watch the rain? If there's no one in the living room, the cat will be more apt to come out."

"You could be right."

Gabe opened the front door, and Melinda followed him outside.

"I hope Cinnamon's okay," she murmured. "He's probably as frightened as Snow seems to be."

"Maybe so, but you need to remember that the critter's a wild animal. I'm sure he'll be fine on his own."

"I suppose. His foot's nearly healed, so he should be okay even if he ran into the woods." Melinda leaned on the porch railing and stared into the yard. "Some party this turned out to be."

Gabe slipped his arm around her waist. "It'll be one you won't likely forget, that's for certain sure."

She nodded. "You're right about that."

"Uh—Melinda, I've been wanting to ask you a question."

Melinda turned to face him. "What did you want to ask?"

He reached up and stroked the side of her face with his finger. "I love you, Melinda. I have for a long time."

"I—I love you, too." Melinda could barely get the words out, her throat felt so dry.

"Would you marry me this fall?"

Melinda swallowed around the lump in her throat. She had to think—had to stop this roaring rush of emotions and hold on to reason. If she accepted his proposal without telling him about Dr. Franklin's suggestion that she become a vet, it would be even harder to tell him later on. *I must tell Gabe now. I shouldn't wait any longer.*

Before Melinda could get the words out, Gabe leaned down and kissed her so tenderly she almost melted into his arms. When the kiss ended, he whispered, "If you marry me, I'll be the happiest man in the world."

Her eyes filled with tears and splashed onto

her cheeks. He reached up to wipe them away. "I hope those are tears of joy."

She nodded. "I do want to marry you, Gabe, but—"

"I'm glad, and I promise to be the best husband in all of Webster County." He reached for her hand. "The rain's letting up, so let's take a walk now."

As the rush of water in the drainpipes became mere drops from the eaves, Melinda's resolve to tell Gabe about Dr. Franklin's suggestion for her future melted away. All she wanted to do was enjoy the time they had together.

"Think I'll ask Aaron to be one of my attendants at the wedding," Gabe said as they headed down the driveway, hand in hand. "Will you ask Susie to be one of yours?"

Melinda nodded. "Probably so, since I have no sisters."

"We'll each need one more person to stand up for us. Maybe we could ask one of our cousins."

"There's plenty of time to decide."

"Jah."

As they walked on, Melinda noticed the misty clouds that seemed as if they were clinging to earth. On both sides of the driveway, leaves littered the ground where the wet wind had spun and stuck them in place. It almost seemed as if she were in a dream. *What would Gabe say if he knew what I was thinking of doing? Would he break our engagement as quickly as he'd proposed?*

"Did you get everything you wanted for your birthday?" Gabe asked, breaking into her thoughts. "Or is there some secret present you were hoping to get and didn't?"

"Well, I—" Melinda halted.

"What's wrong? Why'd you stop walking?"

"Don't move a muscle."

Gabe froze. "Is there a poisonous snake underfoot?" he rasped.

"Relax; it's not a snake." She nudged his arm. "Aren't they sweet?"

"What?"

"Twin fawns, to your left."

Gabe turned his head just as two young deer walked out of the bushes, not three feet away.

Melinda inched closer to the deer.

"Wh–what are you doing?"

"Shh. . ."

She took a few more steps and dropped to her knees.

One of the fawns held back, but the other deer moved closer.

Melinda held her breath. Then the most surprising thing happened. The fawn came right up to her and licked the end of her chin.

When the deer moved away and disappeared into the brush, she touched the spot on her chin where the fawn had licked. "Did you see that, Gabe?" she murmured. "The little deer gave me a birthday kiss."

Chapter 9

Over the next several weeks, Melinda's emotions swung from elation over Gabe's marriage proposal to frustration because she hadn't yet told him that she was considering leaving the Amish faith to pursue a career in veterinary medicine. She knew she needed to say something soon. Although they'd agreed not to tell anyone about their betrothal until they had set a wedding date, speculation about their courtship was bound to get around. And a few weeks before their wedding, they would be officially published during a church service; then everyone would know of their plans.

To make matters worse, Dr. Franklin had recently given Melinda another orphaned raccoon she'd named Rhoda, and every day at work, the doctor continued to tell Melinda what a God-given talent she'd been given when it came to working with animals. Melinda felt that way, too. More and more she felt the pull to become a veterinarian so she could help as many animals as possible. Yet she loved Gabe and wanted to be his wife. She also loved her family and knew how hard it would be if she decided to leave them. Sometimes Melinda felt like a rope during a game of tug-o-war, being pulled first one way and then the other.

As Melinda bent over the rhubarb patch in their garden one Friday morning in early June, she made a decision. *I must find out if Gabe would be willing to leave the Amish faith with me. If we leave together, it will be a little easier, but if I have to do it on my own, I'm not sure I can.*

"Melinda, have you got enough rhubarb yet?" Grandpa called from the back porch, where he stood with a pot holder in his hand.

Melinda smiled and waved. "Almost. I'll be there with it soon!"

Grandpa waved back at her and returned to the house. He was doing better these days, and Melinda was pleased.

Two weeks ago, Papa Noah and Mama had taken him to see a specialist in Springfield. After numerous tests had been run, it was determined that Grandpa's loss of memory was due in part to a malfunctioning thyroid. The doctor said it could be treated with medication, which was good news. Grandpa also had low blood sugar, which could be controlled by his diet. Those two things, coupled with the fact that he'd never gotten over Grandma's death, had put him in a state of depression and caused some occasional memory loss.

Melinda was sure things would be better now. Grandpa had recently begun helping Mama make jams and preserves to sell at the farmers' market, which seemed to ease his sadness. His mind appeared to be sharper already, too. It was a real surprise to see Grandpa spending time in the kitchen, though. Melinda remembered how he used to avoid doing anything related to cooking. She'd heard him tell Papa Noah how odd he thought it was that his youngest son enjoyed baking so much. But now that Grandpa was making delicious jams and jellies, he acted like he'd been interested in working in the kitchen for a good long time.

Melinda chuckled to herself. "It just goes to show, no one's ever too old to change their mind about some things."

When Melinda had picked the last stalks of rhubarb, she ran up to the house. As soon as she had deposited the rhubarb into the kitchen sink, she headed back outside to check the birdhouse Papa Noah had given her as a birthday present.

"Maybe there will be a note from Gabe," she

murmured. It had been several days since she'd heard from him, and she was eager to know when they would be going on another date. Seeing him only at their every-other-week preaching services didn't give them any privacy, and they needed to talk without anyone overhearing their conversation.

When Melinda reached the double-sided birdhouse, she was pleased to hear some baby birds peeping from one end. Careful not to disturb the little sparrows, she lifted the lid on the side that was now her and Gabe's message box. She was equally pleased to see that a note was waiting for her.

> *Dear Melinda,*
>
> *Since the weather has been so warm, I thought it would be nice to go for a drive this evening after supper. Let me know if you'll be free or not. I'll be back to check the message box later this afternoon.*
>
> *Happily yours,*
> *Gabe*

Melinda reached inside the box to retrieve the pencil and tablet they kept there and then scrawled a note in reply.

> *Dear Gabe,*
>
> *Tonight should be fine. Come by around seven. I'm looking forward to our time*

*together, as we have some important things
to talk about.*

Yours fawnly,
Melinda

"What do you think of this hunk of walnut for the gun stock I'm planning to make?" Gabe asked as he held the item in question out for his dad's inspection.

Pap nodded and ran his fingers over the block of wood. "Looks like it'll work out fine. Always did like to have a hunting gun with a well-made stock."

Gabe smiled. *Maybe this will show him I'm able to make more than simple cabinets, birdhouses, and feeders.*

"Are you expecting to do some hunting this fall?" his father questioned.

"Jah, and I hope to use my new gun."

"Sounds good, but any hunting you want to do will have to be done on your day off or after the shop is closed for the day." Pap picked up a stack of work orders and thumbed through them quickly. "We need to get busy with these jobs. You'll have to work on your gun stock during your free time, too."

Gabe frowned but set the piece of wood aside. If he worked on his own projects after hours, he would have less time to court Melinda.

He thought about the note he'd left her earlier, saying he would be by this evening to take her for a buggy ride.

Guess I could run over to her place during lunch and leave her another note saying I can't take her for a ride after all. Gabe pondered the idea a moment then shook his head. *No way! Melinda comes first. Hunting season is several months away. I can work on the gun stock some other time.*

Melinda had just started setting the table for supper when Papa Noah entered the kitchen wearing a worried expression on his face.

"Where's your mamm?" he asked.

"Over at Grandpa Hertzler's side of the house. They're finishing up with the rhubarb-strawberry jam they've been making today."

"Do you know if we've got any hydrogen peroxide in the house?"

"I think there's some in the cupboard above the sink. What do you need it for?"

"That horse I bought a few days ago has a cut on her back leg. At first, I thought I'd have to call the vet, but after checking things over real good, I realized the cut isn't too deep. I think it's something I can tend to myself."

"She didn't have a cut leg when you bought her, I hope."

He shook his head and ambled across the

room to the cupboard. "I believe she may have gouged it on the fence. Probably trying to get out."

Melinda felt immediate concern. "She's not happy here? Is that what you think, Papa Noah?"

He pulled the bottle of peroxide down and turned around. "Looks like it. If I had more free time to spend with her, she might feel calmer and at home already. Between my job at the tree farm and all the chores I have to do here, there aren't enough hours in the day."

Melinda placed the last glass on the table and moved toward her stepfather. "I could doctor the wound and work with the horse to get her calmed down and more comfortable here. I'm good with animals, Papa Noah—you know that."

"Of course you are, but I don't think—"

"Please, let me try. I'll show Nellie some attention so she learns to like it here, and I'll tend that cut on her leg. She'll be good as new in no time."

Papa Noah's furrowed brows let Melinda know he was at least thinking on the idea.

"I'll squeeze it in between chores here and my job at the veterinary clinic." She clasped his arm. "Please, Papa Noah."

He finally smiled and handed her the bottle of peroxide. "Okay, then, you can start right now."

Melinda sprinted for the door. "Tell Mama I've got the burner on the stove turned to low, and I'll be back in time to help her serve up the stew that's cooking for supper."

"Did Papa Noah tell you that I'll be tending his new horse that's got a cut on its back leg?" Melinda asked Faith as they sat at the table eating supper later that evening.

Faith grimaced and glanced over at Noah. "Don't you think you should ask the vet to take a look at the horse rather than allowing Melinda to play doctor?"

"I don't think it's anything too serious." Noah shrugged. "Besides, I know what a way Melinda has with animals, and I figured I'd let her see what she can do first."

"She'll probably end up bringing the horse into the house." Isaiah nudged Melinda in the ribs with his elbow. "First a chicken then a squirrel. I figure a horse must be next on your list."

"I have no intention of bringing Papa Noah's horse into the house." Melinda pursed her lips and squinted at Isaiah. "I think you need to eat what's on your plate and mind your own business."

Isaiah scrunched up his nose and glared at her. "You ain't my boss, sister."

"Never said I was."

"But you're always bossin' me around."

"Am not."

"Are so."

"No, I—"

Noah clapped his hands together and

everyone jumped. Noah rarely got upset, but when he did, he meant business.

"I don't want to hear any more silly bickering," he said. "I've given Melinda permission to doctor the horse, and she'll be doing it in the barn. So this whole conversation you two have been having is just plain *lecherich*."

"I agree," Faith said with a nod. "For that matter, most arguments are ridiculous."

Isaiah gave Melinda one more scathing glare; then he grabbed his fork and popped a hunk of stew meat into his mouth.

Faith didn't know why Melinda had become so testy lately. It made her wonder if there was more going on than just the usual bickering between brother and sister. Well, now that Noah had laid down the law, maybe they could eat in peace.

⁂

Gabe whistled the whole way over to Melinda's house. He could hardly wait to spend time with her and talk about their future. The summer months would go by quickly; soon it would be time for their wedding. Of course, they hadn't set a date yet, so he didn't know exactly which month it would be.

"If I had my own business, I would feel more prepared for marriage," he mumbled. "I wonder how long I'll have to keep working for

Pap before I have enough money saved up to go out on my own." Gabe had looked at a couple of places to rent, but the owners of the buildings were asking too much, and he didn't think his dad would take to the idea of him building a shop right there on the same property as his place of business.

I need to be patient and pray about this more, Gabe decided.

When Gabe pulled into the Hertzlers' front yard, he spotted Isaiah on the lawn playing with his beagle hound, Jericho. The boy had received the dog as a birthday present last year from Noah's boss, Hank Osborn, who raised hound dogs, as well as acres of pine trees. Gabe used to enjoy visiting there when he was a boy, but he hadn't gone to the Christmas tree farm in sometime.

Isaiah waved when he spotted Gabe, and Gabe lifted his hand in response. "Where's Melinda? I hope she's ready for our date."

The boy turned his palms upward. "Don't know nothin' about no date, but Melinda's out in the barn with Papa's new horse."

Gabe figured Melinda had probably gone there to pass the time while she waited for him. He guided his horse to the hitching rail and pulled on the reins. Then he jumped down, secured the animal, and sprinted for the barn.

He found Melinda inside one of the stalls on her knees next to a nice-looking gray-and-white mare. "Are you ready for our ride?" he called.

She stood and smoothed the wrinkles in her long green dress. "Oh, Gabe, I don't think I can go with you tonight."

"How come?"

"Didn't you get my two notes?"

His face warmed. "Uh—I forgot to check the birdhouse on my way in. What did your notes say?"

"The first note I wrote said I could go, but since then, something has come up, so I wrote you a second note, figuring you'd look in the birdhouse before coming up to the house."

His eyebrows drew together. "What's come up that would keep you from going for a ride with me?"

She pointed to the horse. "Nellie has a cut on her back leg. I tended it before supper. She's been acting kind of spooky and hasn't adjusted to her new surroundings yet, so after we ate, I came back to the barn to see that she remains calm and doesn't start her wound bleeding again."

Gabe folded his arms as they exchanged pointed stares.

"I hope you understand," she said with a lift of her chin.

"I don't."

"Have you no concern for Papa Noah's horse?"

"It's not that I don't care. I just don't see why it's your job to nursemaid the animal. Shouldn't the vet be doing that?"

"Now you sound like my mamm." Melinda

stroked the horse's ears. "If the cut were deeper and needed stitches, Papa Noah would have called Dr. Franklin. But it's not bad enough for stitches, which is why he asked me to tend Nellie's leg."

"That's fine," Gabe said through tight lips, "but how is staying here going to help her?"

Melinda left the stall and moved to his side. "The horse is calmer when I'm here, and I'm just starting to gain some headway with her."

Gabe shrugged as frustration and disappointment boiled inside his chest like a kettle of hot water left unattended on the stove. "Sure, whatever. If your daed's horse is more important than me, then I guess that's just the way it is." He turned and started to walk away, but she grabbed hold of his arm.

"Please don't leave mad. You could stay and help me with the horse."

He swung around. "I can't believe you'd expect me to spend this warm summer evening cooped up in the stuffy barn with a sweaty animal that isn't even mine."

Tears gathered in the corners of Melinda's eyes, and it was nearly Gabe's undoing. He hadn't meant to make her cry. Hadn't meant to be so harsh or unwilling to help, either. One of the things that had originally attracted him to Melinda was her caring attitude and sensitivity toward hurting animals, and here he was scolding her for it.

Gabe pulled Melinda into his arms. "I'm sorry. Let's not fight, okay?"

She sniffed. "I don't want to. I want us to always be happy. But if you don't understand my desire to work with animals, then I don't see how—"

He stopped her rush of words with a kiss, and any shred of anger he'd felt earlier fell away like wood chips beneath the sander. "I love you, Melinda."

"I love you, too."

"How about tomorrow night? Will you be able to go for a buggy ride with me then?"

"I—I hope so."

Gabe motioned toward the horse's stall. "How about if I stay and help you cross tie the horse so she won't move around so much?"

She grinned up at him. "That would be *wunderbaar*."

Chapter 10

Melinda sat at the kitchen table, reading a passage from her Bible out loud. " 'Peace I leave with you, my peace I give unto you: not as the world giveth, give I unto you. Let not your heart be troubled, neither let it be afraid.' "

She closed her eyes. *In my heart there is no peace, Lord. Help me make this agonizing decision about becoming a vet, and give me the courage and opportunity to speak with Gabe about it on our buggy ride tonight. I can't decide what I should do until I know how he feels about things.*

Melinda knew she should have told Gabe last night when they'd spent time in the barn with Nellie. But after having that one disagreement, she'd been afraid to bring up anything that might cause more dissension.

"Are you about ready to help me and Grandpa make jam?" Mama asked, pulling Melinda's thoughts aside. "He would like us to go over to his place as soon as we can."

Melinda nodded. "I'll be able to help for a while, but Dr. Franklin needs me at the clinic this afternoon."

"I'm sure we can get most of it done by noon."

Melinda had just closed her Bible when Isaiah bolted through the back door, grinning from ear to ear. "Look what I found!" he said, holding out his hands.

Mama's face turned pale, and she trembled. "Isaiah Hertzler, get that snake out of my house!"

He glanced at the reptile and frowned. "It's dead, Mama. Found it down in the root cellar, and it wasn't movin' a lick."

"So that was a reason to bring the creature in here?"

"I don't see why you're afraid of a dead garter snake. It can't hurt ya none."

"Isaiah—" Mama's tone was one of warning, and Melinda held her breath and waited to see what her little brother would do.

"All right, all right." Isaiah turned toward the door but suddenly whirled back. "I'm thirsty and need a glass of water. I'll get one real quick and be gone, okay?" Without waiting for Mama's reply, he plopped the snake on the floor, grabbed a glass from the cupboard, and headed for the kitchen sink. He had no more than turned on the faucet when Mama's shrill scream ricocheted off the walls.

Melinda's attention was immediately drawn to the creature Isaiah had dropped. Not only was the snake very much alive, but it was slithering across the linoleum toward the table.

Mama hollered again and jumped onto a chair. "You said it was dead, Isaiah!"

"Guess it was only sleepin'." Isaiah stood there laughing until tears rolled down his cheeks.

"It's not the least bit funny," Mama said. "I want you to pick up that snake and haul it back outside where it belongs."

Isaiah took a few steps backward and shook his head. "No way! I ain't about to touch him."

"Why not?"

"He might bite me."

"You weren't worried about that when you lugged him into the house."

"I thought he was dead."

"Garter snakes aren't poisonous," Melinda put in.

"Maybe not, but its bite could still hurt," Isaiah retorted.

"If you're not going to do as I say, then go on up to your room. And don't come out until I say you can," Mama said, shaking her finger at Isaiah.

Isaiah frowned. "But that might be hours from now."

"Would you rather go to the woodshed and

receive a *bletsching*?"

"No, Mama." He turned and fled from the room.

Melinda could hardly believe her brother was acting like such a baby. If she'd been Mama, she would have given him that spanking she had threatened.

"It's bad enough that we have to put up with all your critters. We sure don't need your bruder lugging snakes into the house." Mama squinted at Melinda. "See what kind of example you've set for Isaiah?"

Melinda cringed. Why was she being blamed for this? She opened her mouth to ask that question, but Mama cut her off.

"Are you just going to stand there, or did you plan to help me get rid of this horrible creature?" Mama asked, pointing a shaking finger at the snake.

Melinda bent down, grabbed hold of the snake, and hurried out the door. Once outside, she set the snake on the ground and watched it slither toward the woods. *If I leave home to become a vet, Mama won't have to put up with all my critters or worry about me influencing Isaiah in the wrong way.*

She stood staring at the stately pine trees behind their place and breathing in the fresh outdoor scent. *I wish I didn't have to go back inside and help Mama and Grandpa make jam. I'd much rather spend my morning in the woods where I can draw, watch for deer, and think about my future.* Melinda sighed and turned around. Her responsibilities came first, despite her deep longings.

With a feeling of anticipation, Gabe headed down the road in his buggy toward the Hertzlers' place. He'd been busy in the shop all day and hadn't been able to get away long enough to leave Melinda a note to confirm their buggy ride.

"I hope she's not still doctoring that horse's leg," Gabe muttered.

When Gabe pulled into the Hertzlers', he jumped down from the buggy and hitched the horse to the rail near the barn. As he stood on the front porch, ready to knock on the screen door, he heard loud voices coming from inside the house.

"Melinda, how many times have we told you about bringing your critters into the house?" Gabe recognized Noah's voice, and he sounded upset.

"Only your kitten is allowed inside," Faith chimed in. "And sometimes even she causes problems."

"I've told her that already, but then she never listens to nothin' I have to say," Melinda's little brother added.

It sounded like Melinda's folks were miffed at her. If that was the case, Gabe figured she probably wouldn't be allowed to go out with him.

Would he suffer another disappointment tonight? *Maybe I should turn around and head back home.*

"Reba and Rhoda were fighting in the cage they share," Melinda said.

"Why wasn't Reba in her own cage?" her stepfather questioned.

"The latch won't stay shut, and she keeps chewing the wire and getting out, the same way the squirrel did the night of my birthday party."

Gabe drew in a deep breath and blew it out quickly. *I knew I should have had a talk with her about releasing that raccoon into the woods. I'd better see if I can help in some way.*

He lifted his hand and knocked on the screen door.

"Someone's at the door," Isaiah announced. "Want me to see who it is?"

"It's probably Gabe," Melinda said, moving in that direction. "He said he'd be coming over tonight to take me for a buggy ride."

Mama frowned. "What about the raccoon? She belongs outside."

"Can I at least answer the door?"

"Jah, sure. If it's Gabe, maybe he can help capture the critter." Papa Noah's face was red as a tomato, and a trickle of sweat rolled down his forehead. They'd all been in on the chase to catch Reba, but so far, the quick-footed raccoon had managed to escape everyone's grasp.

Melinda rushed to the door and was glad to see Gabe standing on the porch.

"I came to pick you up for our buggy ride, but I have a notion this isn't such a good time."

"We've been trying to catch one of my raccoons," she explained.

His forehead wrinkled. "Seems like every time I come over here you're either chasing some critter or tending to one."

"It has been kind of hectic lately," Melinda admitted, opening the screen door for him. "Come in. Maybe you can help us catch Reba."

"If you do catch the coon, are you planning to let it go?"

She tipped her head. "Go?"

"Release it into the woods."

"I can't do that, Gabe. Reba's half blind, and she needs to be somewhere safe."

"What about the other raccoon?"

"Rhoda's an orphan, too."

"But she's not sick or anything?"

"No."

"Then why not let her go free?"

"Because she's been keeping Reba company."

Gabe released a huff and stepped into the house just as the raccoon darted into the living room from the door leading to the hallway. Before Melinda had time to respond, the coon snatched one of her mother's slippers, growling and shaking it like a dog would do.

Melinda bent down and grabbed one end of the slipper, tugging it free from Reba's mouth. Gabe came around behind the animal and nearly had it in his grasp when Melinda's cat showed up on the scene. Reba growled. Snow hissed. Then each of them took off in opposite directions.

Melinda watched in horror as the raccoon darted around the living room, bumping into pieces of furniture and acting disoriented.

"What's wrong with that coon?" Gabe asked, scratching the side of his head. "It's carrying on like it's been drinking hard cider or something."

"As I said before, Reba has limited vision. She does seem to be able to follow movement, though."

Gabe snapped his fingers. "That's good news. Open the front door, and I'll see if I can get the critter to follow me outside."

"I'll help you, Gabe," Papa Noah said when he entered the room, followed by Mama and Isaiah.

Melinda wasn't sure Gabe's plan would work, but she figured she should be prepared just in case. "Let me go out to the barn and get Reba's cage. If she does run out the door, I'll need to be ready for her."

"Okay, but hurry," Mama said, fanning her flushed face with her hands.

Moments later, Melinda stood on the front porch holding the cage. She set it in front of the door and hollered, "Okay. I'm ready!"

Mama held the door open, and as Melinda watched the scene unfold, she didn't know who looked funnier—the raccoon, who continued to bump into things, or the menfolk, as they took turns diving after her.

After several more attempts, Reba was finally ushered out the door and into the cage. Relieved that the chase had ended, Melinda flopped into a chair and doubled over with laughter.

"I don't see what's so humorous," Mama grumbled. "This is the second time in a month that one of your critters has gotten into the house and caused an uproar, and I'm getting tired of it."

"Your mamm's right," Papa Noah added firmly. "This kind of commotion has got to stop."

Melinda was tempted to remind her folks that she wasn't the only one in the family responsible for bringing animals inside, but she didn't want to start anything with Isaiah. She glanced over at Gabe, hoping he would say something on her behalf, but he merely stood there with a placid look on his face. Was he on their side, too?

"Gabe and I had planned to go for a buggy ride," Melinda said. "That's why he dropped by."

Mama shook her head. "Until you can find some way to keep your animals locked in their cages and out of my home, you won't be going anywhere to socialize."

"But Mama, that's not fair—"

"And neither is tearing up the house! You're nineteen years old, Melinda, which means you should be more responsible." Papa Noah frowned. "And one more thing: As long as you're living under our roof, you'll do as we say. Is that clear?"

Melinda nodded slowly and blinked back tears. One crept from the corner of her eye and into her hairline. She wiped it away with a sniff. *Maybe I shouldn't be living under your roof.*

Chapter 11

Melinda was on her way to Seymour to deliver some of Grandpa's rhubarb-strawberry jam to the owner of the bed-and-breakfast when she decided to stop and see Gabe. She planned to ask if he would make some new locks for her cages, because as long as her animals kept getting out, her folks would be irritated and might ask her to stop taking in strays altogether. If that happened, she would feel as if she had no other choice but to leave.

When Melinda pulled up to Swartz's Woodworking Shop and hopped down from the buggy, she noticed Gabe's mother in her vegetable garden, working with a hoe.

"Nice day, isn't it?" Leah called with a friendly wave.

"Very pretty."

"Have you got a minute?"

"Jah, sure." Melinda headed up the driveway and joined Gabe's mother at the edge of her garden. "It looks like things are growing well. How are you able to keep up with all the weeds?" She knew Gabe's parents were both in their sixties and figured with no children except Gabe living at home, it would be harder to get things done.

Leah pushed a wayward strand of grayish-brown hair away from her flushed face. "My daughters Karen and Lydia often drop over with their kinner, and everyone helps me weed."

Melinda did a mental head count. Leah and Stephen Swartz had five children and twenty grandchildren. Since all of their offspring were still young enough to have more kinner, they could likely end up with several more grandchildren. She wondered if she and Gabe would be blessed with many children when they got married. *If we get married,* she corrected her thoughts. *What if he changes his mind about marrying me after I tell him about Dr. Franklin's suggestion that I become a vet?*

Melinda still struggled to make a decision, but with her folks not understanding her need to care for animals and refusing to let her go out with Gabe, she wondered if it might not be best if she did leave home and pursue a career in veterinary medicine. Truth was that the longer she worked for Dr. Franklin, the more she desired to become a vet. It would mean great sacrifice and a lot more schooling, but she'd almost convinced herself that it was God's will. Of course, she would still need to convince Gabe.

"I've got a question for you," Leah said, bringing Melinda's thoughts to a halt.

"What is it?"

"I know you work at the vet's and care for lots of animals at home."

"That's true."

"I've been having some trouble with deer getting into my garden and wondered if you had any ideas on keeping them out."

Melinda knew firsthand that the deer and other wildlife in the area could take over a garden if certain measures weren't taken. She also knew some folks used that as an excuse to shoot the deer.

"The best thing would be to build a tall fence, but we've had fairly good luck at keeping the deer out by hanging tin cans around our garden so that when the wind blows, the noise from the cans scares the deer away," Melinda said. "My mamm has also shaved some strong-smelling soap and sprinkled it around the outside of the garden. Another idea would be to put some feed out for the deer close to the edge of your property. If they're getting enough to eat, they won't be as likely to bother your garden."

Leah smiled. "I appreciate the suggestions. You're real *schmaert*, Melinda."

"I'm only smart about things pertaining to animals."

Eager to see Gabe, Melinda glanced toward the woodworking shop.

"I won't keep you any longer. I'm sure you came to visit my son," Leah said. "And if I know Gabe, he'll be pleased to see you."

Melinda nodded. "I did want to speak with him. Guess I'll head out to the shop and do that now."

"Tell Gabe I'll have lunch ready in an hour or so."

"Okay. It was nice talking to you, Leah."

"Same here."

Melinda entered the woodworking shop and spotted Gabe sanding a cabinet door. "Nice job you're doing," she said with a smile.

"Danki." He set the sandpaper aside and leaned on his workbench. "You're just the person I was hoping to see today."

She felt a warm sensation spread over her face. "That's nice to know."

"I've been planning to make new cages for your critters but haven't had the time yet." Gabe smiled. "I have been able to make a couple of new doors for the cages you already have, though. I thought if it was okay, I'd bring the doors by your house this evening and test them on your sneaky raccoons."

"That would be great," Melinda said with a burst of enthusiasm. Gabe's solution was better than her idea of getting new locks for her cages. "I'll be home all evening, so feel free to come by anytime after supper."

"Where are you headed to now? Or did you drive down this way just to see me?" he asked with a hopeful-looking smile.

She grinned in response. "I did come by to see you, but I'm also on my way to Seymour to take some of Grandpa's jam to the bed-and-breakfast. The owners will probably serve some of it to their customers, and I think they're planning to sell a few jars in their gift shop."

"I'm glad your grandpa's doing better these days and has found an outlet for his jam." Gabe motioned to the door. "My daed's outside cutting a stack of lumber that was delivered yesterday afternoon, but I think he's planning to head for Seymour soon, too. He has some finished cabinets he wants to deliver to an English woman who works for the chiropractor there."

Melinda made a sweeping gesture with her hand. "If they look anything like the ones I see here, I'm sure she'll be real pleased."

Gabe blew the sandpaper dust off the cabinet, and it trickled through the air, causing Melinda to sneeze.

"Sorry for sending all that dust in your direction," he said with a look of concern.

"I'm all right."

"I guess you'll have to get used to sandpaper dust if you're planning to marry a carpenter."

She shifted her weight from one foot to the other. "Gabe—there's—uh—something I need to tell you."

"What is it, Melinda? Are you having second thoughts about marrying me?"

"It's not that."

"What is it, then?"

She was about to reply, when Gabe's father stepped into the room. "Herman Yutzy's here to pick up the table and chairs his daed ordered," he announced. "I need your help loading them into his wagon, Gabe."

"Jah, okay." Gabe smiled at Melinda. "Duty calls."

"That's all right. I need to get going anyhow. I'll see you this evening, Gabe."

"You can count on it."

"It's good you didn't have to work today," Mama said to Susie as the two of them finished up the breakfast dishes. "Maybe the two of us can get some baking done."

Susie wiped her sweaty forehead with the back of her hand and groaned. "It's hot in here, and I don't feel much like baking."

"What do you feel like doing?"

"I don't know, but anything that will get me outside would be a welcome relief. My job at the store keeps me inside way too much, and my face is paler than goat's milk."

Mama clucked her tongue and reached for another clean dish to dry. "How you do exaggerate, girl."

"I'm not exaggerating. When I looked in the mirror this morning, I could hardly believe how pasty I looked."

"If you think you need more sun on your face, then why not spend the day weeding the garden?"

"Since Grace Ann and Faith were here last week helping you work in the garden, it's almost weed-free."

Mama nodded. "That's true. They were a big help to me that day."

Susie glanced out the window and noticed an open buggy pulling into their yard. "Looks like Melinda is here," she said, motioning toward the window with her soapy hand. "I wonder what she wants."

"Probably stopped to say hello."

A few minutes later, the back door opened, and Melinda stepped into the kitchen. "Wie geht's?" she asked with a cheery smile.

"We're doing fine," Mama replied.

"What brings you by so early this morning?" Susie asked.

"I'm on my way to Seymour to take some jars of Grandpa's rhubarb-strawberry jam to the bed-and-breakfast," Melinda replied. "I decided to drop by here first and see if you wanted to ride along."

Susie smiled. "A trip to Seymour sounds like a fun way to spend my day off. If we stay around long enough, maybe we can go somewhere for lunch."

Melinda nodded. "I wouldn't mind getting some barbecued ribs at Baldy's Café."

Susie licked her lips. "That does sound good."

"If you're going into town, maybe you could drop by the grocery store and pick up a few things for me before you head back home," Mama said.

Susie looked over at Melinda to get her approval.

"Sure, that shouldn't be a problem." Melinda slipped one arm around her grandmother's waist and gave her a squeeze. "Would you like to go with us?"

Mama shook her head. "I appreciate the offer, but I think it would be good for the two of you to do something fun together. With Susie working at the store, and you helping out at the vet's part-time, you don't get much time together anymore."

"And when you're not working for Dr. Franklin, you're either with Gabe or taking care of some injured or orphaned critter," Susie put in as she finished the last dish and turned to face Melinda.

Melinda's forehead wrinkled. "You make it sound as if I don't have time for my family anymore."

"I never said that."

"Not in so many words, but—"

"I'm ready to go if you are," Susie said, cutting Melinda off in midsentence. She wasn't in the mood to argue this morning, and it seemed that every time she and Melinda discussed her need to be with animals, they ended up in a disagreement.

"Let's go then." Melinda opened the back door. "See you sometime this afternoon, Grandma."

"Jah, okay. Have a good time."

Susie dried her hands on a towel, grabbed her black handbag from the wall peg, and rushed out the door behind Melinda.

❧

"Sure is a nice day, isn't it?" Melinda asked as she and Susie headed down the road in her open buggy.

Susie nodded.

"You've been awfully quiet since we left your house. Is something bothering you?"

Susie shrugged.

Melinda nudged Susie with her elbow. "There is something bothering you, isn't there?"

Susie released an extended sigh. *"Es is mir verleed."*

"Why are you discouraged?"

"Every time I find a fellow I'm interested in, he either has no interest in me, already has a girlfriend, or is going back to Montana."

Melinda glanced over at Susie as she lifted

her eyebrows. "How many fellows do you know who are heading to Montana?"

"Just one. Jonas Byler."

"Ah, I see." Melinda brought her gaze back to the road and gripped the reins a little tighter as they crested the top of a small hill. "I saw Jonas at the last young people's gathering and heard someone mention that he'd come back to the area for a visit." She nudged Susie again. "I didn't know you had an interest in him, though."

"For all the good it does me." Susie grunted. "I doubt he knows I'm alive. And even if he did, he won't be sticking around Webster County long enough to spend any time with me."

"Maybe you could go to Montana and visit Jonas sometime," Melinda suggested. "It would probably be an exciting trip."

"Jah, right. Like Mama and Papa would ever give their permission for me to go off by myself like that."

"They might. I know a lot of Amish young people who like to travel around and see some sights before they get married and settle down."

Susie leaned closer to Melinda. "Say, I have an idea. Why don't the two of us plan a trip to Montana? Think how much fun it would be to catch the train or a bus and go out West to see the sights."

Melinda shook her head vigorously. "I can't go on any trips right now."

"Why not?"

"For one thing, I've got my job at the veterinary clinic."

"It's only part-time, Melinda. I'm sure Dr. Franklin would give you a few weeks off so you could go on a little vacation."

"Even if he did give me the time off, I have responsibilities at home."

"Such as?"

"Taking care of my animals."

"Couldn't someone else in your family do that in your absence?"

"No way! Mama and Papa Noah are too busy with other things, and I wouldn't trust Isaiah to feed my bussli, let alone take care of any of the orphaned animals I have in my care." Melinda drew in a deep breath and released it quickly. "And then there's Gabe."

"Oh, I see how it is," Susie said in a wistful tone. "You're in love with Gabe and don't want to leave him for a few weeks. Isn't that right?"

Melinda nodded. But while it was true that she didn't relish the idea of being away from Gabe, she wasn't about to tell her aunt that the main reason she didn't want to leave home right now was because she was on the verge of making one of the biggest decisions of her life. If she decided to prepare for a career in veterinary work, she would have to begin by taking her GED test, and for that, she needed to be at home, studying.

"So, where would you like to go after I drop off Grandpa's jam at the bed-and-breakfast?"

Melinda asked, changing the subject.

"I thought we were going to have lunch at Baldy's."

"We are. But I thought maybe you'd like to do some shopping first."

"We can do that afterwards, when we pick up the groceries for my mamm."

"Oh, that's right." She looked over at Susie again. "Did she give you a list?"

Susie's eyebrows drew together. "A list?"

"A list of the groceries she wants."

Susie clamped her hand over her mouth. "Ach! I hurried out of the house so quickly, I forgot to ask what she needed."

"Maybe she'll send Grandpa after the items she needs."

"Either that, or as soon as you drop me off at home, she'll give me the list and I'll have to head right back to town."

Melinda snickered. "Oh, well. Then you'll have two good doses of sunshine and fresh air."

Chapter 12

When Melinda arrived home later that day, she was greeted with a sorrowful sight. Isaiah's dog had gone on the rampage, killing a female rabbit that had gotten out of its cage. Melinda was sure it had happened because the door wouldn't stay latched. She was heartsick when she discovered the dead rabbit's four orphaned babies, knowing they might not survive without their mother.

"I'll need to feed them," she murmured, reaching into the open cage.

"Sorry about this," Isaiah said, stepping up beside her. "Don't know what came over Jericho to do such a thing."

"If you kept him tied up like I've asked you

to do, he wouldn't have had the opportunity." Melinda lifted the rabbits gently out of the cage and placed them inside a cardboard box. "I'll take them into the house where I can better care for their needs."

"Mama won't like it," Isaiah asserted. "She's gettin' sick of your critters and the messes they make."

Melinda wrinkled her nose. "You'd best let me worry about that." She hurried out of the barn before her brother could offer a retort.

When she stepped onto the back porch a few minutes later, she spotted Grandpa sitting in the wicker rocking chair outside his living quarters. He waved at her. "Did you get my jam delivered?"

She nodded. "Every last one is gone."

"Then what have you got in the box?"

"Four baby rabbits." Melinda moved closer to his chair and held out the box so he could take a look. "Isaiah's dog killed the mother. Now it's my job to save them."

Grandpa fingered his long, white beard. "It doesn't surprise me that you'd be willing to do that. You're such a caring young woman."

She leaned over and kissed his wrinkled cheek. "I'd best get these little ones inside and find a way to feed them."

"I hope they make it."

"Me, too." Melinda opened the back door and stepped into the house.

When the back door opened and banged against the wall, Faith turned from her task at the kitchen sink, where she'd been peeling some carrots. She fully expected to see Isaiah standing there, but found Melinda holding a box in her hands instead.

"Mercy, daughter, can't you be a little quieter when you enter the house? And for goodness' sake, please shut the door."

Melinda placed the box on one end of the counter, turned, and closed the door with her hip. "Sorry, Mama. I was in a hurry to get the *bopplin* inside."

Faith dropped the carrot into the sink and hurried across the room. "Babies? What kind of babies have you got in that box?"

"Baby rabbits." Melinda's forehead wrinkled as she frowned. "Thanks to Isaiah's mutt, these poor little critters are orphans now."

"Jericho killed the mother rabbit?"

Melinda nodded solemnly. "So now it's my job to raise them."

"You can take care of them out in the barn, but not in here," Faith said with a shake of her head.

"How come?"

Faith blew out an exaggerated breath. "Do you really have to ask? You know how I feel about having animals in the house."

"But you allow Snow to be inside."

"That's different. Snow's a pet, not a wild animal."

Melinda peered into the box and stared at the tiny bunnies. "These little *haaslin* aren't wild, Mama. They're helpless, hungry, and without a mamm."

"Be that as it may—"

"Can't I keep them in my room? I promise they won't be any trouble to you. They'll be inside a box, so there's no chance of them running all over the house or making a mess."

Faith slipped her hands behind her back and popped two knuckles at the same time.

Melinda winced. "Are you upset with me, Mama? You always pop your knuckles whenever you're upset."

"I'm not upset. I just don't want you turning our home into a zoo."

"I'm not trying to." Melinda peered into the box again. "I only want to take care of these orphaned bunnies because they won't make it on their own."

Faith released a blustery sigh. "Oh, all right. But as soon as they start trying to get out of that box, they're to be put in a rabbit cage inside the barn. Is that clear?"

Melinda nodded and gave Faith a hug. "Danki, Mama." Then she grabbed the box and scurried out of the room.

Faith lifted her gaze to the ceiling. "Oh, Lord, please give me the wisdom of Solomon and the patience of Job."

That evening after supper, Melinda sat on the front porch swing, waiting for Gabe to show up. She had just fed the orphaned bunnies with an eyedropper and put them back inside the cardboard box.

A slight breeze came up, whisking away some of the oppressive, muggy July air that had hovered over the land most of the day. A horse and buggy trotted into the yard just then, and Melinda smiled when she saw that it was Gabe. She left the porch and hurried out to greet him.

Gabe climbed down from his buggy and retrieved two wooden cage doors from the back. He motioned to the barn. "Let's go see how they work, shall we?"

As soon as they entered the barn, Melinda took Reba and Rhoda out of their cages and placed them inside an empty horse stall. Gabe removed the old cage doors, and a short time later, he had the new doors set in place.

"The latches can't be jimmied from the inside," he explained. "I don't think the coons will be able to escape, and as soon as I find the time, I'll make you a couple of new cages with doors just like these."

"That would be wunderbaar." Melinda retrieved Reba and Rhoda and put them in their respective cages.

Gabe closed the doors and clicked the locks shut. "I dare either of you critters to get out now," he said, squinting at the animals.

"If it keeps them in, I'll be happy, and so will my folks."

Gabe lifted Melinda's chin with his thumb and lowered his head. His lips were just inches from hers when her brother burst into the barn. "Yodel-oh-de-tee! Yodel-oh-de-tee! My mama taught me how to yodel when I sat on her knee. . . ." Isaiah halted when he saw Gabe and Melinda, and his face turned cherry red. "Oops. Didn't know anyone was here."

"And I didn't know you could yodel," Gabe said. "I thought only Melinda and your mamm were the yodelers in the family."

"He *can't* yodel." Melinda tapped her foot impatiently. "He only does that to mimic me."

Isaiah glared at her. "Do not. I came to the barn to see if Jericho was here."

"He's not." Melinda clenched her teeth. "That mutt had better not be running free again, either."

"He can't be chained up all the time, and it's not his fault your goofy pets are always gettin' out of their cages."

"I think that problem's been solved," Gabe said. "I just put new doors with better locks on the coons' cages, and if it keeps them in, I'll be making more cages for Melinda's other animals."

Isaiah peered at Reba's cage door. "If Papa ever gets around to buildin' Jericho a dog run, maybe you can put a door like this on his cage."

Melinda poked her brother's arm. "Is that any way to ask a favor? Gabe doesn't have a lot of time on his hands and shouldn't be expected to make a cage door for your dog."

"I'll make the time for it," Gabe said with a wide smile. "Fact is, I'll build the whole dog run for Jericho. It will give me a chance to build something on my own without Pap looking over my shoulder and telling me how it's done. Not only that, but it will keep your dog from hurting Melinda's critters."

"That'd be great." Isaiah gave Gabe a wide grin. "Danki, Gabe. You're a right nice fellow."

Melinda moved toward the barn door. "Come on, Gabe. Let's go tell my folks about the cage doors and see if they mind if we go for a buggy ride."

Chapter 13

Melinda drew in a deep breath and prayed for the courage to say what had been on her mind for the last several weeks. Gabe deserved to know what Dr. Franklin wanted her to do, and now was the time to tell him.

"I've been wanting to discuss something with you," she said as they headed down Highway C in his open buggy.

"What's on your mind?"

Melinda moistened her lips with the tip of her tongue. "You know how much I enjoy working with animals."

"Jah."

"And I want to help as many of the sick and hurting ones as I can."

He nodded.

"The thing is—" She paused and drew in a quick breath. This was going to be harder than she'd expected. No wonder she had put off telling him for so long.

"The thing is what?" Gabe prompted.

"Well, Dr. Franklin says I have a special way with animals. He called it a 'God-given talent.'"

"He's right about that. Look how well your daed's horse has responded to you. And those baby bunnies are doing well under your care. Animals have a sixth sense and know when a human being cares for them."

Melinda felt relief that Gabe realized her capabilities. Maybe he would be receptive to the idea of her becoming a vet.

"I do care a lot," she admitted, "but unfortunately, I'm not able to do as much for wounded or sick animals as I would like."

"That's why Doc Franklin's available." Gabe flicked the reins, and his horse picked up speed. "When you find an ailing critter or somebody brings an animal over to your place that has more wrong with it than you can handle, you take it to the vet."

Melinda clasped her hands tightly in her lap. Her throat felt so dry all of a sudden.

"Well, if that doesn't beat all," Gabe said, pointing to the other side of the road. "It's another dead *hasch*. Probably some car or a truck ran into it."

Melinda flinched. She hated to see dead deer, whether they were lying alongside the road after being hit by a car or hanging in someone's barn during deer hunting season.

"If the deer aren't thinned enough during hunting season," Gabe said, "they overpopulate and will soon overrun our area." He glanced over his shoulder and pointed to the deer they'd just passed. "I'd rather see 'em shot for meat than go to waste that way, though. Wouldn't you?"

Melinda formulated her next words carefully. She wanted to be sure Gabe didn't take anything she said the wrong way. "To tell you the truth, I don't like to see *any* deer killed. We raise hogs, sheep, and cows for food, so why would anyone need to kill the deer?"

He shrugged. "Some folks in our community prefer the taste of deer meat, and even if we do have other animals to butcher, a change is nice."

Melinda didn't like the way this conversation was going, so she decided to get back to the subject she needed to discuss with Gabe. "Dr. Franklin thinks I have what it takes to become a vet." There, it was out, and Melinda should have felt better, but she didn't.

A muscle in Gabe's cheek quivered as he stared straight ahead. Was he mulling things over or trying to stay focused on the road? The buggy rolled along, and the horse's hooves made a steady *clip-clop, clip-clop* against the pavement, but Gabe remained quiet.

Unable to stand the silence, Melinda reached over and touched his arm. "Awhile back, the doctor gave me some information on the necessary college courses I would need to take. He told me about a couple different schools of veterinary medicine, too."

Gabe jerked on the reins and guided his horse and buggy to the side of the road. When they were stopped, he turned in his seat and stared hard at Melinda. "Just how far have you gone with all this? Have you already made up your mind to leave the Amish faith? Have you made application to a college?"

She shook her head. "No, no. I would need to get my GED first, and then—"

"So you have decided."

"Not yet, but Dr. Franklin says if I want something badly enough, I should be willing to make whatever sacrifices are necessary. Even if it means giving up those things that are dear to me in order to reach my goal."

"If you were to get the training you needed to become a vet, it would mean leaving the Amish faith and everyone you love behind." Gabe's shoulders slumped as he stared at the floor of his buggy. Apparently he thought this would mean the end of their relationship.

Melinda clasped his hand. "Would you be willing to leave here with me?"

"What?" His mouth dropped open. "How could you even suggest such a thing?"

"I—I thought if you loved me—"

A vein in Gabe's temple began to throb. "You know I love you, Melinda. But I'm happy living here, and I don't want to leave the Amish faith." He squinted as he stared at her long and hard. "I can't imagine you wanting to leave, either."

"I don't really want to leave, but in order for me to—"

"I asked you once if you ever missed the English world or thought you would want to go back to it someday, and you said you were happy being Amish."

"I—I am happy being Amish, but I can't become a veterinarian and remain part of our faith."

"So I guess that means you'll have to choose between me and the modern world."

Frustration welled in Melinda's soul as she fought to keep her emotions under control. Gabe didn't understand the way she felt at all. "It's not the modern world I'd be choosing," she said. "Becoming a vet would mean I could help so many animals."

"You're helping some now, aren't you?"

"Jah, but in such a small way."

He shrugged. "Seems to me you ought to be happy with what you can do for the animals you've taken in and quit wishing for something that goes against our beliefs."

She lowered her head. "My folks don't approve of my desire to care for animals. They're always hollering at me for spending too much time caring for animals."

Gabe grabbed both of Melinda's arms as a look of frustration crossed his face. "You've been baptized and have joined the church. You've made a vow to God to adhere to our church rules. If you left to become part of the English world, you'd be shunned. Have you thought about the seriousness of that?"

"Of course I have, and it would hurt to leave my family behind." Tears seeped out from under her lashes, and she swallowed around the constriction in her throat.

"What do your folks have to say about this? Are they letting you go with their blessings?"

Melinda shook her head. "I haven't told them yet. I wanted to discuss it with you first and see if you'd be willing to—"

"I don't want to leave the Amish faith." Gabe sat for several seconds with a pained expression; then his features softened some. "I've been working real hard and saving up money so I can start my own place of business," he said, taking hold of her hand. "I'm doing it for us so that I can make a good living and provide for the family I'd hoped that we would have someday."

Confusion swirled in Melinda's brain like a tornado spinning at full speed. She did love Gabe, but if he wouldn't leave the Amish faith, then she would be completely on her own if she decided to get the necessary schooling to become a vet. And how would she pay for her classes? College was expensive, not to mention the additional training at a veterinary school. What she made working for Dr. Franklin wasn't nearly enough, and she sure couldn't ask her folks to help out.

Melinda squeezed her eyes shut as a sense of shame washed over her. *That was a selfish thought. I'm not asking Gabe to leave the Amish faith so he can help me financially. I want him to support my decision because he loves me and wants to be with me no matter which world I choose to live in.*

She opened her eyes and looked at him. "Would you do me one favor, Gabe?"

"What's that?"

"Would you at least pray about the matter?"

His forehead wrinkled as his eyebrows drooped. "You want me to pray about you becoming a vet?"

She nodded. "And ask God what His plans for you might be, too."

Gabe gathered up the reins. "I will pray about this, but I think right now I'd best take you home. I don't feel like riding any farther tonight."

Melinda placed her hand on his shoulder. "Gabe—"

"Jah?"

"Please don't say anything to my folks or anyone else about what we've discussed this evening, okay?"

He gave a quick nod. "It's not my place to do the telling. I'll leave that up to you."

Chapter 14

Melinda's hands shook as she stood in front of the birdhouse by their driveway, holding the note she had discovered from Gabe. Had he been thinking about what she'd told him concerning Dr. Franklin's suggestion that she become a vet? Had Gabe decided that he would be willing to go English with her?

She focused on the words he'd written:

Dear Melinda,

I spoke with your daed yesterday, and he said it would be fine if I want to help Isaiah build a dog run, since he still hasn't found the time. He also said he thought I would do a much better job than he could,

*since I'm a carpenter and have the skills and
proper tools.*

*So I plan to come by after work today
and begin the project. If you don't have
anything else to do, maybe you can keep me
company. If not, then I hope we can get in
a few minutes to visit when I'm done for
the day.*

*Always yours,
Gabe*

Melinda frowned as she tucked the note inside the front of her apron. Gabe hadn't said a word about her becoming a vet or made any mention of whether he'd made a decision regarding their situation or not. Maybe he planned to discuss it with her tonight. That could be why he'd mentioned her keeping him company and hoping to have a few minutes to visit when he was done at the end of the day.

Melinda bent down and picked up her cat, who had been sunning herself on the grass. "You've got life made, you know that, Snow?"

Snow's only response was a soft *meow* as she opened one lazy eye and snuggled against Melinda.

"I wish all I had to do was lie around and soak up the sun," she said as she walked toward the house.

"You wouldn't be happy, and you know it."

Melinda smiled when she heard her

grandfather's deep, mellow voice. He sat in his wicker rocking chair on the front porch snapping green beans into a bowl wedged between his knees.

"You're right, Grandpa. I wouldn't be happy if I wasn't busy," she said as she stepped onto the porch and stood beside him. "I enjoy caring for my animals too much to sit around all day and do nothing."

"Speaking of your animals, have you let either of the coons go yet?"

She nodded and sat in the chair beside him, nestling Snow in her lap. "In all fairness to Rhoda, the healthy raccoon, I released her into the woods the other day. But Reba is really lonely without her."

"Maybe you should let her go, too."

"I can't. She's partially blind, and I'm sure she wouldn't make it in the woods on her own." Melinda stroked the cat behind its left ear. "Gabe's coming over later to help Isaiah build a dog run, so maybe once my brother's mutt is locked away, I can let Reba roam around our place whenever I'm at home and am able to keep an eye out for her."

Grandpa's bushy gray eyebrows drew together. "Do you think it's fair to confine Isaiah's dog so your raccoon can run free?"

Melinda shrugged. "I suppose not, but Jericho's been known to attack other animals, too. Don't forget the baby bunnies I'm caring for.

Jericho killed their mother, you know."

"That was a shame, but the dog was only doing what comes natural to him. Maybe when Gabe's done with the dog run, he can build some other kind of pen for the coon."

"You mean something bigger than the cage I keep her in now?"

"Jah. Maybe he could make it more like the cages I've seen at the zoo." Grandpa dropped another bean into the bowl. "Some of those zoo cages are real nice—tree branches, scrub brush, and small pools of water inside."

Melinda's heart pounded as a host of ideas skittered through her mind. How wonderful it would be if she had larger cages that were similar to the animals' natural habitat. The critters would feel more at home until it was time to let them go free.

Why am I even thinking such thoughts? If I leave home to go to college, I won't be caring for any of my animal friends until I become a vet, and then it will be in a much different way. Besides, that could be several years from now.

Gabe clucked to his horse to get him moving. He was tired after a long day at the shop. Even so, he looked forward to going over to the Hertzlers' to build the dog run for Isaiah. It would be something different to work on for a change, and it would give him a chance to speak with Melinda. Maybe he could talk some sense into her—make her see more clearly what the consequences would be if she left the Amish faith.

He thought about his own plans to open a woodworking shop where he could make a variety of things. What would be the point in doing that if Melinda left and he stayed behind? Without her by his side, nothing would ever be the same. He felt sure he could never be happy if he left the Amish faith, because he was Amish through and through. For Melinda, though, it might be different because she had been born into the modern world and her father had been English. Maybe Melinda didn't have the same commitment to the Amish faith as Gabe did. Maybe she could leave it behind and never look back.

He swallowed hard. *Why'd I have to go and fall in love with a woman who isn't satisfied with the plain, simple life? Why can't I set aside my feelings for her now?*

Gabe flicked the reins to get the horse moving faster. He knew the answer to that question. He loved Melinda and didn't want to lose her. But did he love her enough to give up the only way of life he'd ever known and go English?

Gabe pulled into the Hertzlers' yard sometime later and parked his buggy next to the barn. Since he would be there a few hours, he decided to unhitch the horse and put him in one of the stalls.

As Gabe led the gelding through the barn

door, he spotted Melinda standing on the other side of the building in front of an animal cage with her back to him.

He hurried to get the horse situated in a stall then strolled over to where she stood. "Hey! What are you up to?"

Melinda turned, and Gabe saw that she held a raccoon in her arms.

"You shouldn't carry that coon around like that," he admonished, wishing he'd said something sooner about her taking such chances. "What if the critter bites or scratches you real bad?"

Melinda lifted her chin and looked at him as if he'd taken leave of his senses. "Reba's as tame as my cat. And for your information, she likes it when I hold her."

"Humph! She's a wild animal. You can't be sure of what she might do."

Melinda's eyes narrowed. "I don't want to argue with you, Gabe. I've been taking in wild animals since I was a young girl, and I think I know what I'm doing."

Gabe blew out his breath in a puff of air that lifted the hair off his forehead. She was right; they shouldn't be arguing. Besides, his irritation had more to do with what she had told him about wanting to leave the Amish faith and becoming a vet than it did with the silly raccoon. He needed to handle this situation carefully so he didn't make Melinda mad. If she became angry with him, she might jump the fence and go English just to spite him. Even so, Gabe knew he'd have to tell Melinda that he didn't want her to leave; nor did he want to leave with her.

"I didn't mean to upset you," Gabe muttered.

"All's forgiven." Melinda put Reba back in her cage and turned to face him. "I was wondering if you've thought any more about what we discussed the other night."

He glanced around nervously. "Are—are we alone?"

She nodded. "Papa Noah's still at work, Mama and Grandpa are inside the house, and the last time I saw Isaiah, he was digging in the dirt out behind the barn."

Gabe plunked down on a bale of straw, and Melinda seated herself beside him. "In answer to your question," he said, "I have thought more about what we discussed the other night, and I've also been praying."

"Have you made a decision?"

"I'm hoping you'll change your mind and decide to be content with being Amish."

"As I told you before, I am content being Amish. I'm just not content being unable to properly care for any animals I find that are hurt." She frowned. "And I'm sure not content with always being scolded by my folks for helping my animal friends."

"So what it boils down to is that one of us has to give up something we feel is important in order for us to be together." He hurried on before he lost his nerve. "If you left home to get the schooling you would need to become a vet, and I went with you, then I'd be giving up a way of life I love and respect."

She nodded slowly.

"And if you stayed Amish to please me, then you'd be giving up your desire to care for more animals than you're doing now."

She nodded again. "That's true, but if I leave home, I'll also be giving up my family and the way of life I've become accustomed to, same as you. Sacrifices would have to be made on both our parts if we decided to go English."

Gabe massaged the bridge of his nose as he contemplated their problem. As far as he was concerned, it was a no-win situation. No matter how it turned out, one of them would be unhappy. Truth be told, he figured if they left the Amish faith together, they both would be unhappy. Melinda might think being a vet was what she wanted, but he knew one thing for sure—if they went English, Melinda's relationship with her family would be greatly affected.

"We don't have to make a decision right now," Melinda said, touching his arm. "However, I need to get registered for classes at the college in Springfield before the end of August. In the meantime, I'm going to see about getting my GED—graduate equivalency diploma."

"I know what a GED is, Melinda." He slowly shook his head. "I'll bet your folks would be upset if they knew what you were planning to do. Are you going to tell them soon?"

She grunted. "I plan to, but it needs to be said at the right time, in the right way. Maybe after I pass the GED test I'll tell them."

Gabe stood, feeling the need to end this discussion. He didn't want Melinda to take the GED test, but he figured there was no way to stop her from doing so, since she seemed to have her mind set on it. The best thing he could do was continue to pray that she would change her mind.

"I'd best round up Isaiah so we can get busy on that dog run." Gabe took a few steps toward the door but turned back around. "Do you know where your daed had planned to build it?"

"He cemented some posts in an area to the left of the barn."

"Are you coming out to keep us company?"

"I've got a few things I need to do inside the house right now. Then some corn needs to be shucked."

"Maybe I'll see you later then." Gabe hurried out of the barn, grabbed some tools from the back of his buggy, and went to look for Melinda's brother. He hoped a few hours of hard work would get him calmed down.

Gabe found Isaiah digging in the soil just as Melinda had said. Streaks of dirt covered the boy's pale blue shirt and dark brown trousers, and several murky-looking smudges were smearing his face.

"What are you doing out here?" Gabe asked, squatting beside Isaiah.

"Lookin' for an old bone Jericho buried some time ago."

Gabe squinted. "Why would you be doing that?"

"My dog's bored and needs somethin' to do. Thought if he had a bone to chew on, he might be happier." Isaiah's mouth turned down at the corners. "Since I'm not supposed to let Jericho off his chain during the day, I figured it wouldn't be good to let him loose in order to look for the bone himself."

"Why not just give him a new bone?"

"Don't have one," Isaiah said with a shrug. "Mama hasn't made any beef soup in a while, and those are the only kind of bones Jericho likes."

Gabe chuckled as he rose to his feet. "How about you and me getting busy on that dog run, and you can worry about finding Jericho a bone later on?"

"Jah, okay." When Isaiah stood and slapped the sides of his trousers, dirt blew everywhere. Gabe stepped quickly aside, and the boy sneezed. He pulled a dusty hanky from his pocket and blew his nose. "You think Jericho will be happier once he has a pen of his own?"

"I believe so."

"It's important for dogs to be happy, same as people, jah?"

"I suppose." Gabe clenched his fingers. *I'd be happy if I had my own business, stayed right here in Webster County, and married Melinda. I've got to figure out some way to make her see how foolish it would be to leave the Amish faith. Doesn't she realize how many people will be hurt if she goes English? Me, most of all.*

"How are things going with you these days?" Noah's boss, Hank, asked as he lowered himself to the ground where Noah knelt, studying a struggling pine tree.

Noah looked over at Hank and smiled. "You mean how are things going here or at home?"

"Both."

"Here, things are going well enough, but at home I'm not so sure."

Hank pulled his fingers through the sides of his reddish-brown hair. "What's going on at home?"

"It's the same old thing. Melinda's critters stirring up trouble, and Faith getting perturbed with Melinda for shirking her duties because she's preoccupied with her animals."

Hank thumped Noah on the back. "At least you know where your daughter is, and you don't have to worry about her running all over creation in some fancy souped-up car, like some of the

English kids who live in this area are doing."

"That's true. I guess we should be grateful that Melinda spends most of her time in the barn tending to some critter or working at the veterinary clinic with Dr. Franklin."

"When does she find the time to be courted? I heard that Gabe Swartz has an interest in her."

"Oh, she manages to fit that into her schedule. But whenever Faith needs something done, Melinda has a dozen excuses." Noah groaned. "Sometimes I wish Faith and I could have had more children, but then there are days when either Isaiah or Melinda does something foolish that I think maybe the Lord gave us all the children He knew we could handle."

Hank snickered. "I hear you there. When Sandy and I first decided to adopt, we talked about getting four or five kids. But after we got Cheryl, and then Ryan, we knew we were blessed and decided two children were enough to make our family complete."

"I guess God knew what each of us needed." Noah leaned closer to the fledgling pine tree and squinted. "Raising children is a lot like taking care of the trees you grow here on your Christmas tree farm."

"How so?"

"They both need lots of attention and plenty of nurturing in order to make 'em grow. I just hope I've nurtured my children enough."

Melinda sat in a wicker chair on the back porch, shucking corn and watching Gabe and Isaiah work under the sweltering sun. She could hear the steady *thump, thump, thump* as they pounded nails to hold the wire fencing that was being connected to the wooden poles Papa Noah had previously put in.

I wish I could make Gabe understand my need to become a vet. If only he loved me enough to. . .

A piercing scream halted Melinda's thoughts. Had Gabe been hurt? Was it Isaiah?

She dropped the corn, leaped off the porch, and dashed across the yard.

When Melinda arrived at the dog run a few seconds later, she discovered Isaiah holding his thumb and jumping up and down. "Ouch! Ouch!" he hollered. "Ach! That hurts me somethin' awful!"

"What happened? Are you seriously injured?"

"He smacked his thumb with the hammer," Gabe explained. "But he won't let me get a good look, so I don't know how much damage was done."

"Give me your hand," Melinda ordered, grabbing hold of her brother's arm.

"Don't touch me!"

"I need to see how bad it is."

"You'd better let her look at that," Gabe put in.

Isaiah whimpered but finally released his thumb for Melinda's inspection.

She held it gently between her fingers. The skin was red and swollen, and the nail was beginning to turn purple. "You might end up losing that nail," she said with a click of her tongue.

Isaiah sniffed, and a few tears trickled down his cheeks. "How can ya tell? You ain't no doctor."

"No, but she'd like to be."

Melinda glared at Gabe then looked quickly back at her brother. What was Gabe thinking, blurting out something like that in front of Isaiah? "What Gabe meant to say is that I've doctored enough animals to know many things. Besides, I lost a couple of nails myself when I slammed two fingers in my bedroom door when I was a girl."

Isaiah rocked back and forth on his heels, moaning like a heifer about to give birth.

"You'd best go up to the house and ask Mama to put some ice on your thumb. If it's cared for right away, the nail might not come loose," Melinda instructed.

"Guess I won't be able to help ya no more, Gabe. Sorry about that," the boy mumbled.

Gabe patted Isaiah on the shoulder. "It's okay. I'll do what I can on my own. We probably wouldn't have gotten it all done today anyway. I'll come back in a few days to finish the project."

"I can help you," Melinda volunteered after her brother had scurried away. "After I'm done shucking corn, that is."

Gabe's expression was dubious at first, but then he nodded. "I'll take any help I can get."

"Please hold still, Isaiah," Faith instructed as she dabbed some peroxide under the nail of his thumb. "I want to be sure you don't get an infection."

"It hurts like crazy, Mama." Isaiah wiggled back and forth in his chair and groaned.

"I know, son."

"Do you think I'm gonna lose my nail?"

"Time will tell." Faith reached for the ice bag lying on the table and handed it to Isaiah. "You'd better keep this on your thumb awhile. It'll help the swelling go down and should help ease the pain, too."

Isaiah positioned the bag of ice over his thumb and leaned back in his chair. "I think I might feel better if I had some of Papa's lemon sponge cake to eat while I'm sittin' here."

Faith chuckled and ruffled her son's hair. "You think that would help, huh?"

He grinned. "I surely do."

"All right then. I'll fix us a slice of cake and some cold milk to wash it down."

A few minutes later, Faith was seated at the table across from her boy, with a piece of Noah's delicious lemon sponge cake sitting before them.

"This sure is tasty," Isaiah said after he'd

taken his first bite. "I think Papa's the best cook in all of Webster County."

"Melinda thinks that, too."

Isaiah's eyebrows furrowed. "Speaking of Melinda, do you wanna know what I heard Gabe say about her?"

"Not if it's gossip."

"It ain't."

"Isn't."

"That's what I meant." Isaiah took a drink of milk and wiped his mouth with the back of his hand.

Faith reached into the wicker basket sitting in the center of the table and handed him a napkin.

Isaiah swiped it across his mouth. "As I was saying, when Melinda was lookin' at my sore thumb, and she said I might lose my fingernail, I said to her, 'How do you know? You ain't no doctor.' And then Gabe said, 'No, but she'd like to be.' "

Faith pursed her lips. "What did he mean by that?"

"Beats me. I never got the chance to ask, 'cause Melinda sent me up to the house to have you take a look at my thumb."

"Gabe probably made that comment because Melinda's always playing doctor on some sick or hurting animal."

Isaiah shrugged. "Maybe so. She does think she can fix every critter that's ailin'."

Faith reached for her glass of milk and took

a sip, letting the cool liquid roll around in her mouth. *I hope that's all it meant. I don't know how I would deal with it if Melinda decided to leave the Amish faith and pursue a career in the English world the way I did when I was her age.*

Chapter 15

For the next few weeks, Melinda struggled for answers as to what she should do about becoming a vet, but no clear direction came. She'd helped Gabe finish Jericho's dog run, and Gabe had agreed to make Reba a larger cage when he found the time. But every time Melinda broached the subject of them leaving the Amish faith, they ended up in an argument. Before she left for work on Thursday morning, she had found a note from Gabe in the birdhouse. He wanted her to go with him to the farmers' market on Saturday after the woodworking shop closed at noon. She'd written him back, saying she could go because she wouldn't be working at the veterinary clinic.

Now Melinda sat on the porch swing waiting

for Gabe and hoping things would go all right between them. She had to make a decision soon and needed Gabe's final answer. Thursday after work, she'd spoken with Dr. Franklin again, and he'd explained the necessary procedure for getting her GED. Without her folks' knowledge, she had gotten the information she needed in order to study for the test and was scheduled to take it at the college in Springfield in two weeks. Dr. Franklin's wife, Ellen, had agreed to drive her there.

Melinda jumped up when she heard a horse and buggy pull into the yard, figuring it must be Gabe. Instead, she recognized Harold Esh, one of their Amish neighbors.

"Wie geht's?" the elderly man called as she approached his buggy.

"I'm doing fine, and you?"

"Oh, can't complain."

"Are you here to see my daed?"

Harold shook his head and stepped down from the buggy. "Found some pheasant eggs in the field this morning, and their mamm was lyin' dead beside them." He motioned to the cardboard box in the back of his buggy. "Don't believe she'd been gone too long, because the eggs were still warm."

"What do you think happened?"

"Looked to me like she'd been shot with a pellet gun."

Melinda gasped. "It's not pheasant hunting

season yet. I can't understand who would do such a thing."

He shrugged. "Probably some kid usin' the bird for target practice."

Melinda's heart clenched. To think that someone would kill a defenseless animal for the mere sport of it made her feel sick.

"I thought you might like to try and get the eggs to hatch," Harold said.

"I may be able to keep them warm under the heat of a gas lamp, but it would be better if I could get one of our hens to sit on the eggs."

Harold grunted. "I've read about such things but have never attempted it before." He reached for the box and handed it to Melinda. "With all the interest you have in animals, you'd probably make a good vet. 'Course, you'd have to be English for that, I guess."

Melinda's throat constricted. Did Harold know what she was considering? Had Gabe let it slip, or had Dr. Franklin mentioned the idea of her becoming a vet to someone?

"I'm taking some of my pencil drawings into Seymour today," she said, hoping Harold wouldn't pursue the subject of her making a good vet. "In the past, I've sold a few pictures to the gift shop at the bed-and-breakfast there, so I'm hoping they'll want to buy more."

Harold reached under the brim of his straw hat and swiped at the sweat running down his forehead. "Wouldn't think there'd be much money to be made selling artwork around these parts."

"The owner of the bed-and-breakfast told me that tourists who stay there are usually looking for things made by the Amish."

When Harold made no comment, Melinda said, "Well, I'd best get these eggs out to the chicken coop. Thanks for bringing them by, and I'll let you know how it goes."

Harold climbed into his buggy and gathered up the reins. "Have a nice time in Seymour, and drive safely."

Melinda hurried off as Harold's buggy rumbled out of the yard. Now if she could only get one of the hens to adopt the eggs he had brought her.

⁂

Gabe was glad his dad had gone to Springfield and decided to close their shop for the rest of the day. That gave him the freedom to take Melinda to the farmers' market without having to ask for time off. Pap was a hard worker and didn't close up any more often than necessary. Whenever Gabe wanted a break from work, Pap usually made some comment like, "Them that works hard eats hearty."

"I work plenty hard," Gabe mumbled as he headed for the house. He planned to grab a couple of molasses cookies his mother had made yesterday, chug down some iced tea, and be on his way to Melinda's.

Inside the kitchen, Gabe found his mother standing in front of their propane-operated stove, where a large enamel kettle sat on the back burner. Steam poured out, and the lid clattered like Pap's old supply wagon when it rumbled down the graveled driveway.

"What are you cooking, Mom?" he asked, washing his hands at the sink.

"I'm canning some beets."

He sniffed deeply of the pungent aroma. "I wondered if that was what I smelled. Some tasty beets will be real nice come winter."

Gabe poured himself some iced tea. "Sure is hot out there today."

His mother turned and wiped her damp forehead with the towel that had been lying on the counter. "It's even warmer in here. That's the only trouble with canning. It makes the whole kitchen heat up."

Gabe grabbed a molasses cookie from the cookie jar on the counter and stuffed it into his mouth. "Umm. . .this is sure good."

She smiled. "Help yourself to as many as you like. Your sister Karen is coming over tomorrow, and we plan to do more baking."

Gabe took out six cookies and wrapped them in a paper towel. "Guess I'll eat these on my way over to the Hertzlers' place."

"Going to see Melinda?"

He nodded. "I'm taking her to the farmers'

market in Seymour."

"Sounds like fun. Melinda's a nice girl."

"I think so."

"She and I had a little talk one day not long ago before she stopped by the woodworking shop to see you."

He tipped his head to one side. "Was it me you were talking about?"

Mom chuckled and reached behind the kettle to turn down the burner of the stove. "I was asking her advice on how to keep the deer out of my garden."

"What'd she tell you?"

"She suggested a couple of things. One was to put some feed out for the deer along the edge of our property." Mom gestured to the pot of boiling beets. "As you can see, it worked, because I have plenty of garden produce."

"Melinda's pretty schmaert when it comes to things like that." *She's just not so smart when it comes to making a decision that would affect the rest of her life.* Gabe glanced at his mother. *Sure wish I could talk this over with Mom. She's always full of good advice and might have some idea on how I can get Melinda to see things from my point of view.*

"Are you troubled about something, son?" his mother asked. "You look a bit *umgerennt.*"

Gabe shook his head. "I'm not upset. Just feeling kind of confused about some things."

"Do you want to talk about it?"

Of course Gabe wanted to talk about it, but

he thought about his promise to Melinda not to mention her plans to anyone, and he couldn't go back on his word. "Naw, I'll figure things out in due time."

Mom smiled. "I'm sure you will. Now run along and have yourself a good day at the market."

"I will," Gabe said as he hurried out the door.

A short time later, he was headed down the road toward the Hertzlers' place. As he gave his horse the freedom to trot, he thought about Melinda and prayed she would change her mind about becoming a vet. He'd been reading his Bible every night and asking God to show him if leaving the Amish faith was the right thing for either of them to do. So far, he'd felt no direction other than to keep working toward his goal of opening his own woodworking shop. If only Melinda would be content to marry him and stay in Webster County as an Amish woman who looked after needy animals, the way she was doing now. It didn't seem right that she'd want to follow in her mother's footsteps and leave the Amish faith to pursue a strictly English career.

By the time Gabe pulled into the Hertzlers' driveway, he was feeling pretty worked up. What he really wanted to do was tell Melinda exactly how he felt about things, but he didn't want to spoil their day at the farmers' market by initiating another argument. With a firm resolve to hold his tongue, he hopped out of his buggy and secured the horse to the hitching rail near the barn. He glanced up at the house, hoping Melinda would be on the porch waiting for him, but no one was in sight. He scanned the yard, but the only thing he saw was Isaiah's dog, Jericho, pacing back and forth in his new pen.

Gabe meandered over to see Jericho, and the mutt wagged his tail while barking a friendly greeting.

"You like your pen, boy?" Gabe reached through the wire, gave the dog a pat on the head, and then headed for the house. He was almost to the back door when he heard the sound of yodeling coming from the chicken coop.

"That has to be Melinda," he said with a chuckle.

He strode toward the coop and found Melinda on her knees in front of some eggs that were nestled in a wooden box filled with straw.

"What are you doing?" Gabe asked, shutting the door behind him.

Melinda lifted her head and smiled. "I'm watching to see if one of our hens will sit on some pheasant eggs Harold Esh brought by awhile ago."

Gabe squatted beside her. "How come he brought you those?"

"The mother pheasant had been killed, and since the eggs were still warm, Harold thought I might be able to get them to hatch."

Gabe shook his head. "You may as well become a vet, because everyone in Webster County thinks they should bring their ailing, orphaned, or crippled animals to you."

Melinda looked at him pointedly. "You really think I should become a vet?"

Gabe could have bit his tongue. Of course he didn't think she should become a vet. "It was just a figure of speech," he mumbled.

"I really do like caring for animals," she said in a wistful tone.

"I know you do."

"Are you're still thinking and praying about it?" He nodded.

"Any idea how long it will be before you give me your final answer?"

He shrugged. "Can't really say. I've got to be clear about things before I can make such a life-changing decision."

"I understand. I feel that way, too. I don't want either of us to make a hasty decision." Melinda pointed to the pheasant eggs lying in the nest of straw. "I wonder how I can coax one of the chickens to sit on these."

In one quick motion, Gabe reached out, grabbed a fat red hen, and plunked her on top of the eggs. He didn't know who was the most surprised when the chicken stayed put, him or Melinda.

"She's accepting them!" Melinda clapped her hands. "Oh, Gabe, you're so schmaert. I should have thought to do that."

Gabe took Melinda's hand as they stood. "Are you ready to go to Seymour?"

She nodded toward the hen. "I'd better wait and see how things go. She might decide not to stay on the nest."

Gabe's face heated as irritation set in. "You'd give up an afternoon at the market to stay home and babysit a bunch of pheasant eggs that may never hatch?"

She shrugged.

"If your animals are more important than me, then I guess I'll head to Seymour alone."

Melinda's eyes were filled with tears. "Please don't be mad."

Gabe hated it when she cried, and he pulled her quickly into his arms. "I'm not mad—just hurt because you'd rather be out in the chicken coop than spend the afternoon with me."

"That's not true." Her voice shook with emotion. "I do want to go to the farmers' market with you today."

He glanced at the setting hen. "Does that mean you'll go?"

She nodded. "Jah, okay. I'll check on the eggs after we get back."

⁂

"Since I don't have to work today, I thought I'd go into Seymour and check out the farmers' market," Susie said to her mother as they finished cleaning up the kitchen.

Mama turned from washing the table and

smiled. "I think that's a good idea. You're always complaining that you don't get to do anything fun, but going to the market should be enjoyable."

Susie smiled. "Would you like to go along?"

"I appreciate the offer, but I've developed a headache, so I think I'll go to my room and lie down awhile."

Susie felt immediate concern. "Are you *grank*?"

"I don't think I'm sick; just have a headache is all." Mama reached up and rubbed the back of her neck. "Probably slept wrong on my neck."

"Maybe it would be best if I stayed home." Susie placed the broom she'd been using into the utility closet and shut the door. "That way if you need anything, I'll be here to see that your needs are met."

Mama shook her head. "Don't fret about me, daughter. I'll be fine once I lie down and rest my head. You go along to the market and enjoy your day." She patted Susie's arm. "I insist on it."

Susie sighed. "Oh, all right. Is there anything you'd like me to pick up while I'm in town?"

"Hmm. . ." Mama pursed her lips. "Maybe some peanut brittle if anyone's selling it at the market. I haven't had time to make your daed any for quite a while, and it's his favorite."

Susie nodded. "All right then. If I see any peanut brittle, I'll be sure to bring some home." Feeling a sense of excitement, she scurried around to clean off the kitchen counters and wipe them dry. She could hardly wait to hitch up a buggy and head for town. Maybe she would see Melinda at the market. Maybe they could go out for lunch together.

Chapter 16

When Gabe and Melinda pulled into the parking lot at the farmers' market, Melinda felt a sense of excitement. She'd always enjoyed coming here and remembered several times when she was a little girl and had spent the day with her mother. She thought about one time when she and Mama had met Papa Noah at the farmers' market, before her parents were a couple. After leaving the market that day, the three of them had gone to lunch at Baldy's Café, and Melinda had enjoyed Mama's jokes and listening to country music on the radio.

"Maybe we can eat at Baldy's today," she suggested to Gabe.

"Or how about Don's Pizza Place?"

"Either one is fine, I guess," she said. "We can look around the farmers' market awhile, eat lunch, and head over to the bed-and-breakfast where they sell Grandpa's rhubarb-strawberry jam and some of my drawings. I want to see what's sold and ask if they want me to bring any more in."

"That's fine by me." Gabe jumped down to help Melinda out of the buggy. "So where shall we start first?" he asked as they walked toward the tables on the other side of the parking lot.

"Wherever you like."

He took her hand and gave it a gentle squeeze. "I like it when we're not arguing."

"Me, too."

They walked hand in hand until they came to a table where an English man had some wooden holders for trash cans for sale. They resembled a small cupboard, but the door opened from the top, and the trash can was placed inside.

Gabe seemed quite impressed and plied the man with several questions. They soon learned that he lived near Kansas City and had been heading to Branson to sell some of his wooden items to a gift shop there. He said he'd heard about the farmers' market in Seymour and decided to rent a table before he went to Branson.

"I think I could make something like those and probably sell them for a lot less money than his are going for," Gabe whispered to Melinda as they moved away from the table. "I believe I'll make one to give Mom for Christmas this year."

"Have you ever thought that you could make and sell wooden items if you lived in the English world?" Melinda blurted without thinking.

Gabe frowned so deeply his forehead was etched with wrinkles, and Melinda knew she had spoiled their day together.

Gabe gritted his teeth as he and Melinda walked away from the English man's table. Melinda had obviously not given up her idea of going English, and it seemed as if she was trying to convince him that he would be happy giving up the only way of life he had ever known. *Could I be happy living in the English world?* he wondered. *Would I have more opportunity to have a woodworking shop of my own there, and would I be successful at it if I did?* The English man who had wooden trash holders for sale was obviously doing all right. Of course, that didn't mean Gabe would do well, but it did mean there was a need for well-crafted wooden items in the English world, as well as here in his Amish community.

Gabe grimaced. *Why did Melinda suddenly have to decide she wanted to become a vet? Why couldn't she be happy with the way things were?*

Maybe I should go see Dr. Franklin and ask if he'll try to talk Melinda out of leaving the Amish faith.

"Let's look over there at the table where Mary King's selling peanut brittle," Melinda suggested, nudging Gabe's arm.

"Jah, sure," he mumbled. Maybe a hunk of peanut brittle would help brighten his spirits. He sure needed something to make him feel better right now.

"Wie geht's?" Melinda asked, stepping up to Mary's table.

Mary smiled, her brown eyes looking so sincere. "I'm doing well. How are you?"

"I can't complain." Melinda scanned the table full of baked goods, candy, and fresh produce. "Are you here alone, or is the rest of your family around someplace?"

"Ben's got our two oldest boys, Harvey and Walter, helping him do chores around our place today," Mary replied. "And the younger children are with Ben's sister, Carolyn."

"Is it hard for you to be on your own here today?"

Mary shook her head. "To tell you the truth, it's kind of nice. If Dan and Sarah were here, I'd be dealing with them wanting to run around, and then I'd probably end up having to work alone at the table anyhow."

Melinda chuckled. "That's how my little brother is, too. He always wants to run around and play when he should be working."

Gabe cleared his throat a couple of times. "I thought we were going to buy some candy, Melinda."

"Of course we are." Melinda picked up a hunk of peanut brittle that had been wrapped in cellophane paper. "If we break it in two, this one should be big enough for both of us."

"Whatever," he muttered. Melinda sure wanted to be in control of things. She couldn't even let him pick the peanut brittle he wanted. Well, there were some things she couldn't control, and him going English was one of them!

As Melinda and Mary continued to visit, Gabe glanced around the market area. He spotted his friend Aaron across the way, talking to his younger brother, Joseph.

Gabe cleared his throat, hoping to get Melinda's attention, but she kept right on yakking. Finally, he nudged her arm. "I'm going over to speak with Aaron."

"Okay. I'll join you there in a few minutes."

When Susie stepped down from her buggy and secured the horse to the hitching rail, she spotted Melinda on the other side of the market talking to Mary King. She was about to head that way when she noticed another buggy pulling in. Her heart skipped a beat when she saw Jonas Byler sitting in the driver's seat.

"I'm surprised to see you," she said when he jumped down from his buggy. "I figured you'd probably gone back to Montana."

"Nope, not yet. I thought it would be good if I stayed awhile and spent some time with my family."

A sense of excitement bubbled in Susie's chest. If Jonas wasn't going back to Montana right away, maybe there was a chance he might take an interest in her. "What can you tell me about Rexford, Montana?" she asked, hoping to let him know in a subtle way that she had an interest in him.

"What do you want to know?"

"What's the weather like, how many Amish people live in the area, what do the homes look like—"

Jonas held up his hand. "Whoa! One question at a time, please."

Susie's cheeks warmed. Ever since she'd been a little girl, she'd had a habit of running off at the mouth. No wonder she still had no boyfriend. Who would want a *blappere* woman for a girlfriend?

"You don't have to be embarrassed for asking questions." Jonas leaned against his buggy and smiled. "I just can't answer more than one at a time."

Susie felt herself begin to relax. Maybe Jonas didn't think she was a blabbering woman after all. "Let's start with the weather," she suggested.

For the next several minutes, Susie listened with rapt attention as Jonas told her about the cold, snowy winters they had in Montana, and how he went deer hunting every fall. He said most of the Amish homes there were built from logs, and that many of the Amish men in the area made log furniture.

"Even though we're a small community, I still enjoy living there," he concluded.

I wish you would stay here, Susie silently cried. *If you'd only take an interest in me, I'd do my best to make you happy.*

Jonas cleared his throat a couple of times. "Guess I'll wander around the market now and see what's for sale."

Invite me to join you. Oh, if you'd only ask. Susie knew she couldn't boldly suggest such a thing, but she might be able to drop a hint. "I was about to start looking, too," she said with a smile. "It's always interesting to see what others from our community are selling."

He shuffled his feet a few times then gave his horse a pat on the neck. "Well, I'll be seeing you around." Before Susie could open her mouth, he strode off toward a group of tables.

Should I follow him? No, that might seem like I was being pushy. With a frustrated sigh, Susie headed for some tables in the opposite direction.

Melinda had just left Mary's table when she noticed Susie heading her way. "I didn't know you were going to be here today," she said when Susie reached her.

"I didn't know I was coming until this morning." Susie glanced around. "Are you here alone?"

"I came with Gabe." Melinda pointed across the way. "He's over there talking to Aaron."

"Oh, I see. Then I guess you'll be hanging around with him the rest of the day."

Melinda nodded. "We're going somewhere for lunch soon." She gave Susie's arm a gentle squeeze. "Why don't you join us?"

Susie shook her head. "I've told you before: I don't like being the fifth wheel on a buggy."

Melinda thought a moment before responding. "Maybe Gabe could invite Aaron, too. That way there will be four of us instead of three."

"No way!"

"Why not?"

"It might seem like you're trying to match me up with Aaron, and I'm sure he wouldn't like that any more than I would."

"Don't be silly," Melinda said with a shake of her head. "Everyone knows you and Aaron are only friends."

Susie grunted. "We're not really that much. I just know him is all."

"We've both known Aaron Zook since we were kinner, so it shouldn't seem to him or anyone else as if you're a courting couple."

Susie glanced over at the table where Jonas stood talking to a man who had some wooden products for sale, and Melinda couldn't help but notice her wistful expression. "I'm surprised to see Jonas Byler here today. I thought he was going back to Montana."

"I spoke with him a few minutes ago, and he said he had decided to stick around awhile longer so he can visit with his family."

"Is that so?"

"Jah, that's what he said."

"Maybe there's another reason he hasn't gone back to Montana yet."

"What other reason could there be?"

"Maybe some pretty woman has caught his eye."

Susie frowned. "You really think so?"

Melinda nudged Susie again. "You're smitten, aren't you?"

Susie's cheeks turned bright red, and her eyes darted back and forth as if she was worried someone might be listening to their conversation. "Okay, so I do have an interest in him." Susie grimaced. "For all the good it'll do me."

"What's that supposed to mean?"

"Jonas isn't interested in me. If he was, he would have asked me to walk around the market with him instead of going off by himself."

"Maybe he's shy." Melinda smiled. "Say, I have an idea. How about if I ask Gabe to invite

Jonas to join us for lunch? Then you and Jonas can spend time together, and it'll give him the chance to see how wunderbaar you are."

"Puh! I'm not wonderful, and I don't want Jonas to think he's being set up." Susie shook her head. "If it's meant for us to be together, then Jonas will come to me on his own." Before Melinda could comment, Susie turned and hurried away.

"My poor aunt Susie," Melinda mumbled. "She wants a boyfriend so badly, and I've got one who doesn't see things my way. Maybe we'll both end up being old maids."

As Gabe sat at a table across from Melinda in Baldy's Café, he struggled to find something to say. It seemed as if every time they'd been together lately they had ended up in a disagreement. He still couldn't believe that while they were at the farmers' market, Melinda had suggested he make wooden items while living as an Englisher in the modern world. Didn't she realize he was happy living here, close to his family and friends? Didn't she realize how selfish she was being, asking him to leave all he loved behind?

But you love Melinda, a little voice niggled at the back of his mind. *Would you be happy living without her if she goes English and you stay Amish?*

"What's wrong?" Melinda asked, reaching across the table to touch Gabe's hand. "You look so *verwart*."

"I am feeling a bit perplexed," he admitted.

"About what?"

"You and me going English."

"Are you still struggling with a decision?"

He nodded. "It would be hard to leave my family and friends."

"But we'd have each other, and we can come home for visits."

Gabe shook his head. "It wouldn't be the same, and you know it. Since we've both joined the church, if we leave, our ties to the church would be broken, and it would affect our relationship with our families, too."

"I know," she said with a slow nod. "But then, there are always concessions to be made when making a major change in one's life."

Gabe reached for his glass of iced tea and took a drink. "Let's change the subject, shall we?"

"What do you want to talk about?"

He plunked his spoon into the tumbler and stirred the ice around, making it clink against the glass. There didn't seem to be much they could talk about without arguing. If they talked about him wanting to hunt, Melinda would get defensive. If they talked about her wanting to become a vet, Gabe would be upset. If they talked about her preoccupation with animals and her lack of interest in other things, they would probably go home not speaking at all.

"Let's talk about the weather," he finally said. "It seems to be the safest subject of all."

Melinda smiled, but it appeared to be forced. "Jah, sure, we can talk about the weather."

Chapter 17

Melinda lounged against a log in the woods behind their home, where she'd been sitting for the last several minutes, sketching two does eating some corn she had scattered on the ground.

She thought about the way Gabe had looked at her when he'd brought her home from Seymour earlier today—as if he'd wanted to say something but was afraid to for fear they would have another disagreement. So instead of saying what was obviously on his mind, Gabe had told Melinda good-bye without even giving her a hug or a kiss. When she'd invited him to stay for supper, he had turned her down, saying he had somewhere else to go this evening. She was sure he was using it as an excuse not to be with her.

"We can't continue on like this," Melinda murmured. "We both need to make a decision soon, and it should be Gabe, since I've pretty much made up my mind that I'd like to become a vet."

She glanced back at the deer grazing a few feet away. They looked so peaceful, she almost envied them.

"You're too pretty for anyone to kill," she whispered.

Pow! Pow! Pow!

Melinda jumped at the sound of a gun being fired, and the deer scattered.

"*Was is letz do?* What is wrong here? It's not hunting season yet." She dropped her tablet and pencil into the canvas tote at her feet, slung it over her shoulder, and followed the repeated popping sounds.

As Melinda stepped into an open field, the sight that greeted her sent a shock wave spiraling from the top of her head all the way to her toes. There stood Gabe, holding a gun and firing continuously at a target nailed to a tree several yards away.

Melinda remained motionless, unable to think, speak, or even breathe. Gabe kept on shooting, apparently unaware of her presence. When he ran out of bullets and began to reload, she marched up to him and poked her finger in his back. "Just what do you think you're doing?"

He whirled around. "Melinda, you scared me half to death!"

"Thanks to that noisy gun of yours, you scared the deer away that I had been sketching." Melinda's voice trembled, and her ears tingled.

"Sorry about that, but I'm target practicing— getting ready for fall, when hunting season opens." Gabe's eyebrows squeezed together. As he stared at her, the silence between them was thick like cream, only not nearly as pleasant. "If I'd known you were nearby trying to draw a picture, I wouldn't have shot the gun," he finally mumbled.

Melinda's hands shook as she held them at her sides, trying to gain control of her swirling emotions. "So this is where you planned to come after you dropped me off this afternoon, huh?"

"Jah."

"Why didn't you tell me that you were going to target practice?"

His chest expanded with a deep breath then fell when he exhaled. "I didn't think you'd want to hear it."

"How come?"

"I know how you feel about hunting, Melinda. I figured we'd end up having another argument if I even mentioned using my gun."

Melinda planted both hands on her hips. "The creatures in these woods are dear to me."

"And I'm not?" Gabe's eyelids fluttered in rapid succession. "Do the deer mean more to you than me?"

Melinda stared at the toes of her sneakers.

How could she make him understand? "I do love you, Gabe, but I care about the animals God created, too. That's why I want to become a—"

"God made many animals for us to eat—deer included."

"Jah, well," Melinda huffed, "I'd better not see you on my folks' property with your gun again. I'm going home right now and ask Papa Noah to post some No Hunting signs on our land."

Gabe's mouth dropped open. "You're kidding!"

"I'm not."

"Listen, Melinda, you can't save every deer in the woods."

"I know that, but I can save those in *our* woods."

Gabe's only response was a disgruntled groan.

"And since we're already arguing—I think it's time we both make a decision about me becoming a veterinarian and us leaving the Amish faith."

"I can't leave, Melinda."

"Can't or won't?"

He stared at the ground. "I love you, but—"

"But not enough to help me realize my dream?"

"I want you to be happy, but I don't think leaving family and friends to become a vet will bring you the happiness you're looking for."

"This isn't about happiness, Gabe. It's about helping animals—as many as I can."

"I think you're obsessed with the whole idea,

and I don't believe you've thought everything through."

"For several weeks I've done nothing but think about this. I'd thought that if you were in agreement with me and were willing to start a new life in the English world, I would know it was God's will."

"But I'm not willing, so it must not be God's will. Can't you see that?"

She shook her head. "You're confusing me."

Gabe reached out his hand to her, but Melinda backed away.

"I—I need to go," she murmured.

"Please don't, Melinda. Stay, and let's talk about this some more."

She turned her hands palm up. "What else is there to say? You want to stay Amish, and I want to—no, I *need* to—leave the faith."

"But you don't need to. You can—"

Melinda pivoted away from Gabe before he could finish his sentence. Clutching tightly to the canvas bag slung over her shoulder, she fled for home.

As Gabe watched Melinda run away from him, he wondered how the day could have ended on such a sour note. There had to be some way to make Melinda aware of how much he loved her. If he could get her to realize that fact, she might change her mind about leaving the Amish faith.

Gabe dropped to a seat on a nearby log and stared at his gun. *If I gave up hunting, would that make her happy?* He shook his head. *No, that's not our main problem. Even if I were to promise never to hunt another deer, I think she would still want to leave home and become a vet. Maybe I should talk to Noah about this—let him know what his daughter is thinking of doing.*

Gabe groaned and slapped the side of his head. "That would just make Melinda mad and maybe even more determined to have her way on this."

He sat several seconds, pondering things and praying for guidance, until an idea popped into his head. He jumped up. "I'm going home right now and make Melinda a special gift—something that will let her know how much I care. Something she can't take to any old college."

❧❧

Melinda had just stepped into the yard when she spotted Susie climbing down from her buggy.

"Have you been in the woods again?" Susie asked as Melinda drew near.

"Jah. I was drawing a picture of some deer. Until Gabe scared them off, that is."

Susie's forehead wrinkled. "How'd he do that?"

"He had a gun and was shooting at a target

nailed to a tree."

"You'd better get used to hearing guns go off," Susie said. "Soon it will be hunting season, you know."

"I do know, and it's not me I'm worried about. My concern is for the deer."

"Many of our men hunt," Susie reminded her. "It's just the way of things."

"I know that, too. I also realize I can't save every deer in the woods." Melinda compressed her lips. "I can, however, protect those that do come onto our property."

"So if you know you can't save every deer, then don't be so hard on Gabe. I'm sure he loves you."

"Then he should prove it."

"I think he did that when he asked you to marry him."

Melinda's mouth fell open. "You—you know about his proposal?"

Susie nodded. "I heard it from Gabe's mamm when I was working at Kaulp's Store last week. She dropped by to get—"

"Gabe must have told her," Melinda interrupted with a shake of her head. "I can't believe he'd do that after we agreed to keep it quiet until we had set a date."

"I don't see what the big secret is." Susie leaned against the buggy and folded her arms. "Even if you're not officially published, your close friends and family members should know what you're planning."

"I would have told them if things weren't so *verhuddelt*."

"What things are mixed up?"

"Things between me and Gabe." Melinda drew in a shaky breath. "I'm beginning to wonder if I made a mistake in agreeing to marry him."

"You can't mean that. I think you're just upset about Gabe hunting. You're not thinking straight right now, that's all."

"You're right, I am upset, but there's more involved than just Gabe wanting to hunt. It's a lot more than you realize." Tears trickled down Melinda's cheeks, and she swiped at them with the back of her hand.

"I realize this," Susie said in a snappish tone, "If Gabe were *my* boyfriend, I'd do everything I could to make him happy. He's a good man and will make you a fine husband."

"I know he's a good man, but he doesn't love me enough to—" Melinda's voice trailed off, and she looked away.

"To what?"

"To—to leave the Amish faith with me." Melinda almost choked on her final words.

Susie's eyebrows shot up, and her eyes widened. "Please tell me you're kidding."

Melinda shook her head. "I'm not kidding."

Susie grabbed Melinda's arm and pulled her toward the buggy. "We'd better sit down so you can tell me about this crazy notion."

Melinda took a seat beside Susie in the front

of her buggy and drew in a deep breath. This was going to be harder than she'd thought.

"Now what's all this about you wanting to leave the Amish faith?" Susie asked, nudging Melinda's arm with her elbow.

"I didn't say I *wanted* to leave."

"But you said Gabe doesn't love you enough to leave the faith with you."

Melinda swallowed hard and pulled in another quick breath. "As you know, I've been working at Dr. Franklin's clinic for some time now."

Susie nodded.

"He's been telling me for quite a spell that I've got a special way with *gediere*."

"We all know that. You've been good with animals since you were a kinner."

Melinda moistened her lips with the tip of her tongue. "Which is why Dr. Franklin thinks I would make a good vet."

Susie's mouth dropped open. "But in order to become a vet, you'd need lots of schooling. A lot more than the eight years you've had, that's for sure."

"I know, and in order to get the necessary schooling, I'd have to leave the Amish faith and go English." Melinda paused and waited for Susie's reaction, but Susie just sat with her arms folded, staring straight ahead.

"I've made plans to take my GED test, which is the first step I'll need in order to prepare for college," Melinda continued.

"And Gabe knows about this and doesn't go for the idea?"

"He hasn't exactly said he doesn't go for the idea of me becoming a vet, but in order for us to be together, he'd have to go English with me, and he says he's not willing to do that."

Susie pursed her lips and squinted at Melinda. "And you are?"

"Well, I—"

"I know Gabe loves you, Melinda, but he'll have to break up with you if you go English and he doesn't."

Melinda grimaced. "At first Gabe said he would pray about things. But then we had an argument in the woods over him target practicing so he can hunt in the fall, and he ended up telling me that he won't leave the Amish faith."

"I can't believe this. I just can't believe it," Susie mumbled with a shake of her head.

"Do you think I'm wrong for wanting to take care of animals?"

"Not wrong for wanting to take care of animals. Just wrong for wanting to leave the only life you've ever known."

"That's not true," Melinda corrected. "I lived in the English world with my mamm and my real daed until I was six years old."

"You can't tell me you remember much about that."

"I remember some things."

Susie groaned. "I can't imagine how it would

be not to have you in my life, Melinda. How can you even consider leaving your family and friends?"

"This isn't an easy decision for me, and I know the sacrifices I would have to make." Melinda nibbled on the inside of her cheek. "I feel a need to care for animals, and Dr. Franklin says I can't do it properly unless I have professional training."

"What do your folks have to say about this?"

"They don't know yet."

"You haven't told them a thing?"

Melinda shook her head.

"But they know Gabe's asked you to marry him, right?"

"No. I figured I'd wait until after I passed my GED test to tell them that, too. But since Gabe's not going to leave the Amish faith, there's really no point in telling them about his marriage proposal." Melinda clasped Susie's hand. "You've got to promise you won't say anything about this to anyone. Do I have your word?"

"I still think you should tell them, but until you're ready, I'll keep quiet."

Chapter 18

On Monday morning, Melinda stopped at the birdhouse out front before she headed for work. There she discovered a note from Gabe.

Dear Melinda,
*   I'm sorry about our disagreement*
yesterday, and I hope we can figure out
some way to resolve our differences. I was
wondering if you would be free to go on
a picnic supper with me this evening.
I'll bring the food, and I'll check the
birdhouse for an answer before I pick you
up. If you're willing, we can leave around
six o'clock.

Always yours,
Gabe

Melinda smiled. Gabe had said he was sorry. Did that mean he'd changed his mind about leaving the Amish faith with her? Did he finally understand her need to become a vet?

She removed the pencil and tablet from the birdhouse and scrawled a note in return.

> *Dear Gabe,*
> *I accept your apology, and I hope we can settle things between us. A picnic supper sounds nice. I'll be waiting for you at six, and I'll bring a loaf of homemade bread and some of Grandpa's rhubarb-strawberry jam.*
>
> *Yours fawnly,*
> *Melinda*

With a feeling of anticipation, Melinda slipped the note into the birdhouse and climbed back into her buggy.

Things would be better now that Gabe had apologized, and she looked forward to their date tonight. For now, though, she needed to hurry or she would be late for work.

"Melinda, can you come here a minute?" Dr.

Franklin called from examining room one.

Melinda set the mop aside that she'd been using to clean another examining room. "What do you need, Dr. Franklin?" she asked when she entered the other room and found him clipping the toenails of a little black Scottie.

"Would you mind holding Sparky while I finish cutting his toenails? He's as jittery as a june bug this morning."

"I'd be happy to help." Melinda stood on the left side of the examining table and gripped the little dog around the middle with one hand. With her other hand, she held his front paw so the doctor's hands were free to do the clipping. She had assisted Dr. Franklin several times when he had a dog's nails to trim, and the animals always seemed relaxed and calm in her presence.

"Say, Dr. Franklin, I've been wondering about something."

"What's that, Melinda?"

"Well, actually, it's more Isaiah who wants to know the answer to a question."

He glanced up at her. "What does your little brother want to know?"

"Isaiah told me one day that he'd heard that if a dog has a dark mouth, it means he's smart. But if the inside of his mouth is light, then he'll likely be dumb." She giggled, feeling self-conscious for having asked such a silly question. "I told him it was probably just an old wives' tale, but he said I should ask you about it."

The doctor continued to clip Sparky's nails. "Actually, there's some truth in what your brother told you. It's not documented that I know of, but many animal breeders take stock in the color of a dog's mouth. I've heard it said that a dark mouth means a smart dog."

"Hmm. . .that's interesting."

"Sparky's sure doing well," Dr. Franklin commented. "He's a lot more relaxed with you holding him than he was when I tried working on him alone."

Melinda smiled in response. It made her feel good to assist the doctor, and if she could help an animal relax, it was an added bonus.

"If you were a certified vet's assistant, I'd have you helping with many other things here in the clinic," the doctor said.

"I'd like that."

"And if you ever do become a veterinarian, I might consider taking you on as my partner."

"Really?" Melinda's heart swelled with joy. How wonderful it would be to work side by side with Dr. Franklin as his partner, not just as someone who cleaned up the clinic, helped with toenail clipping, or gave flea baths to the dogs and cats that were brought in.

"I really mean it. In fact, I've been thinking that I'd like to help with your schooling."

"Help?"

"Yes. Financially."

Her mouth fell open. "You—you'd really do that for me?"

He nodded. "As you know, my wife and I have no children of our own. It would give me pleasure to help someone who has such a special way with animals. You've got real potential, Melinda, and I'd like to see you use your talents to the best of your abilities."

"And you think in order to do that I'd need to go to school and become a vet?"

"Let me just say this. If you were my daughter, I would do everything in my power to make it happen." He set the clippers aside. "There you go, Sparky. All done until next time."

"Do you want me to put him in one of the cages in the back room until his owner comes to pick him up?"

"Yes, if you don't mind."

"I don't mind at all." Melinda scooped the terrier into her arms and started for the door.

"Oh, Melinda. . .one more thing," Dr. Franklin called.

She turned back around.

"I know my wife said she would drive you to Springfield next Friday to take your GED test, but her mother, who lives in Mansfield, fell and broke her hip last week. So Ellen will be helping her mother for the next couple of weeks, which means she won't be available to drive you to Springfield after all."

Melinda forced a smile to her lips in order to

hide the disappointment she felt. "That's all right. I'm sure I can find someone else to drive me that day. I'll also need to give my folks a legitimate reason for me going to Springfield."

"You're still planning to wait and tell them after you've taken the test?"

She nodded.

"I hope it works out for you."

"Me, too, Dr. Franklin. Me, too."

As Gabe entered Dr. Franklin's veterinary clinic, his face beaded with sweat. He hoped Melinda had left for the day, because he wanted to speak to Dr. Franklin without her knowing. He found the man sitting behind his desk looking at some paperwork.

"Good afternoon, Gabe. I see you don't have your dog with you today," the doctor said. "Did you need something specific, or did you just drop by for a friendly chat?"

"I was wondering if Melinda is here," Gabe said, stepping up to the desk.

Dr. Franklin shook his head. "She left half an hour ago."

A sense of relief swept over Gabe. "That's good to hear."

The doctor's eyebrows drew together as he squinted. "If you're looking for Melinda, why would you think it's good that she's not here?"

Gabe swiped the back of his hand across his damp forehead. He was already botching things and hadn't even said what was on his mind. "I'm not actually *looking* for Melinda. I wanted to talk to you, but I don't want Melinda to hear what I have to say."

Dr. Franklin leaned forward, his elbows resting on the desk. "What did you want to speak to me about?"

"Melinda and her plans to become a vet."

"Oh, I see."

"She said you were the one who gave her the idea. Is that true?"

The doctor nodded. "Melinda's got a special way with animals, and she could use her abilities much better if she furthered her education and got the right training."

"But she takes care of stray animals at her home." Gabe made a sweeping gesture of the room with one hand. "And she helps you here at the clinic."

"Not the way she could if she were to become a vet or even a certified vet's assistant."

Gabe clenched and unclenched his fingers. This conversation wasn't going well at all. He moved a little closer and placed his palms on the desk. "I was hoping you'd be willing to discourage Melinda from leaving the faith."

"Why would I do that? As I said before, I think Melinda has potential."

"But if she leaves the faith, it will mean we

can't be married. It will also put space between Melinda and her family."

Dr. Franklin stacked the papers lying before him into a neat little pile, pushed his chair away from the desk, and stood. "Have you considered leaving with her? I'm sure you could find a job in the field of woodworking. From what Melinda's told me, you're an excellent craftsman."

Gabe rubbed his sweaty hands along the sides of his trousers. It was obvious that Dr. Franklin didn't understand the way things were. All the man seemed to see was his own perspective, and he obviously had no idea of the consequences involved if Melinda left home. "So, you won't discourage Melinda from becoming a vet?"

The doctor shook his head. "Sorry, but no."

"Guess I'll have to be the one to do it then," Gabe mumbled as he turned and walked out the door.

Chapter 19

When Melinda returned home from the veterinary clinic later that day, she found her mother standing in front of the kitchen sink peeling potatoes.

"How was your day?" Mama asked over her shoulder.

"It was good. Dr. Franklin had me hold a terrier so he could clip its nails. He said the animal seemed calmer with me there."

"I know how much you enjoy working at the veterinary clinic. Do you think you'll miss it after you and Gabe are married?"

Melinda sank to a seat at the table. "Who told you Gabe had asked me to marry him?"

"I heard it from Freda Kaulp when I stopped

by her store earlier today. She overheard a conversation between Susie and Leah Swartz the other day." Mama sounded disappointed, and Melinda knew it wasn't that she didn't want Melinda to marry Gabe. More than likely, Mama was hurt because Melinda hadn't told her the news herself.

"I'm sorry you had to hear it secondhand," Melinda apologized. "When Gabe proposed, we decided not to tell anyone until we had agreed on a date." She sighed. "I guess Gabe must have told his mother. How else would Freda have found out?"

Mama washed and dried her hands then joined Melinda at the table. "So, *have* the two of you set a wedding date?"

"Not yet. We've had a couple of disagreements lately, and I don't want to make any definite plans until we get some things resolved." Melinda cringed. She hated keeping secrets from her mother. It would feel so good to tell the whole story about her wanting to become a vet and Gabe being unwilling to leave the Amish faith with her. But she knew how upset her parents would be if they knew she was thinking of leaving, and until she knew for sure, she didn't see any point in revealing her secret.

Mama reached over and took Melinda's hand. "We're all human, and disagreements come up even between two people who are deeply in love."

Melinda nodded.

"Just keep God in the center of your lives, live each day to the fullest, and after you're married, never go to bed angry at one another." Mama smiled. "It's important to work through your differences and pray about things rather than harboring resentment if you don't always get your way."

"I know that, Mama, but it's not always as easy as it seems."

"I never said it would be easy. A good marriage takes work, just like anything else that's worthwhile."

Melinda fiddled with the stack of paper napkins piled in the wicker basket on the table. Could she and Gabe be putting themselves first? Was that why they'd been having so many problems lately? "Gabe's coming by around six o'clock to take me on a picnic supper," she said. "Maybe we can talk some things through then."

"That sounds like a good idea. Will you want help filling the picnic basket?"

"The note he left in the birdhouse out front said he's going to furnish the food. But I thought it would be nice if I took a loaf of bread and some of Grandpa's delicious jam."

"I baked a batch of honey-wheat bread this morning, so help yourself to a loaf. And we have several pints of Grandpa's rhubarb-strawberry jam in the pantry." Mama popped a couple of her knuckles and smiled.

Melinda winced. "Doesn't it hurt when you do that?"

"To me it feels good. Keeps my fingers from getting stiff."

Melinda didn't think she would ever crack her knuckles, no matter how old she was or how stiff her fingers might become. She stood. "Guess I'd better get my cat's supper ready before I go upstairs to change clothes for my picnic date with Gabe." She cupped her hands around her mouth and called, "Here Snow! Come, kitty, kitty. It's time for your supper."

"That's odd," Melinda said when, after a few minutes, there was no sign of the cat. "Snow usually comes running on the first call. Have you seen her, Mama?"

"Not since early this morning when she was racing around the house like her tail was on fire. I figured she might be after a mouse or something."

"Has she been outside today?"

"Not that I know of." Mama popped two more fingers, with an audible *click, click.* "I've never known a cat that liked to hang around the house the way that one does."

Melinda frowned. "I wonder if Isaiah's playing a trick on me and has hidden her someplace."

"He's upstairs in his room. Why don't you go ask him?"

"I think I will." Melinda turned toward the door.

"I hope you find Snow. I know how much you care for that cat," Mama called.

"I care about all my animals." Melinda

sprinted up the stairs, making her first stop Isaiah's bedroom, where she rapped on the door.

"Come in!"

She found her brother sprawled on the bed with a book in his hands. "Isaiah, have you seen Snow?"

"Not since last winter. Sure hope we get plenty of it this year, 'cause I plan to do lots of sledding."

Melinda shook her head. "Ha! You must get your funny bone from our mamm."

"You're right; Mama can be kind of silly at times."

"Seriously, have you seen my cat today?"

Isaiah closed his book and sat up. "No, but awhile ago I thought I heard her out in the hall."

"Upstairs or down?"

"Up here."

"You heard Snow but didn't see her?"

"Right. I heard meowing, and then it stopped. Figured if it was the cat, she'd probably gone downstairs."

Melinda made little circles with her fingertips across her forehead, hoping to stave off the headache she felt coming on. "I didn't see any sign of Snow downstairs, and when I called, she didn't come. It's not like her to hide when it's time to eat."

"Maybe she ain't hungry."

"Always has been before. And it's *isn't*, not *ain't*." Melinda leaned against the door jamb and gritted her teeth as frustration rolled through her body like a whirling windmill. Why did her little brother have to be so difficult? "Has Snow been in the house all day?"

"Don't know. Haven't seen her at all."

Meow. Meow.

Melinda cocked her head. "Did you hear that?"

"Sounds like the cat's somewhere nearby."

"I'm going to find her." Melinda left the room and followed the meowing sounds until she came to a small hole in the wall at the end of the hallway. It seemed too little for her cat to have gone through, yet she could hear Snow's pathetic meows inside the wall.

The first thing Gabe did when he pulled into the Hertzlers' driveway was to check inside the birdhouse to see if there was a response from Melinda. Sure enough, she had left a note saying she would go on the picnic supper with him.

He grinned and glanced at the surprise he had in the back of his buggy. He hoped she would be so pleased with the gift that she would see how much he loved her and change her mind about leaving home to become a vet.

Gabe hopped back into the buggy and picked up the reins. A few minutes later, he tied his horse to the hitching rail and took the porch steps two at a time. He knocked on the door and waited. It took awhile for someone to answer, and when the door finally opened, Melinda's brother stood on the other side.

"I'm here to pick up Melinda. Is she ready to go?" Gabe asked the boy.

Isaiah shook his head. "I don't think so. She's sittin' in front of a hole in the wall upstairs."

Gabe's eyebrows lifted. "Why would she be doing that?"

"Her cat's stuck in there, and she can't figure out how to get the silly critter out. The hole's too small for Melinda to reach her hand into."

"What does your daed have to say? Can't he cut a bigger hole?"

Isaiah shrugged. "Guess he could, but Papa ain't here. He's workin' late at the tree farm and probably won't be home until it's almost dark."

"I'd better go see what I can do to help," Gabe said, stepping into the house.

Isaiah led the way, and Gabe followed him up the stairs and down the hall until they came to the place where Melinda and her mother were on their knees calling to the kitten.

Gabe cleared his throat, and Melinda looked up at him with a dismal expression. "Snow seems to have squeezed through this tiny hole, but she can't get back out."

"She was probably after a mouse," Faith put in.

"I can cut a bigger hole if you want me to,"

Gabe offered. "Where does Noah keep his saws?"

"Out in the barn." Faith nodded at Isaiah. "Run on out there and get one of your daed's saws, would you, son?"

"Okay." The boy scampered off.

Gabe squatted beside Melinda. "I can patch the hole I make with a piece of Sheetrock, and it'll be good as new."

"What if Snow won't come to me once the hole is bigger?" Melinda asked.

Meow! Meow!

"Does that answer your question?" Gabe smiled. "Sounds like your cat can't wait to get out of there."

"I agree," Faith said. "Once Gabe cuts a bigger hole, you can stick your hand inside. I'm sure Snow will come right away."

Isaiah showed up a few minutes later holding a small handsaw, which he handed to Gabe. It didn't take long for Gabe to make a larger opening, and he was careful not to let the blade of the saw stick too far through the other side. He knew if he cut the cat by mistake, Melinda would never forgive him. She might even see it as one more reason for her to leave home.

Once the opening was made, Melinda put her hand inside. "Here, Snow. Come, kitty, kitty."

There was a faint *meow*, and when Melinda pulled her hand out again, she had Snow by the nape of the neck.

Gabe breathed a sigh of relief. The cat was

okay, and Melinda was smiling again.

"Danki, Gabe," she murmured.

"You're welcome." *Maybe now she'll realize how much she needs me. And when she sees what I have in my buggy, she's sure to know how much I love her.*

"I think I'll take Snow downstairs and feed her while you patch the hole." Melinda stood and hurried off toward the stairs.

"If there's a scrap of Sheetrock in the barn, I can fix the hole now," Gabe said, turning to Faith. "If not, I'll bring some over later on."

"I appreciate that. It's very kind of you. It's obvious you like working with your hands," Faith said. "The little deer you carved for Melinda turned out very nice."

"Danki."

"Speaking of deer, Melinda's been spending a lot of time in the woods lately, drawing pictures of the wildlife she sees there. Has she shown you any of her pictures?"

Gabe grimaced. After the argument he and Melinda had a few days ago over him hunting, just the mention of deer made him cringe.

"You're frowning. Don't you care for Melinda's drawings?"

"It's not that," Gabe was quick to say. "It's just. . .well, she seems so protective of the deer in the woods. She doesn't even want me to go hunting."

"I've heard her complain about others who

like to hunt, too. However, Melinda realizes she can't keep all the deer safe or stop everyone from hunting, but she wants to protect those that are on our property." Faith sighed. "Sometimes I worry about Melinda's preoccupation with the animals. It seems like all she wants to do is sketch pictures of those she sees in the woods and take care of those she's in contact with here and at the veterinary clinic. Sometimes she shirks her duties at home in order to care for one of her animals."

Gabe fought the temptation to tell Faith that her only daughter was contemplating leaving the Amish faith to become a vet. It was Melinda's place to tell her folks, not his. Besides, he'd made a promise not to tell anyone until she felt ready and knew for sure what she planned to do.

"I'd better get out to the barn and see if there's any Sheetrock so I can fix this hole," Gabe said, pushing his thoughts aside.

Faith nodded. "And I'd better head back downstairs and get some sewing done."

Half an hour later, Gabe and Melinda stood in front of his open buggy. He had patched the hole with a piece of plywood he'd found in the barn and planned to come back tomorrow with a new piece of Sheetrock, tape, and the mud he would need to do the job correctly.

"See that piece of canvas I have right there?"

Gabe said, motioning to the back of his buggy.

Melinda nodded.

"Pull it aside and take a look at what I made for you last night."

"Is it a trash can holder like the one we saw at the farmers' market?"

He shook his head. "It's something I hope you'll like even better."

Melinda gave the canvas a quick yank, and when a long wooden object came into view, she tipped her head in question. "What is this, Gabe?"

"It's a feeding trough—so you can feed the deer that come into the woods bordering your place."

"That's a wunderbaar idea. If the deer come to our place to eat, they'll be safe from hunters." Unexpectedly, Melinda threw herself into Gabe's arms and squeezed him around the neck. "I'm so glad you want to care for the deer now rather than kill them."

Gabe swallowed hard. Melinda had obviously misinterpreted his gift. How could he admit to her that he had no intention of giving up hunting? He enjoyed hunting and would continue to do so. He just wouldn't do it on her folks' land.

Chapter 20

With the warm August breeze tickling her nose, Melinda leaned back on her elbows and sighed. She loved being here at the pond where birds and wildlife abounded and everything seemed so peaceful. Gabe's picnic supper of barbecued beef sandwiches, dill pickles, and potato salad had left her feeling full and satisfied. Even though he'd admitted that his mother had made most of the meal, Melinda appreciated the gesture. Gabe seemed to enjoy Mama's homemade bread, too, for he ate several pieces slathered with some of Grandpa's rhubarb-strawberry jam.

Not wishing to ruin their meal with a possible argument, Melinda hadn't asked Gabe if he had told his mother that he'd proposed. She thought it would be best to wait awhile on that. So they'd only had a pleasant chat on the drive from her house to the pond, and for the last hour, they'd been sitting on an old quilt enjoying the picnic supper and having more lighthearted conversation.

Melinda glanced over at Gabe. His eyes were closed, and his face was lifted toward the sky. He obviously enjoyed being here, too. *If I can't get him to change his mind about going English, and I have to leave on my own, I'll surely miss him. It doesn't seem fair that I'm expected to choose between those I love and the joy of caring for animals. I wish I could have both.*

As if sensing her watching him, Gabe opened his eyes.

"Were you sleeping?" she asked.

"Nope." He smiled at her in such a sweet way it sent shivers up her spine. "I was just enjoying the warmth of the sun and thinking about how much I want to make you my wife."

Her cheeks warmed. "Gabe—I—"

"Whatever differences we may have, can't we just agree to disagree?"

A little crease had formed in the middle of Gabe's forehead, and Melinda reached up to rub it away. "I wish it was that simple."

"You love me, and I love you. We shouldn't allow anything to come between us."

Melinda was about to reply, but Gabe stopped her words by pulling her into his arms and kissing her. She couldn't think when she was in his arms. Nothing seemed to matter except the two of them sharing a special time of being alone together.

"Let's go for a walk," he said suddenly. "When we get back, we can have some of that apple crisp my mamm made for our dessert."

Melinda nodded, and he helped her to her feet. As they walked together among the pine trees, she knew all the wonderful moments she had shared with Gabe today would stay with her forever.

"I hate to spoil the evening," Gabe said sometime later, "but there are a few things we need to discuss."

"You're right," she agreed. "I also have a question I want to ask you."

"You can ask me anything, Melinda."

"Did you tell your mamm that you'd asked me to marry you?"

Gabe stopped walking, and so did she. "I hope you don't mind, but Mom came right out and asked how serious I was about you. So I felt she had the right to know that I'd proposed marriage."

"I see. Well, apparently, your mamm told Susie when she dropped by Kaulp's General Store, and Freda Kaulp overheard the conversation, and then she blabbed it to my mamm today." Melinda groaned. "Mama wasn't too happy hearing this news secondhand."

Gabe's forehead wrinkled. "I'm sorry she had

to learn about it that way, but you really should have told your folks yourself. Don't you think?"

"I agree, but we had decided not to tell anyone until we'd set a date and had resolved things between us."

"I know, but—"

Melinda jerked her head. "Did you hear that?"

He shrugged. "I didn't hear anything except the rustle of leaves when the wind picked up."

"Listen. There it is again—a strange thrashing sound." Melinda let go of Gabe's hand and hurried off.

"Where are you going?"

"To see what that noise is."

"Not without me, you're not. It might be some wild animal."

When they came upon the source of the noise a few seconds later, Melinda was shocked to discover a young doe with its leg caught in a cruel-looking metal trap. The poor animal thrashed about pathetically, obviously trying to free itself.

"Oh no!" She rushed toward the deer, but Gabe grabbed her around the waist and held her steady.

"What are you trying to do, get yourself hurt?" he scolded.

"I need to free the deer and make sure her leg's not broken."

"Melinda, I don't think that's such a good idea."

She wiggled free and went down on her knees.

Gabe watched as Melinda crawled slowly toward the deer. He didn't like her taking chances like this but figured if he made an issue of it, she would get mad. All he wanted to do was keep her safe—locked in his heart and loved forever.

The doe lay on its belly with the trapped foot extended in front of her. Strangely enough, when Melinda approached, it stopped thrashing and twitched its ears. It was almost as if the critter knew Melinda was there to help.

I wish there was something I could do, but if I get as close to the deer as Melinda is, it will most likely spook. Except for my dog, most animals aren't as comfortable around me as they seem to be with her. Gabe held his breath as Melinda pressed the sides of the trap apart, freeing the animal's leg. An instant later, the deer jumped up and bolted into a thicket of shrubs.

"I wish I'd had the chance to check it over thoroughly," Melinda said when she returned to his side. "I'm sure the doe's leg must have been cut." She shook her head slowly. "I'll never understand why anyone would want to hurt a beautiful deer like that."

Gabe resisted the temptation to argue that hunting deer for food was perfectly acceptable to his way of thinking. But he knew they would argue if he broached that subject again. Besides, setting a trap was no way to catch a deer or any other animal, for that matter. To make the situation worse, it wasn't even hunting season yet.

Gabe checked the trap to be sure it would no longer work and then buried it in the dirt.

"See why I asked Papa Noah to post No Hunting signs on our property?" Melinda's eyes shimmered with unshed tears. She really was sensitive where animals were concerned. A little too sensitive to Gabe's way of thinking. After all, it wasn't as if the critters were human beings.

"Let's head back to our picnic spot and eat our dessert," he said, hoping to brighten Melinda's mood.

She shook her head vigorously. "I have no appetite for food right now. Besides, we haven't finished our conversation yet."

Melinda and Gabe had gone only a few feet, and hadn't even begun to talk about things, when she spotted a baby skunk scampering out of the bushes. "Oh, look, Gabe! Isn't it cute? I wonder if it's an orphan."

"Don't get any dumb ideas, Melinda."

She halted and held her breath, waiting to see what the little skunk would do next. If it wasn't orphaned, she was sure its mother would show up soon.

"Melinda, let's go."

She shook her head. "I need to see if the skunk's mother is around."

"If she does come on the scene, we could be in a lot of trouble." Gabe grabbed Melinda's hand and gave it a tug, but she pulled away.

"I won't go back until I know the baby's not alone."

"And if it is?"

"I'll take it back to my place so I can care for it."

"No way! I won't allow that skunk in my buggy. What if it sprays?"

"Baby skunks never spray unless they're bothered, Gabe."

"Jah, well, picking up a skunk and hauling it home in a buggy could easily be considered 'bothering.'"

Ignoring his comment, Melinda tiptoed a bit closer to the small creature, but she'd only taken a few steps when the baby's mother trotted out of the bushes. Before Melinda had the presence of mind to turn and run, the skunk lifted its tail and let loose with a disgusting spray.

"Let's get out of here!" Gabe hollered.

Melinda gasped for a breath of fresh air as she and Gabe raced toward his buggy. They were about to climb in when he stopped her with an outstretched arm.

"What's wrong? Why are you blocking my way?"

"It's bad enough that we both smell like a skunk. If we get into my buggy, it will stink to high heavens, too."

She squinted at him. "We can't walk home, Gabe. It's too far."

"You're right, but I'm afraid my buggy will never be the same after this trip to the woods."

Melinda dropped her gaze to the ground. "I'm sorry. This was all my fault. I just wanted to be sure the skunk wasn't orphaned, and—" She stopped talking when her eyes started to water.

"Don't cry, Melinda. I hate it when you cry."

"I'm not crying. My eyes are watering because of this awful odor." She fanned her face and whirled around a few times. "Phew! Did you ever smell anything so awful?"

Gabe shook his head. "Not since we found a batch of rotten eggs out behind our henhouse." He plugged his nose. "Even that didn't smell half as bad as we do now."

"I'll help you wash down the buggy," she promised.

"We've got to get this smell off ourselves first."

She nodded. "Maybe Dr. Franklin has something we can use to get the odor out of the buggy—and us, too."

"My dog Shep got himself mixed up with a skunk once," Gabe said. "We bathed him in tomato juice."

"Did it help?"

"Some, but it took weeks before that animal smelled like a dog again."

Melinda folded her arms. "That's not exactly what I wanted to hear."

Gabe laughed, and so did she. At least it had only been a skunk that had come between them this time. And they'd been able to find some humor in it. That was a sign that things were improving in their relationship. At any rate, Melinda hoped they were, even if she and Gabe hadn't had the chance to discuss things and get everything ironed out between them.

Chapter 21

Melinda awoke on Friday morning, tingling with excitement along with a sense of apprehension. Today she would be going to Springfield to take her GED test at the college. Their English neighbor, Marsha Watts, had agreed to give her a ride, but Melinda had only told her folks that she was going to Springfield to do some shopping. It was true. She planned to shop for a few things after she'd taken her test. She would tell her folks about Dr. Franklin's suggestion that she become a vet after she passed the test.

"*If* I pass the test," she murmured as she stepped into a freshly laundered dress.

Melinda hurried from the room and headed for the kitchen to help her mother with breakfast.

Usually, Mama was already up and scurrying about, but today Melinda found the kitchen empty.

"Where's Mama?" she asked Papa Noah when he came in from doing his morning chores a short time later. "Was she outside with you?"

He shook his head. "Your mamm came down with the stomach flu during the night."

Melinda felt immediate concern. "I'm sorry to hear that. Is there anything I can do?"

"I'd appreciate it if you would cancel your trip to Springfield today," he said, hanging his straw hat on a wall peg near the door. "She can't keep anything down and is feeling as weak as a newborn kitten. I don't think it's a good idea for her to be alone today."

"What about Isaiah? Won't he be at home?"

Papa Noah shook his head. "Hank Osborn is shorthanded because a couple of his fellows also have the flu. So I'm taking Isaiah with me to help at the tree farm today."

Melinda nibbled on the inside of her cheek. "How about Grandpa? Can't he keep an eye out for Mama today?"

"He's got his own share of health problems, Melinda. I don't think it's a good idea for him to be exposed to your mamm when she's sick, do you?"

"No, of course not, but—"

"You can go shopping some other day, right?"

Melinda released a sigh. "Okay, Papa Noah. I'll run over to Marsha's house and tell her I won't need a ride to Springfield after all."

Papa Noah smiled. "You're a helpful daughter, and it puts my mind at ease to know I can go to work knowing that my wife will be in good hands today."

Melinda reached for her choring apron. *I suppose I can wait a few more weeks to take that test. Maybe by then I'll be more prepared.*

Gabe stood in front of his workbench sanding the arms of a wooden rocking chair. It was a nice change from working on cabinets, which was what Pap usually stuck him with. Even so, Gabe would rather have been working on the gun stock he'd promised to make for Aaron. After Aaron saw how nice Gabe's gun stock had turned out, he'd placed an order for one just like it. A couple of other men in their community had also asked Gabe to make them a new gun stock, which meant he had plenty of his own work to keep him busy after regular working hours.

If he kept getting orders for gun stocks, he might be able to open his own business sooner than he'd expected. If he had his own place, Melinda might understand why he didn't want to leave their Amish community and start life over in the English world.

Gabe glanced over his shoulder. His dad was working on a coffee table Bishop Frey had recently ordered for his wife's birthday.

Maybe I should tell Pap what I'm thinking of doing. Let him know I'm wanting to go out on my own. It wouldn't be right to wait and drop the news on him when the time comes.

Gabe set the sandpaper aside and moved across the room. "Say, Pap, I was wondering if I could talk to you about something."

"Sure, son. What's on your mind?"

Gabe shifted from one foot to the other, his courage beginning to waver. "I've. . .uh. . .been thinking that I'd like to have my own place of business."

"Are you saying you'd like to open another woodworking business here in our area?"

"Jah."

Pap crossed his arms and stared hard at Gabe. "Would you mind explaining why you'd want to be in competition with me?"

Gabe shook his head. "It wouldn't really be in competition. I'd be making other stuff—things like gun stocks, animal cages, birdhouses, and maybe some different kinds of household items, like the trash can holder I've made to give Mom for Christmas."

"I see."

Hope welled in Gabe's soul. Maybe Pap understood.

"Do you think you could handle a shop on your own?"

Gabe nodded.

"Guess time will tell." Pap shrugged his shoulders. "In the meanwhile, we've got a job to look at in Branson that will take a couple of weeks to finish."

"What kind of job?"

"A bed-and-breakfast needs some new furniture, and they want it to be made by an Amish carpenter."

Gabe leaned against his dad's workbench. "What part of the job will you expect me to do?"

"That all depends."

"On what?"

"On what all the customer wants made."

"Who'll we get to drive us to Branson?"

"I don't know yet. Probably Ed Wilkins. He's usually available whenever I need to go somewhere outside the area."

Gabe headed back to his own workbench. At least Pap hadn't said he would be stuck doing the menial jobs for the bed-and-breakfast. Maybe he would let Gabe build some of the furniture and not just do finish work.

"Oh, and Gabe, there's one more thing," Pap called over his shoulder.

"What's that?"

"If it turns out you're still working for me after you and Melinda get married, I want you to know that I'll pay you enough so you can make a decent living."

Gabe sucked in his breath. Should he tell Pap that he and Melinda might not be getting married? Would Pap have some good advice if he knew what Gabe was up against right now? Or if Pap knew the whole story, would he be worried that Gabe might decide to leave their Amish community and go English with Melinda?

Gabe grabbed his piece of sandpaper and gave the arm of the chair a couple of good swipes. *I'd best not say anything yet. Better to wait until I know for sure what's what.*

When they woke up Saturday morning, Melinda's mother had said she was feeling better and suggested that she and Melinda pick some produce from their garden. They'd spent most of the morning harvesting tomatoes and green beans. Now they stood at the kitchen sink washing the bounty of produce.

"Why don't you let me finish this up?" Melinda suggested. "You were sick yesterday, and it's probably not a good idea for you to overdo."

Mama fanned her hand in front of her face. "I'm fine, dear one. It was only a twenty-four-hour bug, and I promise to rest once the produce is washed and put away." She smiled. "I appreciated your canceling your shopping trip yesterday and staying home to see to my needs. It proves what a thoughtful daughter you are."

Melinda's face heated with embarrassment. If

her mother only knew that she'd planned to do more than shopping in Springfield, she wouldn't be saying such kind things.

"All these tomatoes make me think about that day a few weeks ago when the skunk sprayed you and Gabe," Mama said.

"The two of us smelled to high heavens, and you wouldn't let me come inside until I'd bathed in the galvanized tub Papa Noah had set up in the woodshed." Melinda grimaced at the memory of it. After several baths, alternating tomato juice and a mixture of hydrogen peroxide, baking soda, and liquid dishwashing soap, she had scrubbed so hard she was afraid she wouldn't have any skin left on her body.

The day after their spraying, she and Gabe had washed his buggy down with something Dr. Franklin had given her that was stronger than what she'd bathed in. Never again would Melinda knowingly go near a skunk.

Mama had just placed another batch of tomatoes on a towel to dry when Isaiah entered the room. "I'm glad I didn't have to go to work with Papa today," he muttered. "Pullin' weeds around them trees was harder than workin' in the garden."

"A little hard work never hurt anyone, and I know your daed and Hank Osborn appreciated the help." Mama smiled. "Both of my kinner sacrificed to help others yesterday, and it pleases me to know we've raised such willing workers. I don't know what I'd do without either of my dear children."

Melinda cringed. *What will Mama say when she finds out what I'm thinking of doing? Will she understand why I feel the need to become a vet? Will I feel guilty and miserable once I leave home? Can I really give up all that I have here with my family and friends? I wish I felt free to tell Mama that I'm going to take my GED test as soon as I can reschedule a time. But if she knew, she would probably try to stop me.*

Melinda closed her eyes and leaned against the kitchen cupboard as confusion swirled in her brain like a windmill going at full speed. *Oh, Lord, please help me to know what to do.*

Chapter 22

Two weeks later as Melinda left the college in Springfield where she'd finally gone to take her GED test, a feeling of weariness settled over her like a drenching rain. The test had been difficult—much harder than she'd expected it to be. But she had studied hard and knew she had done her best. If all went well, by this time next week, she might know the results of her scores.

If I find out I've passed the test, then what? she wondered. *Do I really want to leave everyone I love and start life over in the English world?* So many conflicting thoughts swirled around in her brain. One minute, she wanted to become a vet, and the next minute, she wanted things to remain as they were. Why was it so hard to decide what was best for her? She had been thinking and praying about this for weeks. Why wasn't God giving her any clear direction?

She shook the troubling thoughts aside as she approached Marsha's car. *I'll figure this out after I get the results of my test.*

"How did it go?" Marsha asked when Melinda opened the car door and slid into the passenger's seat.

Melinda shrugged. "It was a hard test, but I think I did okay."

"When will you know the results?"

"In a week or so, I expect."

"And then will you tell your folks?"

Melinda nodded.

"Would you like to go somewhere for lunch now, or do you want to do some shopping first?" Marsha asked.

"I'm kind of hungry, so if you don't mind, I'd like to have lunch first."

"That sounds good to me." Marsha started the engine and pulled away from the curb. "When we get back to Seymour, I'd like to stop by Kaulp's General Store before I drop you off at your house. I want to buy a couple of those large wooden spoons they sell there."

"That's fine by me. Since Kaulp's isn't far from my home, I'll just walk from there." Melinda leaned against the seat and tried to relax. Oh, how she wished she knew the results of that test. She hated being deceitful, but if she had told

Mama or Papa Noah the real reason she'd gone to Springfield today, they would have tried to talk her out of it. She felt grateful that Marsha had promised not to say anything.

"I'm heading out to make a delivery," Gabe's dad said as he plucked his straw hat off the counter near the front door and plunked it on his head. "Can you handle things here while I'm gone?"

"Jah, sure," Gabe mumbled. It always irked him whenever Pap asked that question. And he asked it nearly every time he left the shop. Wouldn't the man ever realize that Gabe was capable and could manage things on his own?

"I'll be back sometime before supper," Pap said as he headed out the door.

Gabe grunted and reached for a hunk of sandpaper. "I can't wait until I own my own shop," he muttered when the door clicked shut. He gritted his teeth and gave the arm of the rocking chair he'd been working on a couple of solid swipes.

Sometime later, the shop door opened, and Noah stepped into the room. "How's it going, Gabe?"

"Fine. We're keeping plenty busy these days."

"It's always good to be busy."

"Jah."

"Is your daed around, or are you on your own this afternoon?"

"It's just me. Pap had a delivery to make."

"I see." Noah leaned against the workbench closest to where Gabe was working. "I was on my way home from work and thought I'd stop and talk to you for a minute."

Gabe stood and brushed the sawdust off his trousers. "Is there a problem?"

"Not a problem, exactly." Noah shifted his weight as he cleared his throat. "I'm. . .uh. . .a bit concerned about my daughter."

"Is Melinda all right? Has something happened to her?"

Noah shook his head. "She's not sick or anything like that. In fact, she had one of our neighbors take her to Springfield for the day so she could shop for some things that aren't available in Seymour."

Gabe grimaced. If Melinda had gone to Springfield, she was probably planning to take her GED test today. Did Noah know about it? Is that why he wanted to talk to Gabe? Did Noah think Gabe had some influence over Melinda and could talk her out of going English? But what if Noah didn't know? Gabe had to be careful about what he said so he wouldn't let the cat out of the bag in case Melinda hadn't told her folks about her plans yet.

"What did you want to say to me about Melinda?" Gabe asked.

Noah drew in a quick breath and released it with a huff. "Her mamm and I think she's spending way too much time with those critters of hers. We're afraid if she doesn't find a happy medium soon, she'll end up spending the rest of her life with her priorities all mixed up."

"What's that got to do with me? As I'm sure you must know, Melinda's and my relationship isn't so solid anymore."

"I know you've had words a few times; Melinda confided that much to her mamm. Even though you don't always see eye to eye on things, I'm sure she cares for you, Gabe."

"I care for her, too."

"I'm hoping you might be able to convince her not to spend so much time with those critters of hers. She needs to spend more time helping her mamm and learning things that will help prepare her for marriage."

Gabe groaned as he pulled his fingers through the sides of his hair. "I'm not sure I'm the one you should be talking to, because I don't have that much influence where your daughter is concerned. Fact is our relationship is slipping so bad that she doesn't much care what I have to say about anything."

Noah placed his hand on Gabe's shoulder. "Do you love my daughter?"

Gabe nodded. "Guess I'll always love her."

"Do you think it would help if I put in a good word for you? Or maybe Faith could invite you and your family over for a meal sometime soon."

Gabe shook his head. "Melinda knows what it will take for our relationship to get better. I don't think a meal or a good word from you will make any difference."

"Is the problem you're having about hunting? Does Melinda expect you to give up hunting?"

Gabe rubbed his chin as he contemplated the best way to reply to Noah's question without revealing the real problem. "Let's just say that Melinda's priorities are different than mine, and unless she changes her mind about certain things, we can never have a future together."

Noah stared at Gabe with a peculiar expression. Finally, he turned toward the door, calling over his shoulder, "I'll be praying for you and Melinda."

"I appreciate that."

When the door clicked shut behind Noah, Gabe dropped to his knees and resumed sanding the rocking chair. Oh, how he hoped Melinda would come to her senses and choose him and her family over her animal friends.

Susie had just put a bolt of blue material on one of the shelves near the back of Kaulp's store when the bell above the front door jingled, signaling that a customer had entered the building. She turned and saw Melinda and

Marsha Watts step up to the front counter where Freda Kaulp stood.

A few minutes later, Marsha and Freda moved over to the shelf where the kitchen items were kept, and Melinda headed in Susie's direction.

"Did you come here with your neighbor, or did you just happen to arrive at the same time?" Susie asked as Melinda joined her in front of the shelves full of fabric.

Melinda leaned close and whispered in Susie's ear. "Marsha drove me to Springfield this morning."

"That's nice, but why are you whispering?"

Melinda gave a quick glance over her shoulder then blotted the perspiration from her forehead with the corner of her apron. "I don't want Freda to know where I've been."

Susie squinted. "Why not? Lots of folks in our community hire a driver to take them to Springfield for shopping and appointments."

"Not the kind of appointment I had this morning."

"What kind of appointment did you have?"

Melinda's voice lowered even further. "I went to the college to take my GED test."

Susie swallowed hard as a sick feeling swept over her. So Melinda really was serious about leaving the Amish faith and becoming a vet. She had hoped it was only a passing fancy and that Melinda would give up the idea when she'd had a chance to pray about it.

"You don't look very happy about me taking the test."

"I'm not."

"Don't you even want to know how it went?"

Susie shrugged. "I figured you'd get around to telling me."

Melinda pursed her lips. "It was a hard test. Much harder than I expected it would be."

Susie bit the inside of her lip to keep from smiling. She'd never say it to Melinda, but she'd hoped the test would be difficult and that Melinda would fail. Flunking the test might be the only thing that would keep Melinda from making the biggest mistake of her life. At least, that's how Susie saw it.

"When will you get the results?" Susie asked.

"I–I'm not sure. I expect I should know something in a week or so."

"I see." Susie's fingers traveled over the bolts of material stacked on the shelf as she mulled things over. If Melinda passed her GED and decided to take some college courses to prepare for her veterinary training, they might never see each other again. Once Melinda moved away and pursued a career, she'd have little reason to come home except for an occasional visit. Susie figured even those times would be strained.

Melinda tapped Susie on the shoulder.

"What?"

"Ever since we were little and Mama and I moved here after she'd been an entertainer, you and I have been good friends and shared everything with each other."

Susie knew full well how close she and Melinda had been over the years. But things were tense between them now, and they would only get worse once Melinda left home. *How does Melinda expect me to be happy about this decision?* She turned to face Melinda. "Does Gabe know you went to take the GED test today?"

Melinda shook her head. "I saw no reason to tell him."

"I'll bet you haven't told your folks yet, either. Am I right?"

"No, I haven't told them. I will, though, as soon as I receive my test scores."

"Will you tell them even if you've failed?"

"I don't know. Probably not, since there would be nothing to tell. I can't make a final decision on what I should do with my future until I've passed that test. So, until I do, mum's the word, okay?"

Susie drew in a deep breath as she slowly nodded. Oh, how she wished she didn't have to keep Melinda's secret.

Chapter 23

Clutching a basket of freshly picked tomatoes, Melinda trudged wearily from the garden to the house. It seemed as if there were no end to the ripe tomatoes, and today she and Mama planned to do up several canner-loads. Dr. Franklin had wanted Melinda to work at the clinic this afternoon, but with so many tomatoes to be harvested, she felt obligated to lend her mother a hand. It was a sacrifice, considering that Melinda would much rather be holding a dog or a cat than canning squishy tomatoes. If she became a vet, she'd have even more contact with animals than she did just working for Dr. Franklin a few days a week.

Melinda couldn't believe it had been a week

already since she'd taken her GED test. She worried about when she would get the results and whether she had passed. All this week, she'd alternated her time between working at the clinic and helping Mama can beans and tomatoes, hoping to keep busy enough that she wouldn't think about the test results.

Melinda glanced out the window at the line of trees bordering the back of their property. If she couldn't be working at the clinic, she would have enjoyed being in the woods on this Saturday morning, sketching some of the wildlife. Even being inside the chicken coop, checking on the baby pheasants that had hatched yesterday morning, would have been preferable to being here in the stuffy house. Maybe when she finished with the tomatoes, there would be time for her to make a quick trip to the woods.

Melinda had just placed the tomatoes into the sink to be washed when Isaiah entered the kitchen waving a stack of letters.

"Mail's here," he announced. "Where do you want it?"

Mama nodded toward the table. "You can put it over there, and then I'd like you to go back outside and pull some weeds in the garden. They're starting to overtake the bean plants again."

Isaiah's forehead creased, making a row of tiny wrinkles. "How come Melinda didn't pull the weeds when she was out there picking tomatoes?"

"I didn't have time for that," Melinda responded before Mama could open her mouth. "As it is, I'll be busy all afternoon helping put up the tomatoes I got picked. So the least you can do is to pull a few weeds."

"Melinda's right," Mama agreed. "So grab yourself something cold to drink and hurry out to get the job done."

Isaiah grunted, ambled over to the refrigerator, and withdrew a jug of lemonade. He poured himself a tall glass of the liquid, drank it down, and headed out the door, letting it slam shut behind him.

Mama clicked her tongue noisily. "That boy! Sometimes I think he was born in a barn."

Melinda smiled. It was kind of nice to hear Mama become riled over something Isaiah did for a change. Usually it was Melinda she was upset with. "Is it all right if I take a break to look at the mail?" Melinda asked.

"Sure. I can handle this on my own for a bit."

Melinda took a seat at the table and thumbed through the mail. Her hands trembled when she spotted an envelope with the college's return address. It had to be the results of her GED test. She was glad she'd been given the opportunity to go through the mail first, and not someone else in the family.

I probably should have had them send it to Dr. Franklin's office, she thought, glancing at her mother, who was still at the sink with her back to Melinda. *But they asked for my home address, and I didn't want to be deceitful by writing down something other than where I actually live.* She cringed as a sense of guilt washed over her. *I've already been deceitful by not telling my folks I took the test or letting them know about my plans for the future. I need to right that wrong—and soon.*

Melinda ripped open the envelope, and as she studied her scores, her heart took a nosedive. She'd failed the test.

She had passed the English part of the exam, but the math section had been much harder and she'd missed too many questions. Her only recourse was to study more then retake the test. Either that, or she would have to give up her dream of going to college and eventually on to veterinary school. Maybe it wasn't meant for her to go. Maybe. . .

"Anything interesting in the mail today?" Mama asked, breaking into Melinda's contemplations.

"What? Uh. . .I haven't looked through all of it yet." Melinda slipped the envelope with the GED results under her apron waistband. If she had passed the test, she would have told Mama her plans. But since she'd failed, she saw no point in mentioning it now.

Maybe the Lord is trying to tell me something. Could He want me to give up the idea of becoming a vet and learn to be content being an Amish housewife?

She grabbed the rest of the mail and quickly

thumbed through it. *Or maybe I'm supposed to be patient and wait until I'm more prepared. Oh, Lord, please show me what I'm supposed to do.*

Gabe stared out the window of the van. He and his father had hired Ed Wilkins to drive them to Branson this morning, and after meeting with the owners of the bed-and-breakfast, Pap had signed a contract to make five new tables with matching chairs for their guest kitchen. Gabe wouldn't know until later how much of that job he would be allowed to do, but he had enjoyed his time in Branson.

As they traveled along the main street, he observed several fancy theaters with parking lots full of cars and tour buses. Melinda had told him that this was one of the towns where her mother used to perform, and he wondered if it had been in any of the theaters along this stretch of road.

What must it have been like for Faith to live here and be up on stage before an audience, yodeling and telling jokes? he wondered. *Does she ever miss it? Would Melinda want to live here if she becomes part of the English world again? I'm sure the reason she wants to leave the Amish faith has more to do with her desire to help animals than it does with the allure of the modern world.*

Gabe grimaced. They still hadn't talked things through, and the truth was Gabe had been avoiding the subject whenever he'd seen Melinda. He wanted her to stay Amish and become his wife, not run off to some fancy school and go English. As much as he wanted to be with her, the thought of leaving the Amish faith turned his stomach sour.

"Did you enjoy the lunch we had at the Country Buffet?" Pap asked, breaking into Gabe's disconcerting thoughts.

Gabe nodded and patted his stomach. "I had more than my share of peach cobbler and vanilla ice cream at the dessert bar, too."

His dad chuckled. "Same here."

"What have you got lined up for us to do after we get home this afternoon?" Gabe asked.

"A couple of doors need to be sanded. But since there won't be many hours left to work by the time we get back to the shop, I think you can take the rest of the day off."

"You mean it?"

Pap nodded. "Said so, didn't I?"

Gabe smiled. He figured if he headed straight for the woods after they got home, he'd have plenty of time to do some target practicing before Mom had supper ready.

Melinda tromped through the tall grass, making her way to the woods behind their house. She was glad to finally have some time to herself.

All day as she and Mama had canned tomatoes, she'd grieved over failing her test. Maybe being in the woods awhile would help her gain some perspective.

As Melinda passed the deer feeder Gabe had made, she wondered if she could survive in the English world without him. She hadn't seen Gabe for a couple of weeks, but he'd left a note in the birdhouse yesterday saying he and his dad would be going to Branson to look at a job today. Melinda wished she could have gone with him. She hadn't been back to Branson since she was a little girl. A couple of times during her growing-up years, she'd asked about going there, but Mama always said Branson was part of her past and that she had no desire to go there again.

As Melinda stepped into the woods, her mind whirled with confusion. *English or Amish? Forget about taking another GED test or try again? Marry Gabe or become a vet?*

She shook her head, trying to clear away the troubling thoughts. Three deer—a buck and two does—showed up on the scene, and she quickly took a seat on a tree stump. Pulling her drawing tablet and pencil from the canvas bag she'd brought along, she watched in fascination as she sketched the beautiful creatures.

Pop! Pop! Pop! Melinda tipped her head. It sounded like a gun had been fired somewhere in the distance. But that was impossible. It wasn't deer season yet. Besides, Papa Noah had posted

No Hunting signs on their property. Someone would have to be pretty dumb to be hunting on their land.

Pop! Pop! The noise came again, a little closer this time.

The deer bolted into the bushes, and Melinda groaned. *Just one more thing to ruin my day.*

She tossed her artwork into the canvas satchel, slung it over her shoulder, and headed toward the gunfire, keeping low and, hopefully, out of danger. Whoever was shooting was in for a good tongue-lashing.

A few minutes later, she came to a halt. Gabe stood next to her little brother, and Isaiah held a gun in his hands!

Melinda marched over to them, jerked the gun away from Isaiah, and thrust it at Gabe. "What are you doing here?"

"I'm showing Isaiah how to shoot."

Her heart pounded, and her mouth felt so dry she could barely swallow. "What would make you do such a thing?"

"Isaiah saw the gun stock I made for Aaron when he was over at the Zooks' playing with Aaron's younger brothers," Gabe explained. "When he and your daed dropped by our shop the other day, Isaiah asked if I'd teach him how to shoot."

"Did my stepdaed agree to that?" Melinda's question was directed at Gabe, but it was Isaiah who responded.

"When I asked Gabe about shootin' a gun, Papa was busy talkin' to Gabe's daed. I didn't think he'd mind since I'm twelve years old now." Isaiah looked at Melinda as though daring her to say otherwise. "I can hunt with a youth permit as long as I'm with an adult who's licensed to hunt."

Melinda's attention snapped back to Gabe. "You said you were giving up hunting."

He frowned. "I never said that."

"You told me you were sorry about our disagreement and that—"

"I *was* sorry. Sorry we had words but not sorry for shooting my gun." His jaw clenched, and the late afternoon shadows shifted on his cheek. "I don't see anything wrong with hunting deer when it's for food, not just a trophy."

Melinda realized Gabe was right. He hadn't actually said he wouldn't hunt anymore. She'd just assumed that's what he meant when he'd apologized. And after he gave her the deer feeder he'd made, she thought he felt the same way about the forest animals as she did. She also knew that many men hunted deer for food, not just the sport of it. Even though she couldn't save every deer in the woods, the ones in these woods were hers, and she didn't want any of them hurt. She also didn't like the idea of Gabe teaching her little brother how to hunt.

"It's obvious to me," she said in a shaky voice, "that you don't care nearly as much about animals as I do, which is probably why you won't—"

Gabe held up his hand and nodded toward Isaiah.

Melinda knew it wasn't a good idea to discuss their problems in front of her little brother. In her irritation with Gabe, she'd almost forgotten Isaiah was still there.

"You'd better head for home," she told her brother.

He jutted out his chin. "You ain't my boss."

Gabe intervened. "Isaiah, I think it would be best if you did go home. Your folks might be missing you by now."

Melinda was tempted to tell Gabe he should have thought about that before he dragged her little brother into the woods and placed a gun in his hands, but she decided to keep quiet. Enough had already been said in front of Isaiah, and she didn't want him going home and spouting off everything he'd heard her and Gabe say.

"Okay, I'll go," Isaiah mumbled. "But it's only because Gabe asked me so nice." He cast a quick glance at Melinda and wrinkled his nose.

Melinda folded her arms and said nothing.

"Maybe we can target practice some other time," Isaiah said, smiling at Gabe.

"We'll have to wait and see how it goes," Gabe replied.

"Jah, okay." Isaiah tromped off toward home.

Melinda waited until he was out of sight before she spoke again. Drawing in a deep breath to steady her nerves, she looked right at Gabe.

"You don't have to worry about me leaving the Amish faith. At least not any time soon."

He blinked a couple of times as though he didn't quite believe her.

"I failed my GED test."

"You. . .you did?"

She nodded solemnly.

"So you've given up on the idea of becoming a vet?" he asked with a hopeful expression.

"Well, I—"

"It's for the best, Melinda. You'll see that once we're married."

Melinda drew back like a turtle being poked with a sharp stick. "You don't even care that I failed, do you?"

"Of course I do, but—"

"You know what I think, Gabe?"

He shook his head.

"Even if I was to stay Amish and we did get married, we would probably always be arguing."

"I don't think so, Melinda."

"Jah, we would. We'd argue about all my pets that you think are silly. We'd argue about whether it's okay for you to hunt or not. We'd argue about—" Melinda's throat felt too clogged to say anything more. All she wanted to do was run for the safety of home. And that's exactly what she did.

Chapter 24

Gabe watched Melinda's retreating form as a sense of despair washed over him. He had made such a mess of things. It seemed as though that's all he did anymore—clutter everything between him and Melinda and make her upset. "I never should have brought Isaiah into the woods to target practice," he mumbled. "Especially not without getting Noah's permission." He gathered up his gun and ammunition. "This whole thing between me and Melinda stinks about as bad as when the two of us got sprayed by a skunk!"

Gabe knew the first thing he needed to do was apologize to Melinda's stepfather. Then he had to come up with some way to patch things up with Melinda. There had to be something he could do to make her realize how much he loved her. Either that or they would have to go their separate ways, which seemed to be what she wanted. But it sure wasn't what Gabe wanted. Why couldn't Melinda just be happy with the way things were? Why would she want to give up her family and friends just to take care of some dumb old animals?

Gabe swallowed around the lump that had formed in his throat as he started walking toward the Hertzlers' place. He'd been in love with Melinda too long to let their relationship go, no matter how much they disagreed on things. No, he couldn't give up on them yet.

Melinda paced the length of the front porch, waiting for Papa Noah to show up. Usually he had Saturdays off, but he had worked at the Christmas tree farm today because Hank Osborn was shorthanded.

Melinda thought about the tree farm and how much she had enjoyed visiting there when she was a girl. It had been exciting to see the rows of various-sized pine trees that would eventually become some English person's Christmas tree. She hadn't visited Osborn's Tree Farm in several years.

I don't need to look at Christmas trees anymore. Not when I've got a whole forest full of beautiful trees

I can gaze at whenever I want.

Melinda glanced at the darkening sky, knowing she needed to go inside and see if her mother needed help with supper. She was about to turn when her stepfather's buggy rolled into the yard.

Melinda bounded off the porch and sprinted out to the buggy in time to see Gabe walking across the open field between their house and the woods. She hurried to Papa Noah's side as soon as he stepped down from the buggy. "I need to tell you something," she panted.

"What is it? You look *verlegge*."

"I am troubled. I've just come from the woods, where I discovered Isaiah and Gabe. You'll never guess what they were doing."

"What was it?"

"Gabe was teaching Isaiah to shoot a gun."

Papa Noah's eyebrows furrowed. "He was?"

"Jah."

Before Papa Noah could say anything more, Gabe stepped between them, all red-faced and sweaty. "I need to speak with you, Noah."

"Is it about you teaching my son how to shoot?"

Gabe nodded. "When Isaiah asked me to teach him to shoot a gun, I figured he'd gotten your permission and that you had a youth permit for him." Gabe gave Melinda a sidelong glance, but she looked away.

"Isaiah has never said a word to me about wanting to hunt or even asked about shooting a gun," Papa Noah said with a shake of his head.

"I'm sorry. I should have asked you first. Please know that it will never happen again." Gabe's expression was somber, but Melinda couldn't help but wonder if he really was sorry. Maybe he was simply trying to keep himself out of trouble with her stepfather.

"I accept your apology, Gabe," Papa Noah said. "I appreciate the fact that you had the courage to come talk to me about this matter."

A look of relief flooded Gabe's face.

Papa Noah glanced over at Melinda. "I need to put my horse away. Would you please tell your mamm I'll be in for supper soon?"

She nodded. "I'll give her the message."

Papa Noah headed for the barn, and Melinda turned toward the house. She'd only taken a few steps when Gabe touched her shoulder. "Listen, about our disagreement—"

She halted and turned around.

"I'm sorry about your GED. I understand how much it meant to you."

Melinda shook her head. "I don't think you do understand, Gabe. If you did, you might be more willing to do some things just for me."

"Like what?"

She pointed to the gun in his hands.

"I wasn't planning to hunt on your property."

"I don't care where you had planned to hunt. You shouldn't be teaching Isaiah to hunt. He's too young."

"Not if he has a youth permit and hunts with your daed."

"Papa Noah doesn't hunt, and to my knowledge, he never has."

Gabe stared at the ground, kicking small rocks with the toe of his boot. "The truth is you don't want me to hunt at all. Isn't that right?"

"I know we need some animals for meat," she said, avoiding his question. "But the deer are special to me."

"I realize that. The deer and every other critter you want to help." He stared at her with such intensity she thought he might break down and cry. "The simple fact is you care so much about animals that you'd be willing to give up your faith, family, and friends in order to care for them the way Doc Franklin does."

"Gabe, I—"

"And you want me to give up all those things in order for us to be together."

Tears welled in Melinda's eyes. Gabe was right. She did want that. She thought if he was willing to leave the Amish faith, it would prove how much he loved her.

"Even if we both left the faith, things would never feel right between us," he said with a catch in his voice.

"What do you mean?"

"I'd be leaving family and friends, and so would you."

"I know that, and the thought of it pains

me, Gabe. But we would have each other, and eventually, we'd have a family of our own."

"I'd have to give up my dream of owning my own wood-working business, too."

She shook her head. "You could do carpentry work in the English world."

He took a step toward her. "I love you, Melinda, and I always will, but it's time I face the fact that your wants and my wants don't mesh. I'd thought maybe we could work things out, but now I realize it's just not possible. So, as much as it hurts me to say this, I've come to realize that it has to be over between us." Before she could comment, Gabe swung around and bolted from the yard.

With tears coursing down her cheeks, Melinda moved slowly toward the house. Gabe was right. They both wanted different things. Even though it pained her to admit the truth, if she decided to leave the Amish faith, they would have no future together because Gabe wasn't willing to leave.

***

It was difficult for Melinda to attend church at the Hiltys' the next day, but she knew that unless she was sick, there was no way she could get out of going. After what had happened yesterday between her and Gabe, she didn't want to face him.

Melinda had just stepped down from the

buggy when Susie rushed up to her. "Is it true, Melinda? Have you and Gabe broken up for good?"

"I can't believe the news is out already," Melinda muttered. "Who told you?"

"Gabe must have told his mamm, and then she told my mamm when they got here a few minutes ago." Susie eyed Melinda critically. "Please tell me it's not true."

Melinda quickly explained the way she'd discovered Gabe teaching Isaiah how to shoot and how they had argued, and then Gabe had broken things off.

Susie's expression was solemn. "I can't believe you'd be so *narrisch*. Don't you realize how much Gabe loves you?"

"I'm not being foolish." Melinda shrugged. "I guess Gabe doesn't love me as much as I thought."

"Maybe there's something you can say or do to make Gabe change his mind."

Melinda shook her head as tears clouded her vision. "I would have to give up caring for animals if we got back together."

Susie's eyebrows lifted. "Why would you have to do that? You're caring for animals now, aren't you?"

Melinda didn't know how to respond. It was true—she was caring for some animals, but in a very small way. The little bit she did for the animals she rescued was nothing compared to how she would be able to help them if she became a vet. "We'd better get inside," she said, moving toward the house. "There's no point discussing this because it won't change a thing. Besides, church will be starting soon."

Susie touched Melinda's arm. "If you've broken up with Gabe, does that mean you won't be at the young people's gathering tonight?"

Melinda nodded. "I had planned on going until our breakup, but not now. It wouldn't seem right."

"But you'll miss all the fun if you don't go."

Melinda shrugged.

Susie stared at the ground. "I guess if you're not going, then I won't, either."

Melinda felt as if a heavy weight rested on her shoulders. Susie had no boyfriend to take her home from the gathering, but she'd obviously been looking forward to going. *If Susie stays home on account of me, she'll be miserable, and I'll feel guilty for days.*

Melinda forced her lips to form a smile. "Jah, okay. I'll go tonight."

"You look like you've been sucking on a bunch of sour grapes," Aaron said to Gabe as they climbed down from their buggies.

Gabe moved to the front of his buggy and started to unhitch the horse. "Yesterday, Melinda and I broke up," he mumbled.

Aaron skirted around his own rig. "You're kidding, right?"

"No, it's the truth."

"But I thought you two were crazy in love."

Gabe grunted. "I used to think that, too."

"What happened?"

"Melinda caught me in the woods behind their place teaching her little bruder how to shoot a gun."

Aaron reached under his hat and scratched the back of his head. "That's all? She broke up with you because you were teaching her brother to shoot?"

"Actually, it was me who broke up with her, but I think she agrees that things could never work out between us." Gabe grabbed his horse's bridle and led him toward the corral, where several other horses milled about.

Aaron followed, leaving his own horse hitched to the buggy. "If you love the woman so much, why don't you fight for her?"

"Melinda's love for animals has come between us," Gabe said. "She doesn't want me to hunt, either." He was tempted to tell his friend the rest of the story but figured Aaron might blab to someone else that Melinda wanted to become a vet. Gabe felt sure it would be better for everyone if he kept that information to himself.

"I think it's ridiculous that Melinda would object to you hunting. She can't save every deer in the woods." Aaron shook his head. "If you want my opinion, Melinda's got *verhuddelt* thinking."

"It might be confused thinking to you and me, but it isn't to her."

Aaron leaned against the corral while Gabe put his horse inside. "What are you going to do about this?"

Gabe turned his hands palm up. "What can I do?" *Besides give up hunting and leave the Amish faith so Melinda can fulfill her crazy, selfish dream.*

"I know what I would do," Aaron said.

"What's that?"

"I'd tell Melinda she's verhuddelt and that she needs to come to her senses."

Gabe shook his head. "That would only make things worse. The best thing I can do at this point is to pray about our situation."

"You never know. Melinda might change her mind about you hunting. Women are prone to that, you know," Aaron said with a serious expression.

Gabe gave his horse a gentle pat and left the corral. "You'd best get your horse in here. Church will be starting soon."

"You're right." Aaron followed Gabe back to his horse and buggy. "You know, this whole ordeal you're going through with Melinda is just one more reason why I'm never getting married!"

Maybe Aaron had the right idea about marriage, Gabe thought. Maybe it would have been better if he'd never allowed himself to fall in love with Melinda.

Chapter 25

Melinda didn't know why she had let Susie talk her into attending the young people's gathering, but there she sat, alone on a bale of straw in Abe Martin's barn. It was hard to watch others engage in playing games and sharing friendly banter. Everyone but her seemed to be having a good time. How could she enjoy herself when she wasn't with Gabe and wouldn't be riding home in his buggy at the close of the evening?

It might have been easier if Gabe hadn't been here tonight, but he was standing in front of the punch bowl talking to Mattie Byler. Had he found a replacement for Melinda so soon? The thought of Gabe courting someone else made Melinda's stomach feel queasy, and unbidden tears sprang to her eyes. She sniffed and swiped them away when Susie plunked down beside her.

"Guess what?"

Susie seemed excited about something, but in Melinda's glum mood, it was all she could do to respond with a shrug.

"I can't believe it, but Jonas Byler asked if he could give me a ride home in his buggy tonight."

"Mattie's brother?"

"Jah. Jonas is five years older than me, and until now he's never given me so much as a second glance." Susie grinned. "Maybe Jonas sees me in a different light now and realizes that I'm not a little girl anymore."

"That could be."

"If Jonas decides he likes me, maybe he will stay here and not return to Montana after all."

"Maybe so."

"I hear tell many Amish folks who have moved to remote settlements like those in Montana don't stay very long." Susie popped a couple of her knuckles, the way Melinda's mother often did. "Jonas says. . ."

Melinda broke off a piece of straw and clenched it between her teeth. She really didn't care about any of this but didn't want to appear rude.

"I've never traveled much and would like the chance to see some of the states out West," Susie went on to say. "Jonas says the Amish who live in northern Montana have log homes, only they're much nicer than those the pioneers used to live in."

Melinda listened halfheartedly as her aunt droned on about Jonas and Montana. It was hard for Melinda to concentrate on anything other than Gabe and Mattie, who stood off by themselves in one corner of the barn with their heads together.

I wonder if he's doing that just to make me jealous. He probably thinks if I believe he's interested in someone else, I'll say it's okay for him to hunt and I'll stay Amish and won't try to retake my GED or become a vet. Melinda clenched her fingers into tight balls and held them firmly in her lap. "Maybe I ought to move to Montana," she muttered.

Susie nudged her arm. "What was that?"

"Oh, nothing." Melinda stood, smoothing the wrinkles in her dark blue dress. "I think I'll go outside for a breath of fresh air."

"Would you like some company?"

Melinda shook her head. "If Jonas plans to take you home tonight, you'd better stay put. I wouldn't want you to miss out on your first date with him because of me."

"I'm sure he won't leave without me. Besides, the gathering's not over yet."

"Just the same, I'd rather be alone if you don't mind."

Susie shrugged. "Suit yourself."

Melinda noticed Jonas heading their way with two glasses of punch, so she hurried off. At least Susie was having a good time this evening, and she deserved to be happy.

Outside, Melinda wandered around the yard, staring up at the sky and studying the bright, full moon and thousands of brilliant stars twinkling like fireflies in the night sky. She thought about an old yodeling song her mother had taught her a few years ago.

With arms folded and face lifted toward the night sky, she quietly sang the words of the song. "O silvery moon, I'm so lonely tonight; to stroll once again in your beautiful light. There's a fellow I adore and a longing to see, in that beautiful Yo Ho Valley. My little yodel-tee-ho yodel tee ho—yodel-tee-ho tee! I'll sing you a song, while the moon's growing low. My little yodel-tee-ho—yodel-tee-ho in the beautiful Yo Ho Valley."

A lump formed in Melinda's throat, and she couldn't go on singing. It hurt too much to be reminded that Gabe was no longer her special fellow. *I probably shouldn't have come here tonight,* she thought regretfully as tears spilled onto her cheeks. *If only Gabe and I could work things out. If only. . .*

Philippians 2:3 popped into her mind: *"Let nothing be done through strife or vainglory; but in lowliness of mind let each esteem other better than themselves."*

More tears came, and Melinda reached up to wipe them away. She knew she hadn't put Gabe's needs ahead of hers, but shouldn't he care about her feelings, too? If Gabe really loved her, why couldn't he see how much she wanted to help hurting animals, and why wouldn't he reconsider leaving the Amish faith with her so she could do it? It would be a sacrifice on both their parts, but. . .

"How come you're out here by yourself?"

Melinda whirled around at the sound of a deep voice. In the light of the full moon, she realized it was Gabe's friend, Aaron.

"I—I'm just getting some fresh air."

He grunted. "Jah, fresh and chilly. Fall's right around the corner, and winter will be here before we know it."

"I assume winter's not your favorite time of the year?"

He shrugged. "I can take it or leave it. To tell you the truth, I prefer the warmer days of summer when I can go fishing."

Melinda rubbed her hands briskly over her arms. Aaron was right. It was kind of nippy.

"I'm sorry about you and Gabe breaking up," Aaron said. "Seems a shame you two can't find some way to work out your differences."

Melinda swallowed hard, hoping to push down the lump in her throat that wouldn't go away. So Aaron knew, too. Probably all the young people here tonight had heard the news. "Gabe doesn't understand how I feel about things," she murmured.

"Seems to me that you don't understand him, either."

Melinda cringed. Had Gabe told Aaron all the details of their breakup? He must have, or Aaron wouldn't have said such a thing. Now everyone would soon know the truth, if they didn't already. She wasn't sure she was ready to deal with that. Especially since she still hadn't told her parents any of the details.

"Uh, Aaron, please don't say anything to anyone about me wanting to leave the faith, okay?"

"Huh?"

"I haven't told my folks I'm thinking about becoming a vet, so—"

"Whoa!" Aaron held up his hand. "You're thinking of what?"

"I thought you knew. From what you said earlier, I figured Gabe must have told you everything."

Aaron let out a low whistle. "Now I know why he seemed so upset."

"You mean he didn't tell you what I'm thinking of doing?"

He shook his head. "Just said you'd broken up because he wants to hunt and you're opposed to the idea."

Melinda grimaced, feeling like someone had punched her in the stomach. Aaron hadn't known the truth until she'd opened her mouth and blabbed the whole thing. Now he might tell others, and then things could get really sticky.

She glanced to the left and caught sight of two people walking toward one of the open buggies. Her heart plummeted when she realized it was Gabe and Mattie. When Gabe helped Mattie into the passenger's seat then climbed up beside her, Melinda's whole body trembled. It hurt to know he had gotten over her so quickly.

She turned away, unable to watch the couple drive off together.

"Sorry you had to see that," Aaron said, touching her arm.

"I'd better get used to it, because from the way things look, Gabe will probably marry someone else and I'll be—" Her voice caught on a sob. "Oh, please, Aaron, don't say anything about what I've shared with you tonight."

He shook his head. "It's not for me to say, Melinda."

"Danki. I appreciate that." She sighed. "I wish the singing was over and I could go home. Papa Noah won't be here to pick me up until ten o'clock, but I've got a headache and don't think I can make it through the rest of the evening."

"I'd be glad to give you a lift home right now," Aaron offered. "It would save your daed a trip and keep you from having to stick around here."

Melinda sniffed. "I'd hate for you to miss all the fun on account of me."

"Nah. I wasn't havin' much fun anyway."

"Are you sure? I mean, isn't there someone else you'd rather escort home?"

Aaron shook his head then chuckled as if he were embarrassed. "If I ever find a woman I'm willing to court, she'll have to be spunky like my mamm. I'd want someone who likes to fish and isn't afraid to get her hands dirty, either."

"Most Amish women I know work in their gardens. Doesn't that count as dirty work?"

"I reckon so, but that's not what I meant." Aaron led Melinda toward his buggy.

"What did you mean?"

He tipped his head to one side. "Any woman I'd even consider courting would have to be willing to do lots of outdoor stuff."

"Oh, you mean she should be a tomboy?"

Aaron shrugged. "Guess that's one way to put it, but that's not likely to happen, because there are no women around here that I'd be interested in." He released an undignified grunt. "Even if there was, I'll never get married."

"Why not?"

"Just won't; that's all."

Melinda didn't argue the point, and she found herself wondering if Aaron might not have the right attitude about staying single. If she left home to become a veterinarian, she would probably stay single unless she met and married some English fellow. That thought did nothing to make her feel better. She'd been miserable since she and Gabe had broken up, but she saw no way they could get back together unless one of them made a huge concession. Gabe would probably be better off with Mattie. She was cute and wanted to remain Amish.

"Well, Aaron Zook," Melinda said as he

helped her into his buggy, "I hope you have better luck at finding love than I've had."

Susie's stomach felt as if it were filled with a bunch of swarming bees as she settled herself on the seat of Jonas's buggy and he reached for the reins. The fact that he'd asked to give her a ride home tonight was like an answer to prayer. She just hoped she didn't say anything stupid that might make him wish he hadn't asked.

"I saw you talking with Melinda earlier this evening. Are you and she still good friends?" Jonas asked as they turned out of the driveway and headed down Highway C.

Susie nodded. "Although we don't see eye to eye on much these days."

Jonas chuckled. "I guess that's true with most friends and even family. My cousins John and Jared, who live in Montana, don't always think alike, and they're identical twins."

He flicked the reins to get the horse moving faster, and Susie gripped the edge of her seat. She had hoped they could take a leisurely ride home so she could spend more time with Jonas.

"Is Melinda still drawing pictures of animals and taking in strays?"

"Jah. She works part-time for our local vet, too."

"That sounds interesting. I admire anyone

who has a way with animals."

Susie's heart gave a lurch. Was Jonas interested in Melinda? Had he offered Susie a ride home only to ask about her niece? Was that why he kept asking questions about Melinda?

"I'll bet Melinda would like it where I live," Jonas continued. "There's more wildlife in Montana than you can imagine."

"Do you hunt?" Susie hoped her question might take Jonas's mind off Melinda.

"Jah. Got me a nice big buck deer last year and also a turkey."

"Some of the menfolk in our community also hunt deer. Melinda's boyfriend, Gabe, likes to hunt." Susie figured mentioning that Melinda had a boyfriend might discourage Jonas from taking an interest in her niece. She saw no reason to mention that Melinda and Gabe had recently broken up. No point in giving Jonas any hope of courting Melinda, if that's what he had on his mind.

"Say, I was wondering about something," Jonas said, breaking into Susie's disconcerting thoughts.

"What's that?"

"I'll be leaving for Montana by the end of next week, and I was wondering if it would be all right if I write to you sometimes."

Susie's heart began to hammer as hope swelled in her breast. If Jonas wanted to write her, did that mean they were courting? *No, of course it doesn't mean that,* she berated herself. *Since I acted so interested in Montana, he probably just wants to write and tell me about some of the things going on there.*

"Well, is it all right if I write to you or not?"

"I'd like that," she said, hoping the excitement she felt didn't show too much in her voice. She didn't want to appear overeager.

He smacked the reins to get the horse moving faster. "I'm kept pretty busy with my job and all, but I'll write as often as I can."

Susie smiled. "I'll write often, too."

"I appreciate you giving me a ride home," Mattie said as Gabe directed his horse onto the highway.

He nodded and forced a smile. Deep down, he felt miserable. When he'd seen Melinda talking to his so-called friend, he'd felt as if someone had punched him in the stomach. It had been only a short time since Gabe and Melinda had broken up. He couldn't believe she'd found someone to replace him so quickly. And Aaron Zook, of all people! Didn't she even care that Gabe and Aaron had been friends since they were boys? How could she have proclaimed her love just a few short weeks ago and suddenly taken an interest in someone else?

"I figured you'd be taking Melinda home tonight," Mattie said, breaking into Gabe's troubling thoughts.

"Why would you think that?"

"Since the two of you are courting, I just assumed—"

Gabe shook his head. "We're not courting. Not anymore."

Mattie's pale eyebrows furrowed. "Did you break up with her?"

"Let's just say it was a mutual decision."

"Mind if I ask why?"

Actually, Gabe did mind. He didn't want to think about his breakup with Melinda, much less talk about it. "We. . .uh. . . decided that since we both wanted different things it would be best to go our separate ways."

"That's too bad. Melinda always seemed so happy whenever the two of you were together. I figured it wouldn't be long before an announcement of your betrothal would be published in church."

"I thought that, too," Gabe mumbled. "But things don't always go the way we want. I've come to realize that some things just aren't meant to be."

Mattie reached across the seat and touched his arm. "I'm real sorry, Gabe."

He gave a brief nod. No one could be any sorrier than he.

Chapter 26

"I came by to check on some kitchen cabinets I plan to give Faith for Christmas," Noah said when he stepped into Swartz's Woodworking Shop on Monday morning, two weeks after Gabe and Melinda had broken up.

Gabe leaned against his workbench and crossed his arms. "My daed's delivering some furniture right now, but I know your cabinets have been made and are waiting to be sanded and stained. I'm sure they'll be ready in time for Christmas." He thought about all the orders they had for holiday gifts and how Pap had allowed him to make some chairs and a table for the bed-and-breakfast in Branson. They'd turned out well, and Pap had said he was pleased with Gabe's work.

"I'm glad to hear the cabinets will be ready soon, because the ones in our kitchen were bought used when we built the house next to my folks' place," Noah said, jolting Gabe out of his musings. "They need to be replaced, and my wife's been wanting new ones for quite some time." Noah shifted from one foot to the other. "I. . .uh. . .wanted to tell you that I'm sorry to hear about you and Melinda breaking up. I like you, Gabe, and was looking forward to having you as my son-in-law." He handed Gabe a plate of chocolate chip cookies wrapped with cellophane. "I made these last night and thought you might like some."

"Danki. That was nice of you." Gabe placed the cookies on one end of his workbench. The truth was, he thought highly of Melinda's stepfather and figured Noah would probably make a good father-in-law.

Noah placed his palms on the workbench and leaned toward Gabe. "Melinda's been acting like a kitten with sore paws ever since you two split up. She spends most of her time with those critters of hers, and Faith is fit to be tied because she has to prod Melinda to get any work done."

Gabe pondered Noah's words before responding. "If she's so concerned about going our separate ways, then why'd she ride home from the last young people's gathering with my best friend?"

"Aaron Zook?"

"Jah, that's what I heard."

"I didn't realize that. I thought one of the girls who had no date had given Melinda a ride home that night. I was supposed to pick her up, but she arrived home way before ten." Noah looked intently at Gabe. "I'm thinking this is something you and Melinda need to discuss. I don't believe she'd like the idea of me butting in on something that's really none of my business."

"There's a lot more going on than just her riding home with Aaron."

Noah nodded. "If you're talking about her not wanting you to hunt, she explained her reasons to me, and I said I thought she was wrong."

Gabe toyed with a piece of sandpaper, pushing it back and forth across the work space in front of him, even though there was nothing there to sand. "That's not the whole issue, but it's not for me to be saying. I'm sure Melinda will tell you everything when she's ready." He drew in a deep breath and released it with a huff. "Short of a miracle, I'm afraid it's too late for anything to be resolved between Melinda and me."

Noah shook his head. "It's never too late. Not as long as you're both still free to marry." He turned toward the door, calling over his shoulder, "My daughter is worth fighting for."

The door clicked shut, and Gabe's gaze came to rest on the cookies Noah had given him. It was then that he noticed a verse of scripture had been attached to the edge of the plastic wrap. He reached for it and read the words out loud. " 'But the wisdom that is from above is first pure, then peaceable, gentle, and easy to be entreated, full of mercy and good fruits, without partiality, and without hypocrisy. And the fruit of righteousness is sown in peace of them that make peace.' "

Gabe scratched the side of his head. *What was Noah trying to tell me? Does he think I should try and make peace with Melinda?* Gabe wasn't sure there was any way they could get back to where they had been before she'd told him that she wanted to become a vet, but he would pray about the matter.

Early that morning, Melinda's mother had hired a driver and taken Grandpa to Springfield for a doctor's appointment, asking Melinda to do some cleaning before she left for work at noon. True to her promise, Melinda was now mopping the kitchen floor.

She glanced at the calendar on the opposite wall. It had been two weeks since she and Gabe had gone their separate ways, and the pain in her heart was still so raw she could barely function. Even spending time with her animal friends didn't hold the appeal it once had.

She took another look at the calendar and realized it had been one week since Jonas Byler had returned to Montana, so she figured Susie was probably also grieving.

Dear Lord, bless Gabe and give him a happy life, even if he ends up being with Mattie Byler. Give me wisdom and direction for my own life, and help me to know whether I should take another GED test. Be with Susie, and help her find someone who will love her. . . .

Loud barking in the backyard interrupted Melinda's prayer. She set the mop aside and peeked out the window, wondering what Isaiah's dog was up to. But it wasn't her brother's hound she saw in the yard. It was Gabe's German shepherd, Shep, running around in circles and barking like crazy.

Melinda opened the back door and stepped onto the porch. "What's the matter with you, Shep? You act like you've been stung by a swarm of bees."

As soon as Melinda spoke, the dog quit running and crawled toward the house on its belly.

"What's wrong, boy?" She stepped off the porch. "Are you hurt?"

Shep's only response was a pathetic whimper.

When Melinda drew closer, she realized Shep had several porcupine quills stuck in his nose. "Looks like you had a run-in with an angry critter, didn't you? We need to get those out right away."

The dog looked up at Melinda with sorrowful brown eyes. "Come on, fella. Let's go to the barn and get that taken care of." She led the way, and obediently, the dog followed.

A short time later after removing the quills with a pair of pliers, Melinda was putting antiseptic on Shep's nose when an unexpected visitor showed up. Gabe stepped into the barn, the stubble of straw crackling under his weight. "I've been looking everywhere for you, Shep." He glanced at Melinda then looked quickly away as though he was afraid to make eye contact. "The critter took off last night. I figured he'd come over here to play with Isaiah's dog, but he didn't return, and this morning I got worried." Gabe's forehead creased as he looked back at her and frowned. "What's wrong with him? Why are you doctoring my dog?"

Melinda set the bottle of peroxide back on the shelf before she answered, hoping the action would give her time to take control of her swirling emotions. Ministering to Gabe's dog and then having Gabe show up made her long for things she couldn't have—unless she was willing to set aside her dream and do what Gabe wanted her to do.

When Melinda turned to face Gabe again, her legs shook so badly she could barely stand. "I found Shep in the backyard barking and running around in circles. Then I discovered the poor dog had a bunch of porcupine quills stuck in his nose."

Gabe's face softened some as he patted his knee. "Come here, Shep. Come here, boy."

The dog went immediately to his side, wagging its tail as though nothing had ever happened.

Gabe clicked his tongue. "You silly critter. I thought you had more sense than to tangle with a porcupine."

Shep licked Gabe's hand and whined in response.

"I appreciate you looking out for him," Gabe said, lifting his gaze to meet Melinda's again. "Guess Shep was smart enough to know who to come to when he needed help."

Melinda smiled as she finally began to relax. "Animals have a sixth sense about things."

Gabe took hold of Shep's collar and led him toward the barn door. "I'd better get back home. Pap's at the shop by himself, and we've got lots of work to do."

"It's kind of chilly this morning. Would you like a cup of hot chocolate before you head out?" Melinda asked, not wanting him to go.

He licked his lips, and a slow smile spread across his face. "Hot chocolate sounds nice. If you've got a couple of marshmallows to go with it, that is."

Melinda's heart skipped a beat. Being here in the barn with Gabe felt so natural—like nothing had ever come between them. "I think there are some marshmallows in the kitchen cupboard. Why don't you put Shep in the dog run with Jericho, and I'll meet you on the back porch in a few minutes?"

"Sounds good to me."

Melinda knew there was no point in letting

her thoughts run wild with things hoped for but not likely to occur, but she couldn't seem to help herself. She gave him a quick nod then hurried into the house.

Gabe's palms felt sweaty, and his throat was so dry he could barely swallow when he joined Melinda on the porch a short time later.

"Here you go," she said, handing him a cup of steaming hot chocolate.

"Danki." Gabe blew on the chocolate drink as he tried to think of something sensible to say. What he really wanted to talk about was their relationship and how they could get it back on track, but he couldn't seem to find the right words.

"How's Mattie Byler?" Melinda blurted suddenly.

Gabe nearly choked on the warm liquid in his mouth. "Huh?"

"How's Mattie Byler?"

He reached up to wipe away the chocolate that had dribbled onto his chin. "I guess she's okay. Why do you ask?"

Melinda's cheeks turned bright pink, and he didn't think it had anything to do with the chilly weather. "I saw the two of you together at the last young people's gathering."

"I didn't hang around Mattie all evening," he said defensively. "I just talked to her a few minutes after we both had some punch."

"But I saw her get into your buggy, and you were obviously driving her home."

He nodded. "That's true. Mattie told me her brother Jonas was planning to ask your aunt Susie if she'd be willing to ride in his buggy after the gathering was over."

"What's that got to do with you taking Mattie home?"

"I'm getting to that." Gabe set his empty cup on the porch floor. "Mattie mentioned that she'd come down with a headache and wanted to go home. Since Jonas wasn't going to leave until the gathering was over, Mattie had no transportation."

"So you volunteered to drive her?"

"That's right."

Melinda stared at her empty cup. "Guess I must have gotten the wrong impression."

"There's nothing going on with me and Mattie. We're just friends, and I was only doing a good deed." Gabe squinted. "While we're on the subject of rides home, I heard you rode with Aaron that night."

She nodded. "It's true."

"Are you two seeing each other now?"

She shook her head so hard the ties on her kapp came untied. "Of course not. Aaron only gave me a ride because I, too, had a headache and wanted to go. Papa Noah was supposed to pick me up at ten, but I didn't want to wait around until then."

Gabe smiled as a feeling of relief washed over

him. "I'm glad to hear that."

"What? That I had a headache?"

"No, that you and Aaron aren't seeing each other."

"I'm not interested in Aaron," she said in a near whisper. "Never have been, either."

Gabe leaned a bit closer as he fought the temptation to kiss her, but a ruckus in the dog run ruined the mood. He decided that was probably a good thing, considering that he and Melinda had recently broken up.

"I hope they're not fighting over the bone I gave Jericho last night." Melinda jumped up and bounded off the porch.

Gabe followed. "I'd best get my dog and head for home."

Several minutes later, Gabe had Shep out of the pen and loaded into the back of his buggy. As he pulled out of the driveway, he waved, and Melinda lifted her hand in response. Even though things weren't back to where they should be, at least Melinda and he were speaking again.

"How'd things go with Grandpa's appointment?" Melinda asked her mother that evening as they prepared supper.

"The results of his blood tests were good," Mama replied. "The doctor was pleased with how well Grandpa seems to be doing."

Melinda smiled. "He sure has made a turnaround, especially where his memory is concerned."

Mama handed her a sack of flour. "Would you mind making some biscuits while I fry up the chicken?"

"Sure, I can do that."

Melinda and her mother worked in silence for a time. Then Mama turned down the gas burner under the pan of chicken and nodded toward the table. "Want to sit awhile and have a cup of tea while the meat cooks and the biscuit dough rises?"

"That sounds good."

"How'd your day go?" Mama asked as she poured them both a cup of lemon-mint tea.

"It was busy and kind of crazy."

Mama's eyebrows lifted. "In what way?"

"It began with me doing the cleaning you'd wanted done, and that went fairly well. But then Gabe's dog showed up with a bunch of porcupine quills stuck in his nose."

"I'll bet that hurt," Mama said.

"I'm sure it did. I removed them with a pair of pliers and put some antiseptic on his nose, and by the time Gabe took Shep home, he was acting his old spunky self."

"Did Gabe bring the dog over for you to doctor?"

"Shep came here on his own, and Gabe showed up later looking for him."

Mama took a sip of tea and blotted her lips on a napkin. "How'd that go? Did the two of you get anything resolved between you?"

Melinda shrugged. "Not really, but we didn't argue, either."

"That's a good thing. Maybe if you give yourselves a bit more time, you'll be able to settle your differences."

Snow whizzed into the room with something between her teeth.

"What's that crazy cat got now?" Mama leaned over and squinted as Snow sailed under the table. "Looks like a hunk of balled-up paper."

Melinda chuckled. "At least it's not a mouse."

"Here, kitty. Let me see what's in your mouth," Mama said, reaching for the cat.

Melinda didn't know who was more surprised, her or Mama, when Snow dropped the wad of paper at Mama's feet.

"Well, what do you know—she listened to me for once." Mama bent down and picked up the paper, pulling it apart with her fingers and laying it flat on the table. "Now, what is this?"

Melinda froze as her gaze came to rest on the item in question. It was the results of her failed GED test.

Mama's forehead wrinkled as she studied the piece of paper, then she looked pointedly at Melinda.

"I—I can explain."

"I certainly hope so."

Melinda moistened her lips with the tip of her tongue. "Uh—as you know, Dr. Franklin thinks I have a special way with animals."

Mama nodded.

"He believes I would make a good vet or certified veterinarian's assistant."

No response.

"And. . .well, he suggested I take the GED test, which I would need in order to sign up for some college classes."

"You want to go to college and become a vet?" Mama's voice sounded calm and even, but Melinda could see by the pinched expression on her mother's face that she was having a hard time keeping her emotions under control.

"As you can see by the scores on that paper, I failed the test."

"Does that mean you've given up the idea?"

Melinda toyed with the handle on her teacup. "I–I'm not sure. I've thought about retaking the test."

Mama released a sigh. "And you've been planning all of this behind your daed's and my back, sneaking off to take the test without ever saying a word about it?"

Melinda's eyes filled with tears as a wave of shame and regret washed over her like a drenching rain. "I was planning to tell you."

"When?"

"After I passed the GED test."

Mama grabbed two fingers on her left hand

and gave them a good pop. "Have you thought about what it would mean if you went off to college and got a degree? Have you thought about how it would affect everyone in this family?"

"Of course I have, and it wouldn't be easy for me to leave." There was a tremor in Melinda's voice, and it was all she could do to look her mother in the face.

"After all the things I've told you about my life as an entertainer, I wouldn't think you would even consider becoming part of the English world—not when all your family and friends are Amish living here in Webster County." Mama sniffed deeply, and her quivering chin let Melinda know she was close to tears.

Melinda stared at her untouched cup of tea. "I—I don't really want to leave home, Mama, but becoming a vet would allow me to care for so many hurting and sick animals. If I have a special way with animals, as Dr. Franklin says I do, then wouldn't it be wasted if I didn't learn how to care for them in the best possible way?"

"I guess you'll have to choose what's more important to you—the animals you think need your help, or your family and friends who love you so much," Mama replied without really answering Melinda's question.

Melinda blinked against the tears blurring her vision but made no comment.

Mama leaned across the table and looked at Melinda long and hard. "I'm not saying these things to make you feel guilty. I just don't want you to make the same mistake I did when I left home." She slid her chair back and stood. "Please know that as much as I would hate to see you go, I won't try to stop you. It's your life, and you will have to decide."

Melinda felt as if she were in a stupor, and seeing the distressed look on her mother's face only made her feel worse. *I should have told Mama sooner—maybe even had Dr. Franklin talk to her and Papa Noah. I shouldn't have let her find out by seeing my failed GED test. That could have been avoided if I'd burned the silly thing.*

"I. . .uh . . .need to check on my animals in the barn," she mumbled, pushing away from the table.

When Mama made no reply, Melinda rushed out the back door and headed straight for the barn.

Faith let her head fall forward until it rested on the table. She'd held up well while Melinda told of her plans, but now that Faith was alone in the kitchen, she could allow herself to grieve. How could this have happened? It was like reliving the past, only this time it wasn't Faith wanting to leave home; it was her own precious daughter.

Is this my punishment for leaving my family behind while I tried to make a name for myself in the fancy, modern English world? It was bad enough that I left home and became an entertainer, but then, after I came home with Melinda, I was planning to go back on the road and leave my home again.

Stinging tears escaped Faith's lashes and dribbled onto her cheeks. "Like mother, like daughter," she murmured as a burning lump formed in her throat. "My selfish desires and wayward ways have come back to haunt me."

"Faith, what's wrong? What are you mumbling about?"

Faith's head jerked up. Noah stood staring down at her with a look of concern. She had been so caught up in her sorrow over Melinda that she hadn't heard him come in.

She rushed into his arms. "Oh, Noah, I don't know how to tell you this, but we've lost our daughter to the world!"

Noah pushed Faith gently away from him so that he was looking directly at her. "What are you talking about? How is Melinda lost to the world?"

Faith drew in a shaky breath and quickly related about Melinda taking the GED test, failing it, and wanting to leave the Amish faith and become a vet. When she finished, she gulped in a quick breath of air and collapsed into a chair at the table.

Noah took the seat beside Faith and reached for her hand. "No wonder our daughter's been acting so *fremm* lately. I'll bet she's been planning this for some time."

Faith nodded. "I thought Melinda's strange behavior was because she was upset over her and Gabe breaking up. I should have realized with her unhealthy preoccupation over animals that something more was on the wind." She sniffed deeply. "Oh, Noah, this is all my fault."

"How can it be your fault?"

"If I hadn't been so hard on Melinda, always scolding her for spending too much time with her animal friends, maybe she wouldn't have become discontent. Maybe—"

"Don't be so hard on yourself." Noah gently squeezed her fingers. "We've both gotten after Melinda, and neither of us figured she'd ever want to leave home to become a vet."

Faith blinked against another set of tears. "What are we going to do? How can we keep Melinda from going English?"

Noah let go of her hand and slipped his arm across her shoulders. "The best thing we can do is try to be more understanding and not push Melinda to do what we want. We also need to pray that the Lord's will is done."

She nodded slowly. "Would you at least speak to her about this? The two of you have always had a special bond, even before you and I were married. If anyone can get through to our daughter, it will be you."

"I'll do what I can, but I won't press Melinda on this or try to make her feel guilty."

"I wouldn't expect you to."

Noah pushed back his chair and stood. "Whatever Melinda decides, she needs to know that we still love her."

"Of course." Faith sniffed. "I'll always love my little girl, even if she does leave home."

As Noah headed for the barn, he prayed that God would give him the right words to say to Melinda. He knew if he said the wrong thing, it could drive her further away and might make her want to leave out of rebellion, the way Faith had done when she was a teenager and thought her folks disapproved of her joke telling and yodeling. If Faith had only known back then that it wasn't her jokes or yodeling they disapproved of. It was the fact that she'd fooled around and shirked her duties so often.

Just the way Melinda's been doing here of late, he thought ruefully. *Oh, Lord, why didn't I see what was going on and do something about this sooner?*

When Noah stepped into the barn a few minutes later, he found Melinda inside one of the horse stalls brushing the mare's mane.

"Hi, Papa Noah," she said, glancing over at him as he approached the stall. "Did you just get home from work?"

He nodded. "I went into the house to say hello to your mamm first and found her sitting at the kitchen table quite upset."

Melinda dropped her gaze to the floor, and her hand shook as she set the brush on the edge of a nearby shelf. "She told you then?"

"Jah."

"Papa Noah, I—"

"Why, Melinda? Why did you keep your plans a secret from us? Wouldn't it have been better if you'd told us right away?"

"I—I didn't want to upset you or Mama. And since I haven't passed my GED test yet or made a definite decision, I saw no point in talking about what I might want to do."

Noah leaned on the stall door and groaned. "I know you have a special way with animals and would probably make a good vet, but have you thought about how your leaving would affect this family—your mamm most of all?"

Melinda nodded slowly as tears slipped from her eyes and rolled down her cheeks. "It's affected my relationship with Gabe, too. That's the main reason we're no longer a courting couple."

"Did you ask Gabe to leave the Amish faith with you?"

"Jah, but he doesn't want to." Her chin quivered. "I guess he doesn't love me enough to want to be with me."

"Maybe Gabe feels the same way about you."

Melinda lifted her gaze to meet his. "Oh, Papa Noah, I feel like my heart's being torn in two. I do love Gabe, and I love my family, but if God has blessed me with a special talent to care for sick and hurting animals, shouldn't I be using that talent to its full extent?"

Noah grimaced, unsure of how best to answer. Just as he enjoyed working with the fledgling trees at Hank's tree farm, he knew Melinda enjoyed working with the animals that came into Dr. Franklin's clinic. Even so, they were just animals, and he didn't understand why she would choose a career that would take her away from her family just to help animals who couldn't really love her in return. And to give up her Amish faith and become part of an English world she barely remembered made no sense to him at all.

He stepped inside the stall and drew Melinda into his arms, knowing a lecture was not what she needed right now. "I want you to know that your mamm and I will be praying that God will reveal His will and show you what you're supposed to do."

"I'm praying for that, too," Melinda said in a shaky voice.

Noah patted her back then stepped out of the stall. As he left the barn, he made a decision. He would not mention the subject of Melinda leaving home again. Not until she was ready to give them her choice.

Chapter 27

On the first day of deer hunting season as the Hertzlers sat around the breakfast table, Noah instructed Melinda and Isaiah to stay out of the woods.

"But, Papa Noah, No Hunting signs are posted all over our property," Melinda reminded him.

"That's true," he said with a nod, "but there's always someone who either doesn't see the signs or refuses to take them seriously and hunts wherever he pleases."

"Your daed's right," Grandpa put in. "I remember when I was a boy someone shot a deer right out in our front yard."

Melinda gasped. "I hope the deer on our property will be okay and stay where it's safe."

Isaiah grunted. "Like you can keep all the deer safe, Melinda."

"I can sure try."

"No, you can't. The deer have a mind of their own, and—"

Noah nudged Isaiah with his elbow. "Why don't you eat your breakfast and quit being such a *baddere* to your sister?"

"I ain't bein' a bother." Isaiah wrinkled his nose. "She's just verhuddelt, that's all."

"I'm not confused," Melinda shot back. "You're the one who's verhuddelt."

Noah lifted his hands as he shook his head. "Enough of the squabbling. You two are worse than a couple of hens fighting for the same piece of corn."

Grandpa chuckled, but Isaiah and Melinda both sat frowning, staring at their bowls of oatmeal.

"Do like your daed says and eat before your food gets cold," Faith said sternly.

Melinda pushed back her chair. "I'm not hungry. If nobody has any objections, I think I'll go out to the barn and see how my animals are doing."

Noah's patience was beginning to wane, but he figured if Melinda wasn't hungry he couldn't force her to eat. "Go ahead to the barn," he said. "But be sure and come back in time to help your mamm do the breakfast dishes and clean up the kitchen."

"I will." Melinda rushed out of the kitchen without another word.

❦

All morning as Melinda did her chores, she worried about the deer. By the time she had finished cleaning the kitchen, she was a ball of nerves.

Maybe a walk in the woods would make me feel better, she told herself as she placed the last glass in the cupboard.

"Stay out of the woods." Papa Noah's earlier warning echoed in her ears.

I'll only be there a short time. Just long enough to check on the deer.

She glanced around the room. No sign of Mama or Grandpa, and she knew Isaiah had gone fishing over at Rabers' pond. Papa Noah had left for work as soon as they were finished eating, and she figured her mother had gone next door to clean Grandpa's house.

As Melinda hung up her choring apron, she thought about how there had been no mention of her failed GED test or plans of becoming a vet since she first told her parents. She wasn't sure if they had accepted the idea of her leaving home or if it was just too painful for them to talk about. Either way, Melinda was glad there had been no mention of it. Until she took another GED test and got her scores, there wasn't much she could do about her future plans.

"I'd better leave Mama a note," Melinda murmured, "so she doesn't worry if she returns to the house and finds me gone." She grabbed a piece of paper from a nearby drawer, hurried over to the table, and scrawled a message saying that she was going for a short walk before it was time to leave for the clinic. Then she rushed out the back door and headed straight for the woods.

A short while later, Melinda stepped into the thicket of trees, wishing she had remembered to bring along her drawing tablet. *It's probably for the best. If I took the time to draw, I'd likely get carried away and be here much longer than I should.*

The sound of gunfire in the distance caused Melinda to shudder. Some poor animal had probably met its fate. At least it hadn't happened on their property. She walked deeper into the woods, savoring the distinct aroma of fall with its crisp, clean air and fresh-fallen leaves strewn all over the ground like a carpet of red and gold.

The rustle of leaves halted Melinda's footsteps. She tipped her head and listened. There it was again.

She scanned the area but saw nothing out of the ordinary. Suddenly a fawn stepped out of the bushes and stood staring at Melinda as though it needed her help.

Melinda took a step forward, then another and another, until she was right beside the little deer. That's when she saw it—a doe lying dead among a clump of bushes. "Oh no!" Her breath caught in her throat.

It didn't take Melinda long to realize that the mother deer had been shot, and this little one must be her fawn. Had someone been hunting on their property despite the signs Papa Noah had posted? Or had the doe been shot elsewhere and stumbled onto their land while it bled to death?

The fawn stood beside Melinda with its nose and ears twitching. Melinda bent down and picked it up, noting that the little deer was lightweight and couldn't have been more than a few days old. It was probably born late in the year, she decided.

She hurried from the woods and entered the barn a short time later, where she settled the fawn in an empty horse stall. "I'll need to find one of my feeding bottles and get some nourishment into you right away," she said, patting the deer on top of its head.

She stepped out of the stall and closed the door, planning to feed the deer and then head for work.

❧

"Guess what, Dr. Franklin," Melinda said breathlessly as she entered the veterinary clinic later that day.

"I can't even begin to guess," the vet said with a crooked smile. "But if it has something to do with an animal, then I'll bet that's why you look so wide-eyed and excited."

She nodded enthusiastically. "I found a baby deer in the woods, and its mother had been killed."

"Sorry to hear that. The fawn probably won't survive without its mother."

"I'm hoping it will. I brought it back to our place and put it in an empty stall inside the barn. I plan to bottle-feed it, and—"

Dr. Franklin held up his hand. "And what, Melinda? Make a pet out of it?"

She nodded again.

He shook his head as deep wrinkles creased his forehead. "That's not a good idea."

"Why not?"

"A deer is a wild animal, and it belongs in the woods, not held captive in a barn."

"I won't keep it in the barn forever. When it's bigger, I'll have Papa Noah build a pen."

The doctor leaned forward with his elbows resting on the desk. "Do you think that's fair to the deer when it should be running free in the woods?"

"It might get shot like its mother."

"That's part of life, Melinda. You can't protect every animal from harm, you know."

"But I don't like the thought of animals being hunted for the sport of it." Melinda frowned. "Some people hunt just so they can brag to their friends about the big set of antlers they got or how good their gun is because they can shoot a deer from a long distance."

"I can see where you're coming from, Melinda. It's your sensitive spirit and caring attitude that would help you become a good vet."

She dropped her gaze to the floor. "That may never happen now."

"How come?"

"I failed my GED test."

"I'm sorry to hear that. Are you planning to take it again?"

Melinda shrugged. "I was, but my mother found my test scores, and I had to tell my folks about my plans to become a vet." She groaned. "They weren't happy about it and offered me no support, except to say they'll be praying that God will show me what I should do."

Dr. Franklin nodded. "I may not be as religious as your folks, but I do believe in God. Therefore, I have to say that your folks are right—you do need to pray about this and trust God to show you the right road to take."

"That's what I plan to do." She smiled. "In the meantime, I came here to work, so I guess I should get busy. Do you have anything in particular that needs to be done?"

He nodded toward the door behind him. "Why don't you clean out those empty cages in the back room? After that, you can help me clip the toenails on Hank Osborn's two beagles."

Melinda gave a quick nod and scurried out of the room.

When Noah stepped into the barn after arriving home from work that evening, he was shocked by the sight that greeted him. A young fawn stood in one of the empty horse stalls, and Melinda was kneeling in the straw beside it, stroking the little deer's head.

"What's that deer doing in one of the horse's stalls?" he asked, pointing at the fawn.

Melinda looked up at him with a worried expression. "I found the poor thing in the woods earlier today, standing beside its dead mother." She groaned. "I'm sure someone must have shot it, Papa Noah."

"I thought I had made myself clear when I told you and Isaiah not to go there today." Noah clenched his teeth. Didn't Melinda ever listen? Sometimes she made it so difficult to be patient and understanding.

"I'm sorry, but if I hadn't gone, this little deer would have died."

"What if the person who shot the fawn's mother had been nearby and took another shot that might have hit you?"

"God protected me, as well as this one," she said, motioning to the fawn.

"Jah, well, don't go to the woods again. At least not until hunting season's over."

She nodded in reply.

Noah glanced around. "Where's your bruder? Was he with you when you found the deer?"

"Isaiah wasn't with me. He went fishing over at Rabers' pond soon after breakfast."

"And he's not back yet?"

"I don't think so. His pole isn't where he keeps it." She pointed to the spot on the wall where Isaiah usually hung his fishing gear.

"It'll be getting dark soon, and I don't like the idea of him being at the pond so late. Some crazy hunters could be out road hunting before dusk. That's when the deer start to move around again."

"Would you like me to go look for him?" Melinda offered. "I could take the horse and buggy."

Noah shook his head. "If he's not here within the hour, I'll go after the boy myself."

Melinda shrugged and patted the little deer's head. "Whatever you think is best."

Gabe leaned his gun against a tree and lowered himself to a log. Soon the sun would be going down; then the deer would likely show themselves.

Sure am glad I could get into the woods this afternoon, he thought, leaning his head back and savoring the last few moments of full sunlight. He had decided to hunt in the wooded area to the left of Rabers' pond, which wasn't posted.

Gabe's thoughts went to Melinda, and he

wondered if hunters were respecting the No Hunting signs her stepfather had put around their place. *I hope Melinda has the smarts to stay out of the woods until hunting season is over. No telling what could happen if someone goes onto their property and ignores those signs.*

He reached into his backpack, checking to be sure he'd brought along enough ammunition. Everything seemed to be in order. Now all he needed was a nice-sized buck to step into the clearing. He knew his folks would be pleased to have some deer meat on the table during the winter months.

A twig snapped, and Gabe leaped to attention. He was about to grab his gun when Isaiah Hertzler stepped out from behind a tree.

"What are you doing here?" Gabe asked. "Don't you know how dangerous it is to be in the woods during hunting season when you're not one of the hunters?"

Isaiah shrugged. "I was on my way home from fishin' at the pond, and I ain't scared of bein' in the woods."

"Well, you should be scared, and you should have taken the road, not cut through the woods."

"Mind if I shoot your gun again?" Isaiah asked, ignoring Gabe's reprimand and eyeing the item in question.

"Not unless we get your daed's permission. I think it'd be best if you went straight home." Gabe started to get up, but his backpack fell to the ground. He reached down to pick it up, and when he lifted his head again, he was shocked to see Isaiah holding the gun.

Before Gabe could open his mouth, the gun went off. A piercing pain shot through his left shoulder, and he toppled to his knees. As Gabe fought to remain conscious, a wave of nausea coursed through his stomach.

"Gabe! Gabe, are you all right?" Isaiah dropped down beside him, his youthful face a mask of concern. "I—I didn't mean to shoot you. I don't know how the gun went off."

"I'm bleeding really bad," Gabe said through clenched teeth. "I need something to put on the wound so I can apply pressure."

Isaiah pulled a hanky from his pants pocket and handed it to Gabe. "Will this work?"

Gabe balled it up and shoved it against his shoulder, wincing in pain. "You need to go for help, Isaiah. If I try to stand, I'll most likely pass out."

The boy blanched. "You're not gonna die on me, are you?"

Gabe moaned and tried to make his voice sound more convincing than he felt. "I—I think I'll live, but I need to go to the hospital. Run home and tell your daed what's happened. Ask him to go to the nearest phone and call for help."

"O—okay."

Gabe felt warm blood soak through the hanky and onto his fingers, and the world started to spin. "Hurry, Isaiah."

The last thing Gabe remembered was a muffled, "I'm goin'." Then everything went black.

Melinda had just stepped out of the barn when her little brother dashed into the yard, yelling and waving his arms. "I shot Gabe! I shot Gabe!"

She rushed out to meet him, her heart hammering in her chest. "What do you mean, you shot Gabe?"

"He needs to go to the hospital. He may be bleedin' to death." Isaiah was clearly out of breath, and his cheeks were bright red and splattered with tears.

Melinda grabbed his shoulders and gave them a shake. "Slow down, take a deep breath, and tell me what happened."

"I—I was walkin' through the woods on my way back from Rabers' pond when I ran into Gabe. I asked if I could shoot his gun, but he said no."

"Then what did you do?"

"When Gabe was bent over his ammunition bag, I picked up the gun." Isaiah's lower lip trembled, and more tears spilled onto his cheeks. "The gun went off, Melinda. I didn't mean for it to, but the next thing I knew, Gabe was lyin' on the ground, and there was blood oozin' out of his shoulder somethin' awful."

"Where is Gabe now?" Melinda asked, trying to keep her voice steady and her hands from shaking.

"He's—he's in the woods. Sent me to get Papa and call for help."

As the metallic taste of fear sprang to Melinda's mouth, she grabbed Isaiah's hand and dashed for the house, pulling him with her. Once inside, she made Isaiah tell their folks what had happened.

"Isaiah can take me back to the woods to see about Gabe." Papa Noah looked over at Melinda with a worried frown. "We don't know how badly he's been hurt, but it doesn't sound good. Why don't you run over to the Johnsons' place and ask them to call an ambulance? Your mamm can head over to Gabe's house and let his family know what's happened."

"Can't I go with you?" Melinda asked as a wave of fear shot through her. What if Gabe's wound was so bad that he bled to death? She had to see Gabe. Had to let him know what was on her mind.

Papa Noah shook his head. "Someone needs to get help, and if your mamm has to go to the Johnsons' and then over to see Gabe's folks, it will take her twice as long."

Mama touched Melinda's shoulder. "Your daed's right about this."

Melinda finally nodded.

"As soon as Isaiah shows me where Gabe is,

I'll send the boy back to the house to wait for the ambulance. That way he'll be able to show the paramedics where we are."

Swallowing against the burning lump in her throat, Melinda rushed out the door. She had some serious praying to do.

Chapter 28

Thankful to be alive, Gabe placed the Bible he'd been reading onto the nightstand next to his hospital bed and closed his eyes. *You were looking out for me today, Lord. Me and Isaiah both, and I thank You for that.*

He thought about what could have happened if Melinda's little brother, who obviously hadn't realized the gun was loaded, had pointed it at himself and accidentally pulled the trigger. Or this afternoon, some hunter in the woods could have shot Isaiah, mistaking him for a deer. The boy hadn't been wearing an orange vest or any bright colors.

The accident was more my fault than his. I never should have taught Isaiah how to shoot a gun.

Leastways not without his folks' permission. He's only twelve years old—not really ready for hunting yet.

Gabe clenched his fists, and a shooting pain sliced through his injured shoulder. *I shouldn't have left the safety off my gun, either. That was a careless thing to do, and it makes me wonder if I should even own a gun.*

Heavy footsteps told Gabe someone had entered the room, and his eyes snapped open. A middle-aged nurse with bright red hair strode toward his bed. "How are you feeling?" she asked.

"My arm's pretty sore, but I'm happy to be alive."

She slipped a thermometer under Gabe's tongue then wrapped his good arm with the blood pressure cuff. "You're lucky that bullet went into your shoulder and not your chest. It could have been much more serious and required lengthier surgery."

Gabe nodded.

A few minutes later, the nurse removed the blood pressure apparatus and the thermometer. "Looks like your temperature is normal, and your pressure's right where it should be."

"That's good to hear. When can I go home?"

"The doctor wants to keep you here overnight to watch for possible infection. If everything looks good by tomorrow morning, he'll probably release you then."

"Glad to hear it. I don't enjoy being in the hospital so much."

The nurse chuckled. "Few do." She nodded toward the door. "There's someone in the hall waiting to see you."

Gabe cranked his head in that direction. "Is it my folks? They were here earlier, but I told them to go home and get some sleep."

"It's not your parents. It's a young Amish woman with blond hair and pretty blue eyes."

Gabe pushed himself to a sitting position as a mixture of excitement and dread coursed through his body. He was pretty sure the nurse had described Melinda, because his sisters all had dark hair, and he couldn't think who else might be here to see him.

Maybe I shouldn't see her right now. She's most likely miffed and probably came here to give me a lecture for allowing Isaiah to handle a gun again. Gabe glanced at the door. *Of course, I never said he could touch my gun, but he might not have if I hadn't shown him how to shoot in the first place.*

"Should I show the young woman in?" the nurse asked, breaking into Gabe's deliberations.

He nodded. "Might as well get this over with."

The nurse quirked one auburn eyebrow and looked at Gabe in a curious way, but then she shrugged and scurried out of the room. A few seconds later, Melinda entered. Seeing her red face and swollen eyelids, Gabe realized she had been crying.

"Are you all right?" they said in unison.

Melinda nodded and offered him a weak smile. "I'm fine. It's you I'm worried about."

She's worried about me. Now that's a good sign. Maybe she's not here to chew me out after all. Gabe nodded toward the chair. "Come, have a seat."

Melinda moved slowly across the room, feeling as if she were in a daze. It was hard to comprehend all that had happened this afternoon, and now here was Gabe lying in a hospital bed in Springfield, recovering from surgery, during which the doctors had removed a bullet from his shoulder.

"Are you sure you're okay?" Gabe asked. "Your face is as white as my bedsheets."

"I was just thinking how pale you looked when the ambulance took you away earlier today and how scared I was of never seeing you again." She flopped into the chair with a groan. "Oh, Gabe, I'm glad you're going to be all right, and I'm thankful God has answered my prayers."

"Me, too." He smiled at her in such a sweet way it was all Melinda could do to keep from throwing herself into his arms. But that wouldn't be a good idea, not with his injury and all. Besides, they needed to get some important issues resolved.

"Melinda, I've made a decision—"

"Gabe, I need you to know something—"

They'd both spoken at the same time again.

"You go first," she prompted.

"No, that's okay. I'd like to hear what you've got to say."

Melinda reached out and took his hand, holding it gently and stroking her thumb back and forth across his knuckles.

"You're just what the doctor ordered," he murmured. "Better than any old shot for pain, that's for certain sure."

She cleared her throat and looked directly into his eyes. "Your accident has caused me to do some serious thinking."

Gabe nodded. "Same here."

"I don't want to spend the rest of my life without you."

"That goes double for me, Melinda."

She smiled as relief flooded her soul. "I've decided that even if I can't become a vet, and even if you continue to hunt, I want us to be together."

His eyes brightened. "Does that mean you still want to marry me?"

She nodded. "While you were in surgery, I was sitting in the waiting room, praying and reading the Bible I'd brought from home. God showed me that family and friends, as well as my personal relationship with the Lord, are more important than anything else."

"I'm glad." Gabe smiled. "Now I have something I'd like to say to you."

"What is it?"

"I've been lying in this hospital bed asking

God what I should do to make things right between us." He squeezed her hand. "For me, hunting should only be done whenever there's a real need—for food, I mean. I don't want to hunt just for the sport of it, the way some folks do."

"I think I could live with that, as long as you don't shoot any of the deer I'm feeding."

"I wouldn't think of doing that. But I believe you'd better hear what else I have to say."

Melinda tipped her head. "What is it?"

Gabe drew in a deep breath. "I've decided that if becoming a vet is really that important to you, then I'll jump the fence and go English with you."

Melinda's mouth dropped open. "You—you would do that for me?"

He nodded, and tears shimmered in his hazel-colored eyes. "I've been miserable since our breakup, and I can't stand the thought of going through life without you at my side. I want to be with you, Melinda, no matter what."

She shook her head. "I thought becoming a vet was what I wanted, but I've changed my mind. I can't ask you to make such a sacrifice, and I know how hard it would be on both of us to leave our family and friends."

Gabe motioned to the Bible lying on the table beside his bed. "I'd like you to read something I read earlier. I marked the page with a slip of paper."

Melinda opened the Bible to the place he

had marked and read the verse out loud. " 'Be ye therefore followers of God, as dear children.' " She paused and sniffed back the tears that threatened to spill over. "Oh, Gabe, I want to follow God all of my days; that's the most important thing."

"That's true for me, as well," he said with a nod.

"As much as I enjoy caring for sick and orphaned animals, I've been wrong to put it before my relationship with the Lord and those I love." Tears coursed down Melinda's cheeks, but she didn't bother to wipe them away. "I know I must learn to be content as I seek after God and try to do His will."

"But what if you could serve God and still take care of the animals that are so dear to you?"

"How can I do that without the proper training or a decent place to keep all my animals?"

"I think I might have an idea about that."

She leaned closer. "What is it?"

"After we're married, I'd like to make you more cages—regular ones for the animals you would keep until time to let go, and larger ones, more like the critters' natural surroundings, for those who aren't able to be set free."

"Grandpa Hertzler suggested something like that sometime ago, but I never mentioned it to you."

"With the new cages, you could continue to care for animals the way you're doing now."

"But I still won't be able to help the animals who are seriously injured."

"You can turn those over to Dr. Franklin, same as you've been doing."

She sighed. "I guess it doesn't have to be me who makes them well. Just as long as they have a place to stay while they're mending or needing a home because they're orphaned."

Gabe motioned her to come closer, and when she leaned her face near his, he kissed her tenderly. "I love you, Melinda. Will you marry me?"

She nodded. "I'd be pleased to be your wife."

Epilogue

Melinda and Gabe sat side by side at their corner table, along with their attendants Aaron, Susie, and two of their cousins. Several of their family members and friends stopped by the table to offer congratulations on their marriage, which had taken place a short time ago. Melinda had never been happier. While she hoped to spend many days ahead caring for her animal friends, her primary goal would be to care for the man she loved.

Gabe leaned over and thumped Aaron on the back. "You're the next one to be married, you know."

Aaron shook his head. "No way!"

Gabe glanced over at Melinda and winked.

"That's what they all say."

Aaron's face turned bright red, but he gave no retort.

Grandpa Hertzler stepped up to the table. "I left my gift for you on the kitchen table," he said, leaning over to give Melinda a hug. "It's a box filled with jars of my homemade rhubarb-strawberry jam." He winked at Gabe. "Melinda's mamm taught her how to make it, but I think mine's much better."

Melinda and Gabe laughed, and Melinda turned to embrace Susie, who sat next to her.

"I'm glad you decided not to leave home," Susie whispered in Melinda's ear. "Although, I may be leaving."

Melinda tipped her head, as confusion swirled in her brain. "Why would you leave home?"

"I got another letter from Jonas the other day, and he wants me to come to Montana for a visit. He said he's hoping I'll like it there." Susie's grin stretched from ear to ear. "Doesn't that sound like a good sign to you?"

Melinda nodded and gave Susie's shoulder a squeeze. "It sounds to me like there might be another wedding in our family soon."

Susie shrugged. "One never knows what the future will hold." She patted Melinda's arm.

Isaiah came by next. He smiled at Melinda; then he turned to Gabe and said, "I'm sure happy you're married to my sister now. Maybe someday, when you think I'm old enough, we can go huntin' together."

Gabe glanced over at Melinda.

She nodded and said, "Just as long as neither of you does any hunting on *our* property."

"Wouldn't think of it," Isaiah and Gabe said at the same time.

Papa Noah and Mama stopped at the table, offering their congratulations. "When I was your age, I was out on my own in the English world," Mama whispered to Melinda. "I'm sure glad my daughter had more sense than me."

Melinda wiped tears from her cheeks and gave her mother a hug. "But you returned home, and because of it, you married Papa Noah. That was a very schmaert thing to do."

Mama nodded. "And now you're married to a wonderful man, which is also smart."

"It took me awhile, but I finally realized what I have right here is more important than anything the world has to offer."

Melinda's folks moved on, and Dr. Franklin and his wife, Ellen, stepped up to the corner table. "I not only wanted to say congratulations to both of you," Dr. Franklin said, shaking Gabe's hand, "but I wanted to apologize to Melinda."

Melinda tipped her head in question.

"It wasn't right for me to push you into taking your GED or try to influence you to become a vet."

Melinda gave Dr. Franklin a hug. "You were

only trying to help me take better care of the animals I care so much about."

"That's true, but I should have realized how important the Amish way of life is to you, and I should have tried to help you find a way to care for your animal friends without having to leave your faith to do it."

"It's all right; that's all behind us now," Melinda said tearfully. "I want you to know that I appreciate all that you've taught me about animal care, and I'm glad you were able to find a replacement for me at the veterinary clinic."

Ellen spoke up. "Yes, my nephew, who just graduated from high school, is quite excited about becoming my husband's new assistant." She patted her husband's arm. "Who knows, maybe Len will enjoy working at the clinic so much that he'll decide to become a vet."

"You never know how things are going to turn out." Dr. Franklin gave Gabe's hand another hearty shake, and he and his wife moved on.

Gabe's parents showed up then. Leah's eyes filled with tears as she smiled at Melinda. "Take good care of my boy, okay?"

Melinda nodded. "I will, Leah. You can count on that."

"I have a wedding present for you that couldn't be put on the gift table," Gabe's dad said.

"Is it a new buggy horse?" Gabe asked with a hopeful expression.

Stephen shook his head. "It's something I

think you'll like even better."

"What is it?"

"I made an important decision the other day." He clasped Gabe's shoulder. "You are now the official owner of Swartz's Woodworking Shop."

Gabe's eyes grew large, and his mouth hung wide open. "You mean it, Pap?"

Stephen nodded. "I'm sixty-five years old, and for some time, I've been wanting to take life a little easier. I'd like to spend more of my days fishing and whittling. But of course I'll be available to help you in the shop whenever you need me."

Melinda could see by Gabe's strained expression that he was on the verge of tears. "I'll do my best to keep the place running smoothly, Pap. I'd count it a privilege to have your help anytime."

When Gabe's folks moved away, Melinda reached over to quickly touch her husband's clean-shaven cheek. Since he was now a married man and would begin growing a beard, there wouldn't be many days left to touch the smooth skin on his face. But that didn't bother her. She had always enjoyed the feel of Papa Noah's and Grandpa's fuzzy beards.

"You know what, Gabe?" she said as he stared lovingly into her eyes.

"What?"

"I've learned many things in the last few months, but one thing stands out as most important."

"What's that?"

"Like an obedient fawn follows its mother, I will always follow God, because I am his dear child. And as I follow God's leading, each day will be blessed because you'll be at my side."

Gabe pressed her fingers into the palm of his hand. "I feel the same way."

Melinda smiled and gently squeezed her husband's fingers. Today was the happiest day of her life. She glanced at Aaron and Susie talking to some other young people. She wondered what the future held for her and Gabe's two best friends. She hoped Susie and Aaron would both find someone as dear to them as Gabe was to her. And most of all, Melinda hoped she and Gabe would be blessed with a whole houseful of kinner so they could teach them the importance of God, family, and friends.

Grandpa's Rhubarb-Strawberry Jam

Ingredients:
    8 cups rhubarb, cut into small pieces
    4 cups mashed strawberries
    6 cups sugar

Wash fruit and cut rhubarb into ½-inch pieces. In large kettle, cover rhubarb with half the sugar and let stand for 1 to 2 hours. Crush berries and mix with remaining sugar, then combine with rhubarb. Place mixture on stove over low heat until sugar dissolves, then boil rapidly, stirring often to prevent burning. Cook until mixture thickens. Remove from heat, pour into sterilized canning jars, and seal while hot.

New York Times bestselling author, Wanda E. Brunstetter became fascinated with the Amish way of life when she first visited her husband's Mennonite relatives living in Pennsylvania. Wanda and her husband, Richard, live in Washington State but take every opportunity to visit Amish settlements throughout the States, where they have many Amish friends.

Let's Keep In Touch!

Want to know what Wanda's up to and be the first to hear about new releases, specials, the latest news, and more? Like Wanda on Facebook!

 Visit facebook.com/WandaBrunstetterFans